IN THE SIXTIES, Harry Stein was the foremost authority on cannabis, writing the book on indoor cultivation and inventing thirteen different hybrids. Nowadays, just cresting fifty, he stays straight to keep joint custody of his daughter, fifteen-year-old Angie.

As an independent contractor at a product liability firm, Stein no longer numbs his mind with weed—counting thousands of empty shampoo bottles in a warehouse is numbing enough. But when a crop of "orchids" goes missing, Stein is invited to re-enter the haze he thought he'd left behind. Brian Goodpasture, a local grower and hospice-supplier, is depending upon the unique properties of the missing plants—a strain Stein perfected in his halcyon days—to make them identifiable at the famous Cannabis Cup.

Stein resists—his ex would take Angie away in a heartbeat at the first hint of smoke. Then a gorgeous model named Nicholette appeals on Goodpasture's behalf, and Stein's resolve weakens. And once his interest is sparked, he may as well inhale ...

STEIN, STONED

STEIN, STONED

HAL ACKERMAN

A HARRY STEIN SOFT-BOILED MURDER MYSTERY

TYRUS BOOKS
MADISON, WISCONSIN

mys
CR
Citrus County Library System

Published by
TYRUS BOOKS
1213 N. Sherman Ave., #306
Madison, WI 53704
www.tyrusbooks.com

This is a work of fiction.
Any similarities to people or places,
living or dead, is purely coincidental.

15 14 13 12 11 10   1 2 3 4 5 6 7 8 9 10

ISBN: 978-1-935562-15-3 (hardcover)
ISBN: 978-1-935562-14-6 (paperback)

For Laura.

Love and gratitude to Cathy and the Wednesday night Catheters.

IN MEMORY OF

Jack Herer

ONE

THE BUD OF SINSEMILLA was long and green and graceful as a Russian ballerina. Its crystallized resins sparkled like perfect dewdrops and reflected the outdoorsy good looks of Brian Goodpasture as he held the bud to the sunlight and inhaled its minty perfume. He had cloned the sproutlings from choice stock, cradled them in crèches of peat moss and potting soil, nursed them in a hydroponic solution of nutrients he had formulated to promote a short growing cycle, robust flowers, and his signature joyful Goodpasture high. Discerning buyers had been clamoring for weeks to purchase his new crop of "orchids" sight unseen; such was the reputation of the brilliant young horticulturist. But this harvest was not for sale.

He snipped off a tiny quarter-moon-shaped wedge and gently crushed it onto the wire mesh inside the bowl of the stone pipe his mother had passed down to him, given to her one starry night in a meadow outside of Woodstock by the replacement drummer for a band that had once opened for Country Joe and the Fish.

This would be the first pipeful of the new batch that Goodpasture would smoke. He lit a match and let it flare a few moments to burn off the phosphorus and sulfur, then placed the pipe to his lips and toked long and slow. The oxygenated smoke passed cleanly through the wire screen, along the smooth stone walls of the pipe, down Goodpasture's trachea and into his lungs. Instantly a feeling of well being infused his senses. He noticed the banana trees dancing in the wind, their jagged leaf tips catching the points of sunlight that leaped from leaf to leaf like balls of mercury. Yes, this crop will do very well, he thought. He visualized the faces of the patients at Dr. Alton Schwimmer's hospice when he arrived there on Christmas Day with his special 'boughs of holly' with which they would deck their halls. It was absurdly sad to him that nature's benevolent palliative should be deemed illegal. They loved Goodpasture up there. They called him Robin Hoodpasture.

He brought his shears and sealing apparatus up to the drying shed on the tiered hillside behind his Topanga Canyon home. The house had been built in the 1920s for a local oil baron, who had commandeered telephone poles and railroad ties and had them pounded into the bedrock as foundations. The back shed had been used to store his extensive collection of pornography. Later it was converted to a studio and atelier for its long-time second owner, the water colorist, Ruth Ashton-Hayes, before evolving into its present incarnation. Goodpasture spun the tumbler of the combination lock and punched in the eight-digit security code. He waited for the electronic response and punched in a four-digit reply. He rolled up the corrugated-steel safety cage and braced himself for the deluge of redolence that would envelop him from the two hundred plants he had hung upside down on the rafters to dry.

The thieves had left the room spotless. Not a leaf remained. Not a bud, not a stem, not a mote of resin. Nothing.

TWO

THE PHONE RANG too early for it to be good news. Stein pulled himself out of a blurry sleep onto one elbow and waited with dread to hear his ex-wife's voice on the answering machine with an urgent message about some appointment she had forgotten to tell Stein about that would require his rearranging his schedule to accommodate her. Their joint custody arrangements were already as gerrymandered as a crooked political district. Angie, their fifteen-year-old daughter, stayed with Stein half the week and alternate weekends, then with Hillary the rest of the time unless something unexpected came up, which it almost always did. All these years divorced and he was still her first call in any crisis. It drove him nuts.

But it was not Hillary calling. It was worse in a different way. It was Mrs. Higgit from the warehouse. Her voice cut through him like a fish knife. There was a serious problem, she was saying. The inventory count of shampoo bottles that Mister Stein had just completed was short by a thousand cases from the amount the computer said should be on hand. Mister Mattingly was extremely upset and wishes Mister Stein-on to call back promptly. Mrs. Higgit put extra syllables into words to emphasize their importance. She pronounced Stein as if it rhymed with lion.

Stein sat perfectly still lest his breathing betray his presence. He had spent the last fourteen days in an airless warehouse hand-counting a quarter-million empty octagonal plastic designer shampoo bottles. His skin reeked of polypropylene. It leeched out of his hair, permeated his sheets. He smelled like he had been stored in Tupperware. So, no. He was not going to call back promptly.

He creaked out of bed and pulled on a pair of sweats. The framed picture of him with John and Yoko taken twenty-five years ago today—on his twenty-fifth birthday—hung on the wall above his dresser. Half his life had passed since then, and nineteen years to the day since John had been killed, December 8, 1980. Stein's beard in the photograph was longer than his hair was now. He felt the ghost of his amputated ponytail. He padded down the hallway to Angie's room and knocked.

"Are you up?" He tried to make the prospect sound pleasant.

Her monosyllabic answer splattered against the inside of her door like a thrown object. "NO."

"And good morning to you, too," he bowed, and continued down the stairs to make her breakfast.

Stein's ancient arthritic terrier, Watson, had peed on the tile floor again, so on Stein's first step into the kitchen his leg skated out from under him and he had to grab onto the counter to keep from wish-boning. His flailing arm knocked over the container of milk that Angie had left out despite Stein's reminding her a dozen times the previous night to put it away, and her assurance that she would. A stream of white lava flowed along the counter toward the rack of washed dishes. Stein lunged from his knees and just managed to swoop the dish rack up before the advancing white liquid tongue lapped over its edge. He knelt there in full extension, holding up the dish rack like an offering from a supplicant at the altar of Chaos. He wondered who those people were whose mornings began with freshly squeezed orange juice, pressed shirts and a crisply folded newspaper.

Watson was asleep alongside the heater vent in the living room. Stein unwound his leash from the front door handle. The sound awakened in him a deep Pavlovian response, and he tried gamely to scramble to his feet. His lame hind legs splayed out behind him like someone trying to use chopsticks for the first time. Stein gently lifted Watson's bony, urine-stinking rear end and wheel barrowed him down the front steps into the semi-circular courtyard of their cozy little fourplex in the Fairfax District. It was a dank and cool morning for Los Angeles. Two joggers in their sixties clomped through the mist discussing their portfolios. One was in diversified mutual funds and wore hundred dollar Reeboks. The other had a headband and rental property. Stein had ten extra pounds around his middle and no investments. Watson could no longer lift his leg and had to squat like a girl.

The phone was ringing again as Stein eased Watson up the stairs and back inside. This time it was the voice of Mattingly himself on the machine. Stein could see the squeezed throat and pinched lips that produced the panic in Mattingly's voice. He was sure the missing bottles had been hijacked and that a knock-off version of his Espé "New Millennium" shampoo was going to hit the streets before the release of the real thing. He implored Stein to please please please please please call in as soon as he could.

People like Mattingly sapped Stein's soul. Wasn't it obvious that a discrepancy as neat as a thousand cases was not going to be the result of a 'hijack' but rather a transposed decimal point in one of a hundred tedious mathematical operations? Stein had enough trouble explaining the world to his daughter; he wasn't going to waste time on strangers. Especially strangers who made fifty times what he made.

Angie's platform shoes clomped across her bedroom floor above his head, and Stein realized he hadn't started her breakfast yet. He poured a teaspoon of olive oil into a cast-iron frying pan and diced an onion to brown. Then he cut up the leftover baked potato from last night's dinner into little squares and threw them in with the onions to make home fries. Getting into a good rhythm, he heated the griddle and whisked the egg white into a bowl of pancake batter then added his secret ingredient, vanilla extract, and ladled the first batch onto the skillet.

"Hey, Dad."

Angie tromped into the kitchen and splayed her books out across the table. Her hair was reddish-orange today. Stein became agitated when he saw her doing homework. "You told me you finished everything last night before I let you watch TV."

"I forgot we had a history paper."

"You *forgot?*"

"Comparing *Woodstock* and *Woodstock II.*"

"Your school legitimizes *Woodstock II? Woodstock II* was a completely bogus event staged by people who were too busy making money to be at the real Woodstock."

"Chill, Dad. It's only school."

"It's not only school. Philosophically, there can't be *anything* 'II.' Every moment is its own discrete event. Would you call ten minutes from now NOW II?"

"What about *Home Alone II?* Or *Shrek II?*"

"That's just my point."

"What about World War II?"

"What about telling the truth when I ask you about school work?"

"Something's burning."

Stein whirled around into the kitchen as the pancakes became galvanized into hockey pucks. "Have your juice, I'll make another batch." A car horn tooted outside. Angie swept her books up into her backpack and clambered to the door. "Bye Watsie," she said, in that sweet voice that Stein remembered was once, long ago, also for him.

"Angie. You can't go to school without breakfast."

She glanced back at him, standing in the doorway with a spatula and a worried look. "You're becoming your mother," she said. Her friends honked again.

"Who's driving?"

"That underage kid who lost his license for driving drunk."

"Angie!"

"Pick me up at three-thirty."

She bounded down the four steps into the courtyard and disappeared through the invisible curtain into her life. Stein didn't want to be disappointed that she had forgotten his birthday. He wanted to be forgiving and tolerant and to blame Hillary for not reminding her. One of the collateral damages of divorce is the loss of the person who explains your shortcomings in a way your children can love. When he saw the envelope sticking partway out of his mail slot he got all gooey inside. Aw. She had remembered after all. Just when you think they've let you down, they come through. He opened the envelope without tearing the flap, preserving every part of the gift as an icon. The card was a reproduction of the cover of Stein's famed underground book on cannabis cultivation from the seventies, *Smoke This Book*. That made him frown. He had tried to hide that chapter of his life from her. Taped inside the fold of the card was a professionally heat-sealed plastic bag. And inside the bag was a long, graceful, sea-green bud of sinsemilla. The card was unsigned. Ok, so this was not from Angie.

He did not find the joke amusing. Anyone who knew him knew of the Joint Custody agreement that Hillary had rigorously enforced enjoining Stein from engaging in any "actions deleterious to the well being of the child." Under the threat of losing Angie, Stein had traded in his VW Bus for a Camry, given up old friends, old habits, a pony tail, had taken on an excruciatingly mind-numbing job with a re-insurance company, and had not smoked dope in seven years. It irked him that whoever thought this was so cute should have known better. When the phone rang yet again Stein was too preoccupied and forgot not to answer. "Thank God I caught you," Mattingly gushed.

THREE

CULVER CITY was depressing even on days you weren't changing decades. Railroad tracks sprang up out of nowhere and disappeared under chain link fences that concealed small factories and warehouses, whose alphanumeric names gave no hint of what they made or did. It reminded Stin of the surly east coast towns you'd have to drive through with your parents on the way to the beach, populated by sullen teenagers who looked like they could beat up your father. Stein leaned his arm out the window. He didn't like air conditioning. He had changed out of his faded New York Giants sweats into the uniform he wore every day, Levis and a blue work shirt. Stein used his card key to open the steel gate allowing him to enter the inner parking lot of Espé Warehouse #23, the five-story structure he had hoped never again to see.

Technically, Stein did not have a boss. Technically he was an independent contractor retained by the product liability firm of Lassiter & Frank, overseen by its CEO, a contemporary incarnation of Oscar Wilde's Lady Bracknell. Mrs. Millicent Pope-Lassiter. Therein, through an intricate contortion of leasebacks and loan outs, Stein's services were dealt to a succession of their clients, of which Espé Cosmetics was the most recent. Sadly, counting a warehouse full of shampoo bottles was not the worst he'd endured. In the wake of the 1994 earthquake, he had been assigned to catalogue the missing limbs of a display yard full of Plaster of Paris statues of Napoleon. He had hand-tested the comparative tensile strengths of ten different brands of dental floss. He had verified the symmetry of a shipment of staples. But he drew the line at doing the same thing twice. He had hurried but not rushed to get this job done before midnight last night. He wanted the business of the first fifty years done. He didn't want anything hanging over.

The atmosphere inside the warehouse was thin with already-breathed air. It made Stein light-headed. From the ground floor looking up it was a gigantic beehive. The walls were honeycombed with hundreds of thousands of compartments, each holding one octagonal shaped bottle that would soon be filled with 12.6 ounces of Espé "New Millennium" Shampoo, the most highly publicized, gigantically hyped liquid since Classic Coke.

Stein took the elevator up to the third floor where the executive offices were housed. "Thank God you're here," Mattingly gushed. "I have such a headache I'm giving birth to my brains." He herded Stein into his office and sat him in the good chair alongside his Lucite kidney slab desk. A cluster of uniformly sharpened pencils stood at attention inside a silver cup alongside his telephone. If there were any justice, Mattingly should look wasted and decrepit for all his fretting. But his skin was smooth and his sandy brown hair was combed into a high school pompadour. He looked easily fifteen years younger than Stein, though they had to be roughly the same age. Their daughters were classmates at The Academy, the annoyingly smug private school that Hillary had insisted upon Angie attending.

Mattingly had struck gold as the result of two blind acts of luck. The first was the arrest and conviction of his erstwhile employer, Mister Rudy Esposito, founder of the Esposito Home Cleaning and Laundering Service. Mattingly had been so naïve, he believed that when he had made the rounds "picking up laundry" he had actually been picking up laundry. When Esposito fell prey to a rare form of pancreatic cancer, ironically induced by the vats of cleaning solvents that were kept on the premises for show, Mattingly, who was the only unindicted employee, was left in charge of a factory that produced no goods and a distribution system with neither outlets nor customers. In this rare moment of karmic equilibrium his abilities were perfectly matched to their responsibilities

The second chime tolled for him in the person of a flamboyant, twenty-three-year-old hairdresser named Michael Esposito. Michael was the distant cousin of the self same Rudy Esposito. He had quit his most recent job as a stylist at Pavane, the trendy Palm Springs beauty salon, after a nasty breakup with his older lover-mentor, Paul Vane, who was also the shop's proprietor. Michael Esposito had brought with him the secret formula for the hair and skin products that had made Pavane famous, and which Paul Vane, either out of generosity or desperation, had conferred upon him as his divorce settlement.

Esposito offered Mattingly an equal partnership in the product he would develop in exchange for use of the dormant facility in which he would manufacture, store and distribute it. Mattingly nearly had turned the offer down, but his pretty blonde wife knew Paul Vane's name from some of her friends whose husbands were on the fringes of show business, and prevailed upon her husband to accept. The new company was born under the single-word name by which Michael Esposito now called himself: "ESPÉ."

Within two years, the Espé flagship product, "New Radiance"

shampoo had grabbed a gigantic thirty percent share of the market. At first Mattingly had been properly embarrassed at his vast unearned success, but when he was declared a marketing genius by *Business Week* and when *Entrepreneurs Today* called him a visionary, he traded in his Ford for something beige and German, he moved his family out of Sherman Oaks into Brentwood, and he became a person who, when eighty dollars worth of empty plastic shampoo bottles were missing, felt that a profound injustice had been done him.

No dramatic gesture would make Stein happier than to walk directly to a corner of the room, lift up a blanket concealing the "missing" thousand cases, and leave without ever changing pace or speaking a word. Instead, he did the second best thing. In a grandiose flourish that only can come when spending someone else's money, Stein authorized full replacement value for a thousand cases of missing bottles, he added in shipping and handling and bookkeeping expenses, thus bringing the total to a whopping three hundred dollars, then threw in a sarcastic wear and tear bonus for Mattingly's injured psyche, and tore off a check on the Lassiter and Frank account for fifteen hundred dollars.

"Okay? Are we happy now?" he said, and spread the check before him. "Is there harmony in nature?" He made for the door.

Mattingly sulked. "I need the bottles back."

"Tell me you're not serious."

"They're valuable."

"Health is valuable. A sense of humor is valuable."

"They have the Espé logo on them."

"They're *empty!*"

"You're missing the point."

"You can't make a point by rubbing two bad ideas together."

"People can fill them with anything and sell it as Espé."

"It's shampoo! It's soapy water. Who gives a flying fuck?"

A thin, oboey voice emerged out of the shadows. "It's not just shampoo. It's a commitment to planetary responsibility."

Stein turned to see a young man in his twenties with a slight, almost furtive, build emerge from the shadows. He cocked his hip and gave Stein the long once-over through his smoky dark eyes. "I know what you're thinking," he said. "That I'm just an opportunistic little whore who fucked Paul Vane and took his formulas."

Stein regarded him with polite disregard. "Perhaps if I knew you better."

"This is Michael Esposito," Mattingly clarified. "Espé himself. The inventor of New Millennium shampoo."

"Ah, the boy-genius," said Stein, with irony whose teeth left no impression. "First of all, the new millennium doesn't start until next year. 2001. The first year was not called Zero." He was weary trying to convince people and let it drop.

Paul Vane's protégé was a back-alley boy who still had some bends in his soul, the kind who never would be happy with anything honestly come by. "You think because he was older than me and established that I had nothing to do with developing the formulas," Espé pouted. "That's what everyone thinks. But you're wrong. I was his inspiration. He made them to attract me. Now he regrets giving it all to me in our divorce and wants some of it back. He wants *me* back. That's why he stole the bottles."

Stein called Mattingly by his first name as though they were friends, a condition Mattingly desperately desired. "John" he said. "I'll go to two thousand but you're way out on a limb."

"I'm sorry. I have to have the bottles."

"You're really going to make me look for them?" He restrained himself from putting into words what his tone clearly implied— You anal compulsive little fuck. When I find those bottles, and I will, I'm going to shove every one of them up your ass. "Go get me your paperwork," he said meaning it as a punishment.

Mattingly smiled at the word *paperwork*, and Stein had the instant feeling of dread that he had said the wrong word to the wrong person. Mattingly had hard-copy documentation of every step of each bottle's life cycle; from bulk plastic to molding to labeling to embossing; from factory to warehouse. He had purchase orders, bills of lading, quality control numbers, computer codes all in sequence. He recalculated his own totals and checked them against Mattingly's.

Still, the missing bottles could not be accounted for.

Additionally, Mattingly had assembled the foremen and shipping managers whose signatures had appeared on each color-coded copy and had them verify that they had indeed received or sent every order that bore their name. All were present with the exception of a loading-dock foreman named Morty Greene. Today was Morty's day off, but a call had gone out for him to report. Mattingly gave Stein a slip of paper with Morty Greene's address and phone number and Stein staggered out of the warehouse looking like the sole survivor of a horrendous mining explosion.

In the parking lot, hot chalky sun assaulted Stein's senses. A well-dressed man in his early thirties was standing alongside Stein's Camry. He had a swimmer's build and his even white teeth sparkled with a sincere greeting. "Do I have the good fortune of speaking with Harry Stein?"

"I don't know about the pleasure part, but I am Harry Stein." His mental picture of Morty Greene had been more in the squat,

Jewish accountant mold. Mattingly's minions had apparently reached him. "How did you know I was here?"

"I followed you," the tanned smile brazenly admitted. "After the birthday gift I left at your door I hoped you'd be glad to see me."

"What are you talking about? You're not Morty Greene?"

The young man reached out a suntanned, blond-haired arm, at the end of which was a robust, respectful, genuinely pleased handshake. "My name is Brian Goodpasture. Could you spare me twenty minutes of your life?" He placed a check into Stein's hands in the amount twenty thousand dollars and nodded toward the vintage Mercedes convertible that was parked alongside Stein's Camry.

"A thousand a minute. Yeah, that's about my usual rate."

EARLY ACOUSTIC DYLAN blasted out of Goodpasture's quadraphonic speakers as they motored through pre-Christmas Beverly Hills. The interior upholstery was creamy leather. The seat back adapted to Stein's contour, and a subtle mechanism massaged his acupressure points. "Nice wheels," Stein said.

"Of course it's not a '69 green-and-white Volkswagen bus with tinted windows and a special air-conditioning system that filtered cannabis smoke clean in seconds, and a steering wheel made from the neck of a guitar busted on stage by Pete Townsend."

Stein regarded the young man warily. Flattery was flattering, but he was uncomfortable with people knowing more about him than he did about them. And Goodpasture was, apparently, a Stein archivist. He fondly recounted the tales of Stein's legendary youthful antics; the cannabis "Victory Gardens" he had planted on the grounds of LA police stations, the "Pot-in-every-Chicken" dinners he had perpetrated on the state legislature, and of course the time he had saved the asses of two icons of British rock and roll by taking the kilo of Afghanistani hash that someone had planted in their guitar cases and molding it into a pair of skis that he carried under the noses of the alerted Swiss customs agents at Zermatt.

Stein had to hand it to the kid. He had done his homework. "It wasn't actually the Liverpool Lads," Stein confessed. "But it tells better that way." A display of Santa's sleigh pulled by eight flying smog deer hung over Wilshire Boulevard, tethered on either side to palm trees. Russian hookers pressed their noses against the windows of Cartier and Armani showrooms. "Beverly Hills Christmas dreams," Goodpasture said.

Stein glanced at the time. "Was there a particular place we were going?"

"I thought anywhere away from the warehouse would be a step up."

"True that."

"It just so blows my mind to be driving with you. I feel like Dylan when he met Woody Guthrie."

"Guthrie was on his deathbed."

"Well, except for that part."

"And he told Dylan to go to hell."

"I hope except for that part too."

They pulled into the elongated parking ramp that lay parallel to Santa Monica Boulevard and waited for a woman in a Lexus to finish a phone call, a manicure and a café latte before vacating the parking place. The eye makeup she could do while driving. Goodpasture shut the engine off and swiveled in his seat to face Stein squarely.

"I lost something valuable. All the people I talk to say you're the man to help get it back."

"People?"

"People who know these things."

"Things?"

"Things agricultural."

"Ah."

Stein felt a nostalgic glow for those elliptical conversations you had when you were worried about being bugged by the FBI. "You must have old information," Stein said. "I don't know those people anymore."

"They still know you."

"If they did, they'd know better than to ask."

Goodpasture went on discreetly. "I'm aware of your *family responsibilities*. There'd be absolutely no danger involved. You would not be abrogating any preexisting covenants."

"What do you know about my preexisting covenants?" Stein felt like his low sperm count had been posted on a billboard.

"No actions deleterious to the well being of the child."

"Who the hell are you?"

"A lot of my clients are attorneys," Goodpasture confessed. "One of them negotiated your divorce."

"My lawyer or hers?"

"You didn't have one."

Stein was getting ready to pop this kid. Except that he was so damn engaging. "I'm good people, Harry. Sorry. I know you don't like to be called Harry. But I don't know you well enough to call you Stein, and *Mister Stein* sounds so, you know. Dr. Alton Schwimmer will vouch for me."

Stein took a step back and surveyed the kid intently. Invoking the name of the legendary Alton Schwimmer carried gravitas. Stein had never met the medical vigilante, but you had to admire anyone who had the balls to bring a little dignity to the dying.

"The crop I grew was earmarked for his hospice," Goodpasture went on. The people who stole it intend to exploit it for commercial purposes. That's wrong. Don't you agree?"

Stein gave a cautious, non-verbal yes

"I'm pretty sure I know where to find it. When I do, all I'd want is for you to authenticate that it comes from the same crop as the orchid I gave you."

"I see. Kind of like an art expert."

"Exactly! With your reputation your word would be law." He wrung Stein's hand. "They all thought you had gotten too old, lost the spark. I *told* them they were wrong." He clenched his fist and quoted Stein's motto that was the ethos of the sixties. "Give 'till it feels good."

He had gauged Stein's response incorrectly.

"You make this hard for me. If I had a son who was a dope dealer I'd want him to be exactly like you. But I have to say no."

Goodpasture persisted with restraint. "Once again, you have my complete assurance that this will be purely an insulated, isolated occurrence."

Stein nodded toward the digital clock on the dash. "You said twenty minutes. Are you a man of your word?"

Goodpasture accepted disappointment with grace. They drove back to the warehouse in not unpleasant silence, and arrived on the stroke of the twentieth minute. Stein handed back the check as he got out of the car. Goodpasture refused to take it. "The deal was your time, not your agreement."

Stein appreciated the gesture. He liked the kid. "It would be interesting to see what happened if I tried to cash it."

"You'd see I'm a man of my word."

"Really."

"Really."

It was deliciously tempting. He again tried to return the check. Again Goodpasture refused.

"When I'm old I'll be able to tell my grandkids that Harry Stein is walking around with an uncashed check of mine."

"I'm sure they'll be impressed. You better take this, too." Stein handed the bud back to him through the driver's side window, still in its plastic seal.

"You didn't open it?"

The next motion happened more quickly than the eye could register. Goodpasture tore open the plastic seal and brought the bud up under Stein's nose. "Tell me what you smell," he exhorted. "Tell me its life story."

It was reflex. Stein inhaled deeply and the genetic secrets of Goodpasture's orchid manifested to him. "Humboldt Super Skunk on the maternal side. Crossed with Shiva Shanti. Grown in a hydroponic mixture of nitrates and organic phosphorus."

"I grew them from heirloom seeds of your *Heavenly Hillary*," Goodpasture exulted. "Then cloned them. These are your grandchildren!" He pushed the bud back into Stein's hand and hit the accelerator.

Stein ran a few steps after him in pursuit. "What am I going to do with this?"

"You'll think of something," Goodpasture sang back. As if they had been friends for years. As if he knew they were already partners. "Happy Birthday."

FOUR

NATURALLY, Morty Greene lived way the hell on the other side of town, in Silverlake. There must be a rule that wherever you are in Los Angeles you're always as far away as possible from the next place you have to be.

He resented freeways and had a low opinion of people who used them. It was like wearing a suit or following a recipe. It existed before you existed. You did nothing but blindly follow a predetermined path. He liked to imagine he was letting the winds take him. He drove east on Pico, past the still unreclaimed buildings that were burned out during the '93 riots, their orange and black steel torsos looking like a junkie's bad teeth. He turned north on La Cienega, underneath the freeway overpass that came down in the '94 earthquake, then east again through Koreatown where another huge sinkhole had caved in under a street where they were trying to dig a tunnel for a subway.

Only in Los Angeles would it seem like a good idea to send electrically powered trains carrying thousands of people through tunnels spanning earthquake faults that were marbled with pockets of flammable methane. It's Pompeii, Stein thought. Years from now, school kids will gawk at the site where the "City of Angels" once had been and they'll ask their teachers, *Why did they stay? Didn't they have enough warning? Were they just stupid?*

Stopped at a light on Beverly, a black and white LAPD cruiser pulled up alongside him. Stein took a casual glance at the typical pairing of rookie and vet. The kid looked about twelve. Crewcut, square jaw. Avaricious chin. His partner was thirty years older and had grown out of all those youthful vices. A whiff from his right side made him suddenly hyper aware of the bag containing Goodpasture's orchid that sat out in plain view on the seat alongside him. His heartbeat accelerated. Very subtly and looking everywhere but at the cops, Stein shifted position and brushed the bag off the seat onto the floor. He knew that rolling up his window or too obviously avoiding eye contact with them would register as a red flag and arouse suspicion. Cop wisdom was that the only people who tried to hide something were people with something to hide. So he ventured a normal citizen's half-nod over his left shoulder to acknowledge them. By this time, the light had changed and they drove away without giving him a glance. Following the flood of relief was the outrage that they had perceived him as so undangerous. Didn't they know who he used to be? He had the urge to buzz up alongside them wave the bag of weed, say, "Look what you missed!" and then disappear into thin air before they could catch him.

He followed Beverly to Temple then hooked onto Silverlake Boulevard. He liked this Silverlake. It was one of the few little enclaves where people still lived un-self-conscious off-camera lives. Mexican car repair shops coexisted alongside Italian family restaurants and neo-grunge gay and lesbian bookstores. Tucked into the hills near downtown, it was well past the invisible line of demarcation, east of which no women of Brentwood dared venture, so there was some hope of its staying uncorrupted.

2992 Linda Vista Place was a Mediterranean style two-story apartment on a winding, hilly street. Stein parked facing uphill and turned his wheels out from the curb; then turned them the other way. He knew that one of them was right, and briefly pondered whether it was of greater virtue to be partially uninformed or completely. The building had an outdoor staircase. Morty Greene's apartment was on the second floor and Stein was panting three steps up. Head down, he plunged onward and did not notice until he was nearly on top of her that a handsome black woman was sitting on the second landing observing his approach. A mop and a bucket rested on the step alongside her. Stein became suddenly aware of the footprints he had tracked on the staircase.

"I'm sorry. Did I just—?"

"Nothing stays clean forever," she said.

"True, but forever sometimes gets to last longer than a second."

"Is there some way I can help you?"

"I'm looking for a Morty Greene. Is this where he lives, do you know?"

The woman looked at Stein without answering. He checked the address again. "Morty Greene? Do you know him?"

"Does anyone truly know another person?" She had a clear, strong voice, and Stein enjoyed being engaged in disputation. So many people these days just told you to fuck off. He amended his question.

"Do you know him well enough to tell me whether he's at home?" Stein asked.

"Does he know you well enough? That's the question."

"You're too good at this." Stein resumed his ascent toward the second landing, mindful of where he stepped. The woman rose to her feet using her mop handle as a cane, effectively blocking his way

"He's not up there," she said.

Stein saw now that she was a good deal older than he had first thought. He was impressed with her loyalty, imagined she had worked for Morty Greene's liberal Jewish mother through all of Morty's schoolboy years and now had been passed down to him. "Are you protecting Mr. Greene or your clean floor?" Stein asked. If he sounded a bit impatient it was not with her so much as this whole Mattingly enterprise that he wanted to be done.

"I might be protecting you." She led his eyes toward an immense pair of boots that leaned against a Ford flatbed pickup truck parked below them in the driveway.

"You're not telling me somebody wears those things?"

"Takes a big man to fill big shoes."

Stein got the picture and had to laugh. "If you knew me, you'd understand how absurd it is you would think I was *the man.*" He showed her the yellow Bill of Lading. "I just have to ask him if this is his signature. Believe me, there's no suggestion of crime."

She never took her level gaze from him. "When a white man comes to a black man's home with a typed piece of paper, there's always the suggestion of crime."

Stein cocked his head at the new piece of information. "Did you say a *black man's* home?"

She mirrored his gesture. "Did you not say you were looking for Morty Greene?"

"Morty Greene is a black man?"

"Oh, my!" Her demeanor relaxed and you could see how she'd be with her grandchildren. "I hope this is your first day out of detective school. Because you may want to choose an occupation where you have a greater natural aptitude."

"Now wait a minute. The name Morty Greene. Does that not sound like a middle aged Jew?"

"Do you have a problem with the name I've given my son?"

"Morty Greene is your son?"

She looked at him the way only a black woman can look at a white man while wondering how they have managed to rule the world. "Why the hell else would I be cleaning his apartment?"

Stein turned around, walked down a step and turned back. "Can we start over, Mrs. Greene? My name is Harry Stein. Forgive the intrusion. Is your son at home?"

Her life expanded in front of her in one long exhalation. "Is my son in trouble, Mister Stein?"

"I really don't think so, Mrs. Greene.

"You may call me Edna."

He bowed slightly.

"Children make us strangers to our own lives," she said.

"I know. I used to have one. Then she turned into a teenage girl."

He sensed her accept him as a kindred spirit. "You want to find Morty, he'll be at the Santa Anita race track. He'll be down by the finish line. You can't miss him."

"Thank you."

"Anyway, most people wouldn't."

He started down the stairs.

"Incidentally, the name I gave him wasn't Morty. It was Duluth."
He stopped and looked back up at her. "See now, Duluth I
would have guessed was a black man."

"Then I predict you'll go far in your trade."

Before he went he had to ask. "How do you get the nickname
Morty from Duluth?"

"You don't. It's short for what everyone calls him."

"Which is what?"

"The Mortician," she said, with exactly the right mixture of
irony, warning and resignation.

THE HORSES WERE COMING onto the track for the second
race as Stein drove into the vast parking lot of the Santa Anita race-
track. He'd have to do this fast. Park. Find Morty. Verify his signature. Drive the twenty-five miles back to the West Side to pick
Angie up at school by three-thirty.

Santa Anita was a beautiful place to lose money. Nestled in the
valley a few miles east of Pasadena, it had for its backdrop the San
Gabriel Mountains. This time of year the snow level was down to
five thousand feet and an ermine mantle of white crested the shoulders of Mount Wilson and its lesser peaks. Flocks of seagulls circled the parking lot and settled on the roof of the 1930's era
grandstand. Stein found this curious. What were seagulls doing
miles from the ocean. But as he watched the throng of players hurrying to get their bets down—men with bellies waddling at heart
attack pace, women carrying bridge chairs, Mexican families with
chains of kids, UPS guys on lunch break—he understood. They
smelled fish.

A big, cheery voice with a Brooklyn accent boomed out as Stein approached the turnstile. "Mister Stein. Tell me that's not you." Stein didn't have to look to know that voice. Woody Avariccio was the purveyor of the tout sheet called "Woody's Winners." Woody had the face of an artichoke, and when he smiled it was like   an artichoke smiling.

"Long fuckin' time no fuckin' see, Mister Stein. You find some alternate source of income?"

"I wanted to leave some for the other guys. How are you, Elwood?"

"Every day in every way younger and wiser. You come out to celebrate your birthday?"

"How the hell do you remember my birthday?"

"Am I just another pretty face or do I know numbers?"

Three Japanese businessmen in identical business suits approached Woody's stand. One of them handed Woody a hundred-dollar bill for a sheet. Woody made change from a huge roll in his pocket. Then the second tourist did the same, and the third. Woody changed all three hundreds without flinching.

"People actually buy these things?"

Woody moved Stein half a step over where they could speak privately. "If you've come here to enhance your investment portfolio, I have some information I know you'll find profitable."

"Just for me and your five thousand closest friends?"

"Don't hurt my feelings." He jabbed his index finger at the program. "This one's private. You wanna go home a happy man, you bet your hotdog money on the seven horse."

Stein glanced down at the program. "Dario's Dancer? Are you

kidding? This guy hasn't won since radio."

"That's why he's 38-1."

"And will no doubt run like it."

"So the uninformed might think."

"I'm actually more looking for a biped, today. A two-legger name of Morty Greene. Any help there?"

Woody's expression turned serious. "Morty Greene is not your type of work, Mister Stein."

"Really. And you say this because—?"

"If that's your level of questioning, it should indicate that you have not handicapped this event sufficiently. And you remember what we call people who chase sucker bets."

"Is he here today, Wood?"

"Let me give you a two-part exacta. One: bet the seven horse. Two: stay away from Morty Greene."

Stein strode through the grandstand lobby toward the finish line where Edna Greene had suggested Morty would be sitting. He happened to glance up at the TV screen at the coincident moment that the horse being led to the gate was the seven horse, Dario's Dancer. His odds had jumped up to 43-1, the longest shot on the board. Stein didn't believe in omens, exactly, although one thing was sure and that was that the universe worked in mysterious ways. Stein thought, not really seriously, about Goodpasture's check in his shirt pocket. He tried to multiply twenty thousand by forty-three-to-one odds but got lost in the zeros.

A year ago, in one of the very few interesting assignments he had gotten through Lassiter and Frank, they had been engaged by the Racing Association to crack a cyberspace betting scheme where a ring of Cal Tech math majors had hacked into the pari-mutuel system and were printing out bogus winning tickets after the races had been run. Stein's instinct was that they were not racing fans and were getting the results online. He concocted a plan of posting fake results on the web page they were using as reference. When they came in to cash what they thought were winning tickets the stewards were waiting for them. A grateful management established a line of credit for Stein.

An invisible umbilical cord seemed to be drawing him toward the Large Transaction window. The teller was a blonde in her forties whose nametag said "Brenda." Stein smiled at her affably. "Just for curiosity's sake, I once had a house account here. I wonder if it's still open."

"Of course, Mister Stein."

"You know me?"

"I'm Wanda." She said it like she expected him to remember.

"Why does your badge say Brenda?"

"Don't ask." A pleasant chime sounded. Brenda or Wanda touched his sleeve with a long false nail. "They're at the post, Mister Stein. Did you wish to place a wager?"

Two films ran side-by-side on the inner eyelids of Stein's mental Cineplex. In *WHAT IF IT WINS?* bales of thousand dollar bills fall on him from above. He buys a real house, Angie grows up problem-free, the sixties return, and Stein, at long last, finds true love. In *WHAT IF IT LOSES?* Stein watches in shame and horror as a team of burly moving men load Angie's furniture out of his apartment and she turns to him with a look that will define him for the rest of his life that says, "*I always hoped Mom was wrong about you.*"

He snapped back into sanity. "No bet. I just came by to say

hello."

"I still have the same phone number."

AN INSTANT LATER, the buzzer sounded locking down the betting windows and releasing the starting gate. Twelve superbly conditioned thoroughbred athletes exploded from the gate in a perfect line. Actually, eleven exploded forward. The twelfth stumbled badly and was only saved from a terrible spill by a heads-up move by its jockey. But he was left eight lengths behind the rest of the field before he had run a step. It was the seven horse. Dario's Dancer. Stein thanked the universe for bestowing the wisdom upon him to resist temptation. He resumed his search for Morty Greene.

As the horses strung out along the back stretch, people all around him were standing on benches, exhorting their horses in English, Spanish, Korean, Chinese. Unburdened by a stake in the outcome, Stein passed through these magnetic fields as unaffected as a neutron sailing through the Van Allen Radiation belt. His radar was locked in on the large, rectangular object the size of a drive-in movie screen that he intuitively knew was Morty Greene's back.

The pitch and timbre of the track announcer's voice rose chromatically at each furlong. As the leaders came out of the far turn into the stretch, he was hitting C-sharp. "Missed The Boat is holding on gamely. Then comes Couldawouldashoulda. Smart Move is third. But from the back of the pack here comes Dario's Dancer. Charging like an express train. They're stride for stride in the last eighty yards. Missed The Boat. Dario's Dancer. Missed The Boat,

Dario's Dancer. At the wire…it's too close to call."

Oblivious to the excitement of the photo finish, Stein tapped the back shoulder of the drive in movie screen in front of him and asked pleasantly if he might be Morty Greene. The gentleman whose shoulder had been tapped rose slowly but continuously from his seat. He was sharply dressed in a tan sports jacket and slacks, hand-painted silk tie, and shoes that wouldn't have left much unused alligator. As he turned around, Stein could see Edna Greene's strength clearly displayed in his eyes. Her other qualities of wisdom and understanding, if present in her son, were far better concealed. Stein greeted him with his charming non-combative smile. He felt a cell memory of the old rhythm returning. It was good to be back in the game.

"How're you doing? My name is Harry Stein."

"I know who you are," Morty Greene said.

"You do?" Then he noted the cell phone on the seat alongside. "Ah. She told you I was coming." His voice sounded rueful.

"Of course she told me. She's my mother. You Jewish boys expect *everyone's* mother to love you the best."

"Anyway, then you know why I'm here." Stein unfolded the yellow copy of the shipping invoice that Mattingly had provided. Another voice interposed before Stein could ask his first question.

"What are you pushing paper at my man? Are you out of your fucking mind?" The source of the second voice stood up. But not very far; He came to the middle of Morty Greene's chest. Standing next to each other they looked like a bar graph depicting the US/Japanese trade deficit. The shorter man had on a blue sports jacket over a tight-fitting silk shirt. His skin was black and smooth, and he had a large bubbling yellow scar on his left cheek that looked like a tomato grub crawling toward his eye.

"This will take all of one second. I just need you to look at this signature and tell me if it's yours. One word, yes/no, and I'm gone."

Morty's full attention was at the giant screen tote board, where the finish of the race was being replayed, and the words PHOTO FINISH flashing repeatedly. "Nope," Morty said.

"No, it's not your signature?" Stein's heart began to race. Had his name been forged? Was there really something going on with these shampoo bottles?

"No, I'm not doing company business on my day off."

"This isn't corporate. It's just you and me."

"Maybe you didn't hear my man over the crowd noise." The smaller man pressed up very close to Stein's ear. He did so by pulling on Stein's arm with such sudden and considerable force that the rest of Stein's body followed in close proximity. "My friend said no."

"I get that it's his day off. I could authorize the company's paying him right now for an hour's overtime."

A roar went up from the crowd as the result of the photo was posted up on the board.

"There's my overtime," Morty said. He pounded his fist into his open palm. The gesture carried the weight of a falling oak. "Damn if that artichoke-face muthafucker didn't have it. Five hundred. Right on his nose!"

Stein looked with disbelief at the tote board. "A friend of mine told me to bet that horse." Stein lamented.

"You should listen to the good advice of your friends," the short man observed. He and Morty high and low fived at their good fortune.

"Morty! You just hit a fifty-to-one shot. Are you really not going to tell me whether you signed this?"

"Forty-five to-one. And yeah. I'm not gonna tell you if I signed it."

☘ ☘ ☘

THE OVERHEAD SUN drove Stein's shadow straight down into the yielding asphalt as he made the long walk back through the parking lot to his car. He berated himself at every step. He had blundered up to Morty Greene without a strategy, without giving himself a way to win. Woody was right. There was a word for people like him. The word was. He had gained nothing, learned nothing, accomplished nothing. It was right that he should have to go back to counting shampoo bottles. That was his level. A man at the top of his game would have gotten what he came here to get.

He leaned for a moment against the polished green hood of a Mercedes Benz. He was startled by the sudden appearance of a man right in front of him, and instinctively catalogued his opponent's weaknesses: What he saw was a man in middle age, looking paunchy and soft, glib but without the bite to back up the bark, speckles of gray in his hair, soft conciliatory body, a man who could be taken. This all registered in a moment, before he realized that he was looking at his own reflection. A mechanized voice ordered him to take three steps back, which he did, and walked rapidly away.

Stein had forgotten where he had parked his car and scoured Aisle D for twenty minutes before he found it in Aisle E. He opened his door and was practically driven to his knees by the rush of aroma that cascaded out. Goodpasture's bud must have come out of its plastic bag when Stein had swept it under the seat, and the sun beating down on the roof for the last hour had turned the car into an oven. Passersby in the next row craned their heads in search of the source. A young boy asked his parents in a loud voice what that smell was. They pretended not to know, but his fifteen-year-old brother looked back at Stein and flashed him the peace sign.

It would mean an extra hour and twenty extra miles, but he had to go home first to air out the car and his clothing. He could not go to Angie's school with the car smelling like this. He could just picture himself getting yanked out of the seat by Sergeant Henley, the 300-pound parking enforcement officer who stood guard at the gate of The Academy, and being dragged by the scruff of the neck to the principal's office.

Weeks later, when he would relate this story and people asked him why didn't he just throw the bud away, he had no better answer than to say he couldn't. It was too beautiful.

🌿 🌿 🌿

Penelope Kim, Stein's tall, slender, twenty-year-old Korean bisexual neighbor, was in the courtyard wearing her blue Spandex yoga togs, bent into her downward-facing dog when Stein arrived home and tried to hurry past her to his apartment.

"Stein!" She called through her legs. "I've been looking for you. I have to pick your brain."

She sprang from her pose and bounded at his heels like a Doberman puppy. Penelope had been an Olympic diving champion at fifteen, and a Paris high-fashion model at sixteen, where under the name "Cambodia" she had posed nude for the famous calendar featuring old and new farm equipment. She had climbed K-2 and had her fortune told by the Dalai Lama. She had been declared clinically dead on two separate occasions, slept with the male and female costars of three major motion pictures and their sequels; and since all that was merely her life, the exotic protagonist of the screenplay she was writing was a middle-aged Jewish insurance investigator, who in her script she called Klein.

"So did you write your five pages today?" Stein asked her.

"No, today's been a thinking day."

"You write and think on different days?"

"They're separate functions. I can't explain it. I need to find out more about what you did at the factory," Penelope said as she followed Stein into his apartment.

"It's a warehouse."

"I changed it to a factory. It's more visual. I can't explain it." Watson was asleep in a shaft of sunlight on the living-room rug. He raised an eyelid, grumbled, and went back to sleep. "Maybe I'll give Klein an old dog. Make the audience worry that he'll die."

"Klein or the dog?"

She giggled. "I hadn't thought of that." She grabbed a ballpoint off his desk and scribbled shorthand notes across the taut pliable skin of her forearm. "Stein, this place looks like a garage sale. Your *feng shui* is all for shit. I'm going to get my friend Fiona to do a complete energy rebalancing for you." Stein looked distractedly from the hand-grouted coffee table to the overstuffed sofa to the fifties pole lamp. "I hate it when you ignore me," Penelope pouted. "I'm too much of a narcissist to take the rejection."

"I'm looking for a place to hide this." He displayed the contents of the plastic wrapping that he had resealed.

"Stein, that's marijuana!"

"I'm aware of that. And now, so is everyone else in the zip code." He explored and rejected several hiding places—under the base of the pole lamp, in the pinball machine, his file cabinet—while giving her an offhand synopsis of the morning's activities.

She looked at him with reverence. "Stein, you pretend to live this boring normal life, but you're out making dope deals, betting horses. Reality *so* kicks fiction's ass."

"Ah!"

He strode triumphantly to the hall closet and tucked the packet in among the helter-skelter shelves of blankets and bed linens.

"No good," said Penelope. "Not enough ventilation. It'll stink up the house."

"It won't stink up the house."

"I vote for the file cabinet."

"It's not a referendum." Her chin and her eyes dropped. "I'm sorry. Penelope, I didn't mean to snap at you." As a penance he admitted, "I can't hide it in my file cabinet. She snoops there."

The phone rang. Stein let the machine pick up.

"I can't believe you still use a landline. Even Klein has a pager."

"You'd give Van Gogh a spray can."

Mattingly's voice came over the machine in a panic. Morty Greene had called in and quit his job. This was enough proof for Mattingly that the bottles had been stolen and he was going to swear out a warrant for Morty's arrest. Stein grabbed the receiver, shouting "Do not!" He didn't know why he would so adamantly defend Morty Greene. It probably had something to do with Edna and that whatever Mattingly thought was right, Stein wanted to be wrong.

Mattingly whispered into the phone. "Something new has come up."

"Do not swear out any warrants. I'll get there as soon as I can."

Penelope had unzipped her legging and was curled into the shape of Infinity writing rapidly down the inside of her left calf. "Stein you are so amazing. You flushed him out! How are you going to bust him?"

"Flushed who out? What are you talking about?"

"Morty Greene?"

"You sure you don't want to change his name to something more visual?"

"Don't condescend to me. I'm vulnerable."

"Then don't jump from one random thought to another and think it's logic."

She watched him resume his search for a proper hiding place.

"Do you know if the bottles have the Espé New Millennium logo embossed on them?" Penelope asked.

"What difference could that possibly make?"

"I know people who were paying three dollars apiece for the *old* New Radiance bottles. New Millennium's would be worth a fortune."

"Ah!" Stein dropped so abruptly to his knees that Penelope might have thought her insight had given him a stroke. He grasped the bottom shelf of the wall unit that housed his stereo equipment—his turntable, cassette tapes, and two hundred albums. "Give me a hand with this."

"I can't believe you still have vinyl," she giggled. "The last living owner of a turntable."

She grasped the sides of the unit, bent her body like a willow, and tugged mightily. The unit creaked toward her, away from the wall. Stein slithered into the space, reached down through the twistings of speaker wire and puffs of Jurassic dust motes. His hand found the mesh door of the unused air-conditioning duct. He opened the gate and reached in. His fingers rooted blindly in the space. He touched something cold and smooth and leaped back, pulling his hand out.

"What!" Penelope screamed.

"It felt like a termite queen."

"You can't have termites in a metal air duct. Let me in there."

She changed places with him, pulled her long black hair back and pushed her lithe, slender body into the narrow space.

"It's like up and behind," Stein guided her.

"I have it. It's not a termite queen."

Penelope withdrew a crumpled cellophane bag. Inside that was another sandwich bag, and inside that a ball of silver foil, and inside that a green, seedy, nickel bag of high-school weed.

"Then I think we can presume your daughter knows about this hiding place," Penelope smiled.

"I'm gonna kill her."

"Like father like daughter."

"That's not funny."

The phone rang again. Stein grabbed the receiver off the hook as if he were grabbing Mattingly's throat. "No warrants! I will BE there!"

"Was that school?" Penelope asked, with her deadpan smile.

FIVE

ALL THE WAY up Sunset into Bel Air Stein carried on a ferocious inner monologue with Angie: Stein as the biblical God of Vengeance hurling bolts of lightning at the offending nickel bag. Stein as the wounded single parent who had given his daughter trust and respect and been deceived in return. She needed discipline of course, but when he trawled back through his own childhood memories for clues of how to dispense it, he came back empty. His own father had been generally tolerant of him from a safe distance, but had never waded through the waters of adolescent fury or attempted to run the gauntlet that led to the heart. Stein senior had been recalled by the cosmic manufacturer with a defective fuel pump after just forty-nine thousand miles. Maybe that was why it felt so weird to Stein, turning fifty. Outdistancing his ancestor made him feel ancient and unprotected with no one out in front blocking the wind.

It was in this agitated frame of mind that Stein drove up the circular driveway of the bastion of smug privilege called The Academy. The white stucco archways, the rolling hillsides of well-mown lawns, the sixteen-year-old kids in their forty thousand-dollar convertibles, the nannies waiting in their employers' Range Rovers, as though their employers ever roved a range—it was like going to a resort. "Club Ed," Stein called it, when he and Hillary argued. He half expected to see an old Negro waiter in a red jacket and white gloves come bustling over the hillside with a rum drink on a tray.

"Hey, Dad."

Angie and her two girlfriends sauntered over. Elyssa, tall, rail-thin, a dancer, and Megan, a vivacious redhead who knew every 18-year-old boy on the West Side. And Angie, her genetics still locked too tightly in the divorce wars for Stein to see her clearly. He recognized too much of himself in her sharp, protective sense of humor, in the ways she contrived not to be an outsider. He wondered if his own desperate needs were so inadequately camouflaged.

"Get in," Stein said, making no attempt to be cordial. He heard one of her friends say "uh-oh," but Angie would not give him the satisfaction of hurrying. She hugged each of her friends, made plans for later, deliberately extending the moment before finally climbing into the back seat, leaving Stein to drive like a chauffeur.

"That was rude," she said.

"What about sitting in the back? Is that rude?"

She mouthed something unintelligible.

"We'll have plenty to talk about it when we get home. I promise you that."

"Whatever."

They drove in silence. Stein occasionally glanced into the rearview mirror to see the effects of his siege. But she had her earphones plugged in, and was no more affected by his feeble sanctions than a sand crab is by the fluctuations of light on Jupiter.

Penelope Kim's door flew open the moment she saw Stein and Angie walking up the courtyard. "I solved it," she exclaimed. "Do you want to hear?"

"Not right now, ok?" He tried not to break stride.

"I changed the Morty Greene character to a woman. But everything else is the same."

"She's a six foot nine inch woman?"

"You are so linear. Do you want to know why the bottles get stolen?"

"Yes, but later."

He fumbled to find the right key.

"The shampoo is just incidental. It's the bottles! This is the packaging generation. As long as people *think* they have Espé, that's all that matters."

He got the door open and pointedly prevented Penelope from coming in. "Later, ok?"

Angie dumped her backpack and jacket over Stein's desk and tromped into the kitchen. "How come there's never any food here?" she peered disdainfully into the refrigerator.

"There's cheese, there's apples. I got Fujis, the kind you like. There's bread. There's pasta. We have to talk."

"I like Galas, not Fujis."

"Last time I got Galas; you told me you wanted Fujis."

"No. Last time you got Fujis."

"What's the difference? They all taste good when you have the munchies."

Everything stopped for a moment. He had taken her by surprise. And himself even more. There was no retreating now.

"What is that supposed to mean?" she asked with hostile nonchalance.

"It means I found your stash."

Her face went through the gamut of adolescent response. From shock through denial and outrage, to defiant attack. "That's a real invasion of privacy. Going through my things."

"The air duct is not *your things*."

"It's not even mine anyway. I'm holding it for someone."

"Oh, that's original."

"Believe what you want."

"What I want is the truth."

"No, what you want is some kind of parental fantasy."

"How'd you even get it in there? That shelf weighs a ton."

"You see? That proves it's not mine. And what were you doing anyway, prowling around the—?"

The phone rang. "Leave it," Stein ordered. He was too late.

"Hello? Yes, he's right here." She handed Stein the phone. "It's Ma."

Stein held the receiver against his shirt. "We're not through talking about this."

Angie took the stairs three at a time. Stein uncovered the receiver and said hello in his talking-to-Hillary voice. He was annoyed to hear Penelope Kim on the other end, and irked at Angie for tricking him. "You're being a pain in the ass now, Penelope. I will call you when I can."

"I'll let that go because I'm large of spirit and you'd regret saying something so unkind to me. I'm calling to tell you that the most beautiful woman in the world is about to knock on your door."

"Don't, Penelope."

"I don't mean me, but thanks."

A moment later Stein heard the click of approaching heels, then a brief pause followed by a tap on his door and a voice as soft as Georgia twilight speak his name. He swung the door open, on guard against whatever potential loveliness that might be waiting there to deter him from his parental task. But even Penelope's warning did not prepare Stein for the shock to his system caused by the intimate presence of such absolute, unadorned beauty. Her eyes were green and vibrant and not afraid to meet his eyes, which fled from her gaze like a squirrel from a fire. She wore a soft white blouse open at the neck, a sixties style peasant skirt and boots. Her hair was the color of a fiery sunset. She offered her hand, which he took. Her skin had an extra dimension of life. "My name is Nicholette Bradley," she said. "I believe you know a friend of mine."

Stein was in near total hypnosis. Still he managed a passable opening line. "That couldn't be possible because if I knew a friend of yours I would know about you. And if I knew you for even ten seconds longer than I already do, I would have asked you to marry me." He counted down without missing a beat. "Nine, eight, seven…"

"I'm Brian Goodpasture's friend."

"Ah." The countdown aborted and he released her appendage.

"I wonder if you'd mind making me a cup of tea." Before he realized that meant she might want to come inside, she had stepped inside. Upstairs, Angie's stereo amped out a Tori Amos CD, her plaintive voice tobogganing through octaves of tortured love.

"Forgive the mess. I have a teenager."

Nicholette moved familiarly through the roomscape as though she had been here many times. Stein became aware of how a person who never met him would perceive the place and the person who lived in it. She found the chair in the breakfast nook where Angie had splayed her books out that morning. "Is this all right?"

"Anywhere you're comfortable. He bustled past her into the kitchen, there rifled through the cabinet above the counter. "I have mint, chamomile, English Breakfast, licorice."

"Or actually, juice would be fine if you have it."

"I think so." Stein knelt at the open refrigerator door, giving Nicholette ample time to come up behind him, drape her arms languidly over his neck, press her breasts against his back, envelop him in the chrysalis of her stupendously luxuriant hair, if that had been any part of her reason for coming here.

"Boysenberry-apple OK?"

"That's fine."

He brought the juice to the table and watched her lips engage with the glass, part slightly to allow the fortunate liquid to pass through, and followed its pilgrimage along the furrow of her tongue down through the shimmer of tiny convulsions below her chin. She put her glass down after a sip and got to her business.

"Brian's disappeared," she said.

He immediately wished that his response had been more clever than "What?"

"He called me right after he left you this morning. We made plans to meet at noon for lunch. He never arrived."

"That was just a few hours ago. Why would you think he's *disappeared?*"

"He's extremely punctual. At twelve-fifteen, when he hadn't arrived, I called him in his car. Then at home. Then on his pager. Then at another private number. I tried them all again at ten minute intervals for an hour. I called friends who always know his whereabouts. As far as I can tell, you were the last person who saw him."

"Miss Bradley, I—"

"Call me Nikki, please." Her fingertips grazed his forearm. The feeling that went through him transcended any trivial concern about whether the act was unconscious or contrived. He would happily live forever in that state of ecstatic anticipation.

"He's lucky to have someone that cares so much about him," Stein managed to say. "But I'm sure he's fine. Why shouldn't he be?"

"You're right. Nobody in the world ever died."

Stein carefully modulated his voice so that its amplitude would not travel upstairs. "Do you think he may have died?"

"I honestly don't know."

"Maybe you ought to go to the police."

"You know Brian's business."

"Still. Death trumps weed."

"He was sure you were going to change your mind. He said if you saw a person in need you would never turn her away. Do you see a person in need here, Mister Stein?"

All of his instincts surged forward to say yes. He could feel the tectonic grinding of his internal plates, knowing that he would have to refuse.

"The thing is, I don't see how I could really *help*. I don't know his friends or anything about him. I wouldn't know where to look, who to call. I don't know what I could *add*."

"If there was something very simple, very specific you could add, would you help?" He came close to touching her hand. He touched the neck of the juice glass.

"What would that be?"

"Would you drive with me to his house?"

Her request was so disarmingly small, calling only for an act of the most basic chivalry and kindness. He made a lame gesture of apology citing the sounds from upstairs. "I'm sorry. I just can't get away."

She took a card from her purse, wrote some numbers on the back and handed it to him. The card was a miniature cover of *Vogue* magazine, with an incredibly sexy photograph of her. "I hope Brian didn't misjudge you," she said.

Stein stood in his open doorway breathing in the wake of aroma that trailed behind Nicholette as she runway-strode beneath the arbor of bougainvillea out of the courtyard to the street. The feeling recalled looking up at the comet Hale-Bopp the last evening it would be visible after its month-long sojourn across the western sky, and the inexplicable ache of nostalgia he had felt knowing that he would never see its light again. Nicholette had written Goodpasture's phone numbers on the back of the card along with her address. Stein had a strong impulse to call him. But that would have to wait until after Round Two with Angie. He climbed the stairs toward her door, which was half open. Tori Amos was still playing and an *I Love Lucy* rerun was on TV. Angie was sprawled out on her bed amongst books and clothes, talking on the phone.

"I thought you were supposed to be studying."

"I am studying."

"We need to talk."

"Fine. Whatever."

"Would you mind? His gesture implied that she turn off the distractions.

"I multi-task."

He waited. And ultimately she hung up, logged out, turned off.

"Tell me about the weed."

"Who was that woman?

"Nobody. A friend of a friend."

"Are you dating her?"

"The weed, Angie."

"You should marry Lila."

"Lila is a friend not a girlfriend. This conversation is about you."

"Of course I've smoked it. Who hasn't? It's not that big a deal."

"It's not that big a deal? Is that what you're saying?"

"If you knew what other people at school were doing."

"This is not about other people."

"But if you knew."

"If I knew I'd be terrified."

"You'd be glad all I was doing was smoking weed."

"I'm not just glad I'm thrilled."

She made that face that said *how much longer into the century do you plan for this to go on?*

"As long as we're being honest, Angie, do you smoke regularly?"

"As long as we're being honest, do you?"

"Do *I?*"

She was giggling at him now. "Mom showed me some of the pictures of you in your hippie days." She grabbed her backpack from the pile of books and clothing and CD boxes on her bed, and after rummaging about in it, found the black-and-white photo she'd been hunting for. "How could you think a beard and a pony tail looked cool?" She draped her arms over his shoulders while they commiserated over the picture.

"Thanks for the Kodak moment. But it doesn't answer my question."

"Which is?

"Do you smoke it regularly?"

"It makes me paranoid and hungry. I don't like it."

"I wish you had a stronger reason."

"You mean like 'Just say no'?"

"If you don't like it and you don't smoke it, why do you have it?"

"I told you. I'm holding it for someone."

"And you promise that is the absolute truth?"

She looked at him balefully.

"Who is it? Who are you holding it for?"

"Right. Like I'm going to tell you."

"I'd like to know."

"Then this conversation has come to an end."

"Do you understand that possession is still a crime in this state?"

"I'll never let them take you alive, Daddy."

WALKING WATSON helped Stein clear his head. Watson was stronger in the afternoons. He could make it down the steps unassisted. His sausage stump of a tail had been a barometer of his personality all his life, pointing straight up as though broadcasting good news to Mars. But last year he had run out into the street and been knocked unconscious by the axle of the mail truck. Though he had recovered most of his functions, he had aged from a fifteen year-old pup to an old dog whose tail was now locked in the permanent down position like it was dousing for water. Stein had always considered Watson to be a four-legged repository of his own spirit, and seeing him so depleted weighed heavily upon him.

Nicholette's visit had left Stein unsettled. He thought of himself as the retired gunslinger in the Western movies who goes out to the barn late at nights while his wife and kids are asleep and unwraps the old Colt .45 from the crèche where he has carefully swathed it in bunting and fur, feeling its heft and weight in his hand, remembering its dangerous, seductive power, but also the promises he made to people who depended on his being alive, and then returning it to its hiding place, along with another tiny little piece of himself.

When Stein mentally replayed the stream of condescending replies he had made to Nicholette he did not feel like a western hero. He felt like an idiot. He wished that someone from the Ministry of Pompous Assholes had come and shoved a pie in his face— a service he had performed during his youth to many others who deserved it.

"You ought to clean up after your pet."

The morally superior voice of a neighbor, a deputy sheriff in the Environment posse, brought Stein back into now. Watson had squirted out a squalid little dump onto a patch of new grass. "What are you feeding him?" she added.

"He's old. Cut him some slack."

"I wasn't blaming him."

Naturally, Stein had neglected to bring the little baggies, the latest industry to thrive on America's obsession with early toilet training. "I have them inside," he muttered. He scooted Watson back into the house and came back out with a baggie, fully intending to perform his civic duty. But when he saw the woman still standing there, marking the spot, he could not give her the satisfaction of having puppeteered him. Before getting to the sidewalk he diverted from his path and knocked on Penelope Kim's door. She lived on the other side of the horseshoe from Stein. Their front doors faced each other across a center courtyard dominated by a tall banyan tree.

"Go away," she pouted from inside. "I'm writing."

"I thought today was a thinking day."

She came to the door wearing slim running shorts and a tank top that clung to her like tracing paper. "I hate when you do this to me, Stein."

"Do what?"

"Make me beg."

"I don't know what you're talking about."

"Nicholette Bradley has been gone for eleven minutes and you haven't told me a word."

"How do you know her name?"

"God. Stein. Do you not exist in the modern world? Have you not seen the last fifty covers of *Cosmo* and *Vogue*?"

Vogue. Stein pulled Nicholette's card out of his shirt pocket. Now the picture made sense.

"Oh my God. Is that what she smells like?" Penelope plucked the card out of Stein's hand and filled her chest with a long Zen breath, one nostril at a time. Stein realized that he had been breathing in that perfume too and was still partially intoxicated.

"She wants to sleep with you, doesn't she?"

"I'm pretty sure."

"You underestimate your power."

Music emanated from Angie's bedroom across the courtyard. Stein felt drawn to obligation. "I should get back."

"Are you still menstruating about her weed? You should send her to Paris, Stein. Let her live on her own for a while. Tend bar. Be an artist's model. It would be good for her. Good for both of you."

"That's so interesting! Her mother keeps suggesting precisely that."

"Her mother has your balls in a bolo."

"Why don't you give Klein a teenage daughter? So I can read it as an instructional manual."

"You say that as a joke."

"Tell me what he does when his daughter forgets *her* father's fiftieth birthday."

"Stein, is it your birthday? Is that why you're depressed?"

"I'm not depressed."

"Oh my God! Of course you're a Sag. How could I not have known that?"

Penelope wrangled him inside and sat him down on one of her silky, cushiony arrangements. Her entire apartment was white. White walls, white curtains, white lampshades, white silk room dividers, white lilies in a white porcelain vase on a white obelisk. She knelt behind him and told him to close his eyes.

"I have to clean up Watson's—"

"Shh."

Her fingertips on his temples felt like butterfly wings that sent sparks of electricity through him. He wondered if being attracted to a bisexual meant that he was partially gay. "Being old is cool," Penelope murmured. Her fingertips manipulated his scalp through the short grey hair. "My high-school teacher told me that it takes a man until he's fifty to realize that his penis is not a weapon but a baton."

"Your *high-school teacher* told you that?"

She was past that and already on to the next thing. "Stein, you just gave me the perfect idea for Klein. The killers use his daughter as bait knowing that he can't help trying to rescue her. She's his kryptonite. That's how they get him."

"What do you mean, *get him*?"

"You know, kill him."

"The character you're modeling on me dies?"

"It's the perfect existential ending, Stein. He's so sixties. Which are so over."

There was a thump and a loud crash from across the courtyard.

"Angie!"

Stein catapulted off Penelope's cushions and out her door. Across the courtyard, Stein's door was wide open. He bounded across the bed of ivy that grew around the circumference of the banyan tree and vaulted up the steps of his landing. "ANGIE!" He bellowed up to the open second story window directly overhead. He grabbed the kryptonite bar lock from his bicycle that rested against the stairs and entered his living room on full alert.

The wooden rack of cassette tapes had been knocked over, and plastic boxes littered the floor. His breath came heavily. There was a noise on the staircase. A leg materialized. Followed by a body in a business suit and a beautiful face. Stein looked up at his ex-wife with a combination of rapidly depleting relief and growing anger. "Hillary?" He allowed his right arm brandishing the iron bar to drop to his side and tried to make his voice sound welcoming,

coming not even close. "What are you doing here?"

"I told you. I was taking Angie Christmas shopping tonight and to see *The Nutcracker.*"

"You never told me that."

She was uninterested in his protest.

"You never even asked."

"I told Angie to tell you."

Nitrogen bubbles popped in Stein's brain. He spoke so civilly he thought his teeth would pulverize. "We agreed not use Angie as a go-between, Hillary. Does this conversation ring a bell? We agreed we would make all parental arrangement directly with each other."

"Are you going to hold me hostage to every word I say?"

"Do you mean are you accountable for what you say? YES! We call that being an adult. Setting an example to our child about integrity."

"Don't spar with me Harry, I'm too tired to pull my punches."

"Anyway, you can't take her to *The Nutcracker* tonight. We have plans."

Angie clomped down the steps at that moment. "What *plans?* We don't have any plans,"

"Well we *should,*" he grouched. "It's my damn birthday." He turned on Hillary. "You should have told her. I remind her when it's yours."

Angie shot Stein a look of pity and mortification a parent never wants to see from his child. "Is *that* why you've been acting so weird today? You thought I forgot your birthday?"

"Don't make it worse by pretending."

Angie strode with purpose to the linen closet, tossed aside the blankets and pillowcases where Stein had momentarily contemplated hiding Goodpasture's birthday bud, then marched back to him brandishing a festively wrapped parcel. "Do you and Watson not have the same birthday?" she demanded. "Does this not prove I remembered?" She tore apart the folds of red and blue tissue paper and thrust the inner contents at Stein. It was a package of twelve rawhide chewies. She knelt and nuzzled Watson. "You see Watsie, I know it's your special day."

"I am humbled in ways I cannot describe," Stein said.

"Why are you still here, anyway? I thought you had gone to the airport to pick up Lila."

Stein blanched. "Is that tonight?"

"Duh.."

He rummaged through a pile of yellow Post-Its stuck to his desk calendar and found the note he was looking for. "Oh God." He looked pleadingly at the clock, whose face was as unforgiving as Hillary's. "She's going to think I forgot."

"You did forget."

"But you know her. She's going to think it's because she's not important enough to remember." He grabbed his wallet and keys, leapt down the four steps, turned his ankle and very nearly went sprawling, recovered and waved back over his shoulder that he was ok as he stumbled toward his car.

"That's your father," Hillary said, "always chasing the six o'clock plane at six forty-five."

At the curb, Stein's neighbor was still eyeing the offending brown blotch.

TRAFFIC on the southbound 405 was tighter than a spastic colon. Stein juked and jived between lanes making up a car length then losing it back. He visualized Lila sitting alone at Baggage Claim, watching the last unclaimed duffel make its five hundredth orbit around carousel. If wishing made it true, he would wish that he loved Lila. Angie was right. She was the perfect woman for him. Goofy and dependable, smart and practical, she had an appreciation of life's fragility and a batty sense of humor. She had been her second husband's second wife. They had had seven good years, then cancer. When the bad end came, it was Lila and not his first wife who changed her husband's bandages and washed him. It was Lila holding his hand as his life ebbed from it, even when his own teenage son and daughter could not. The one deficit that negated all her strong qualities was her obvious poor judgment. She was in love with Stein.

Ninety minutes late, Stein ran raggedly into the United Airlines baggage claim area. Lila was sitting on her suitcase, wearing her red Versace business suit, reading *Cosmopolitan.*

"Good! You're still here," he gasped.

"*Good* I'm still here? No, it's not good that I'm here. It's pathetic. If I had any self-respect I would be home in a hot bath drinking a glass of Merlot."

"You wouldn't believe the traffic."

"You forgot. You can admit it."

"I absolutely did not forget! In fact, I've been making trial runs all week to see which was the best route."

"I called your house. They told me you just left."

"I'm a shit," Stein conceded.

"But you're an *old* shit and you need some pity." She handed him a neatly wrapped little package. "Happy birthday. And thanks for coming up with a really nice lie. I still want to believe it."

She watched hopefully as Stein opened the box. It was the soundtrack to *Woodstock II*. "Angie told me you'd like it."

He nodded yes. "My girls."

🌿 🌿 🌿

DRIVING NORTHBOUND on the 405, Stein was concentrating on eleven different things other than driving, so he didn't see the sixteen-wheeler lumbering into the same lane from the left that he was entering from the right. The blast of its air horn practically lifted his car off the road. Its huge form filled his field of view like an iceberg. He lurched blindly to the right, hit the gas hard, found himself going straight at the median. Lila screamed. Stein hit the brake, skidded and jounced across the steel nubs implanted into the road. The wind draft made the Camry fishtail. The bottom corner of the MERGE LEFT sign sheared off his outside mirror. The truck never slowed. A second blast of its horn dopplered out behind it like a lingering *fuck you*. Heart pounding, Stein pulled to the shoulder and asked Lila if she was ok.

"Am I ok? No, I'm not ok. Look at me." Her voice was tweeting in its upper register. She had been thrown sideways in her seat and her wide brimmed hat knocked askew along with her equilibrium. "If you have a death wish, it's proper etiquette to let your passenger know ahead of time."

"Sorry."

He started up again and drove slowly on surface streets away from the freeway. He was more lightheaded than he realized from the adrenaline rush. He made a few exploratory turns that took them into dark and unfamiliar territory. Lila noticed his uncertainty. "I presume you know where you're going," she said.

"By presume, you mean you hope and wish?"

"Can you drive without your mirror?"

"Who needs hindsight?"

A water tower rose silently out of the darkness; it looked vaguely familiar to Stein and he realized exactly where he was. He had never approached the Espé warehouse from this direction, from the far side of the Ballona Wetlands. He remembered that he had forgotten to follow up with Mattingly about the whole Morty Greene arrest warrant thing and a bad sound emanated from his throat.

"Are we lost?"

He had nearly passed the driveway when he jerked the wheel and careened into a skidding turn.

"Jesus, Stein! Where did you learn to drive?"

"There's a thing I have to do here. It'll only take a second."

"Here? Where is here?"

"Do you mind?"

"Like I have a vote."

He punched his security code into the electronic box at the side of the gate and the wooden barrier arm rose in salute. He came to a hard stop at the glass-doored entrance.

"Do you want to wait here or come in?" He decided for her. "I'll just be a second."

He jumped out of the car and entered the warehouse unchallenged. The outer door was open. The security guard's desk was unoccupied. A game show played on the portable TV alongside the four-inch monitor. It would take a real criminal mastermind to steal anything out of here, Stein thought. Down the hallway leading to the executive offices there were framed posters of the previous years' magazine and billboard ads. The girl was clean cut and heartbreakingly beautiful. Her hair looked too perfect to be human. Except now that Stein had met Nicholette Bradley, he recognized that she was the girl in the photographs. She was the Espé New Radiance Girl.

A light was on in Mattingly's office, and Stein had a foreboding that he was going to walk in on something horrible, like Mattingly romping naked with Mrs. Higgit. He made sure he made a lot of noise and gave ample warning for them to separate and dress. "Hello, I'm here," he called out. "Stop doing anything disgusting." Mattingly was sitting dolefully at his desk. Even the sight of Stein did not cheer him. He extended to Stein the handful of papers he had been clutching.

The sheaf of extortion notes was typed on old-fashioned bond paper. They were short, none more than a line or two. Each alluded to a dire consequence: One threatened to *blow the lid off* the Espé campaign. Another predicted the *Fall of the House of Espé*.

"It's Paul Vane," Mattingly moaned, before Stein had formulated enough interest to ask the question. "The hair dresser. Michael Esposito's ex-whatever. You need to stop him."

"Stop him from what?" Stein was in the dark as to how this related to Morty Greene, if any of it did.

"It's a desperate cry for help." The thin disembodied voice once again emerged from the recesses of the room as Michael Esposito glided out of the shadows. "He sees that he's nothing without me. He wants me back."

"Yes, well I'm definitely the one to settle a battle between ex-lovers. I've done it so well in my own life." Stein bowed and about-faced.

Michael undulated toward him, sniffing the atmosphere around him as if trolling for pheromones, then boldly blocking his path to the door. "I believe someone has already been out to see my ex-lover," Michael declared. "I think we will find that *this* is the business card of Paul Vane." With a theatrical flourish his two long fingers swooped down and plucked the card out of Stein's front pocket. But his yelp of triumph caught in his throat when he saw that the card was not Paul Vane's at all. He turned red as a full-body niacin flush. *"Faltez-moi,"* he gasped. "Mea culpa. Mea *maxima* culpa." He replaced Nicholette's card into Stein's breast pocket and smoothed his shirt.

Stein cut the embarrassment by exaggerating it. "I hope that was as much fun for you as it was for me." And then to Mattingly. "So we have a lover's quarrel … which the interested or disinterested parties will settle on their own. Bottles will be returned. No arrest warrants for Morty Greene. Everybody lives happily ever after and goes to the beach." With a bow and a smile he turned to go, adding a courteous and firm, "Case closed."

The hallway back toward the exit seemed endless. He wanted to be out of here and have this lathering chapter behind him. The security guard was still not at his desk. The TV still played to an empty room. Something caught Stein's attention. A news crew was reporting live from Topanga Canyon where an explosion had demolished part of a home. No injuries or fatalities had been discovered. Luckily no one had been at home. The preliminary investigation put the cause as an outdoor gas line feeding a barbecue pit that had been clogged, leading to a gas buildup. The woman delivering the report had been instructed by her news chief to find some snide humor in this and she did her witless best.

Stein ran back to the car. Lila quickly ended a furtive phone call saying, "He's coming. Tell everyone to stay," and stuffed her phone back into her purse. The next moment Stein pulled the passenger side door open and shoved the keys into Lila's hand. "Take the car. I've got to go."

"WHAT?"

"You're right." He took the keys back. "I need the car. I'll get you a cab."

"Stein!"

He grabbed her cell phone and gave Yellow Cab specific directions and made sure there'd be a taxi here in less than five minutes. "Don't say anything to Angie. I know you guys sometimes talk about me."

"Stein. What is going on?"

His mind was already ten miles away at the top of Topanga Canyon. The photograph of the one known occupant of the demolished house shown on the TV screen had been unmistakable. Despite its having been taken several years ago, and despite the altered appearance caused by the young man's wire-rim glasses and beard, there was not the slightest doubt that the missing occupant of the demolished house was Brian Goodpasture.

SIX

A LONG RIBBON OF HEADLIGHTS skirted the shoreline from its cinched waist at Santa Monica to its sexy outcropping of hip at Malibu. Stein wove through traffic on Pacific Coast Highway like he was running back a kickoff. He saw that he was doing seventy and willed himself to back off the pedal and breathe. The TV news report had said there had been no casualties. Was that the word they used? *Casualties?* No, that was too military. *Injuries.* Yes they must have said injuries. There were no injuries. That was good.

The news report surmised that the explosion had been caused by a clogged gas line to a barbecue. That "some bright [or not so bright] citizen" had kicked dirt over the intake valve while carelessly leaving the gas line open, thereby creating a critical mass that would have required only the slightest spark to combust. Stein knew that was crap. In the twenty minutes he had spent with Goodpasture, he knew that Brian was not a man to make careless mistakes. And anyone who had read Stein's bible on cannabis horticulture, as Goodpasture had bragged that he had done, would grok that the barbecue grill was not there to roast weenies. He didn't know what he could accomplish now that whatever had happened had already happened. He did know he might have prevented what happened had he listened to Nicholette Bradley when she said that Goodpasture was in danger.

He banked right off PCH into Topanga Canyon. For decades this had been a Serengeti of lost souls, a game preserve for old hippies, old bikers, old druggies, old acoustic string players. But lately, a new breed of lawyers and music executives had begun to change the ecology. They were the ones who stayed home from Woodstock and now made enough money to say they had been there. From the hot-tubbed patios of their new big houses that drove the natives back into the hills like coyotes, they gave their friends (one of whom was black) he black power salute, reminisced, delusional, about riding shotgun with Angela Davis at the Marin Country courthouse, leading street demonstrations in favor of The Chicago 7, for Bobby Seale and Bobby Kennedy, McCarthy and King.

The turn-off to Eden Rock Road was completely blocked off by police. Fire engines and TV news trucks orbited in tight rings around them. Lights were flashing all over the place and orange cones closed off the road. Stein drove past the cutoff with assumed disinterest, then parked on the side of the road under a clump of eucalyptus trees. The trudge back uphill had him puffing after very few steps. He would have to take himself in hand, he thought. Longevity was not in his bloodline.

Tucked away at the shank end of the media wall, behind all the sleek vans with their microwave towers, Stein found the converted dump truck that bore the hand-painted logo of NOOZ.COM. Molly Marbery was a complete one-woman crew. Barely five-feet tall and ninety pounds, she was strong as a roadie and lugged whatever equipment she needed on her hip. She was bright and tough, an actual investigative journalist. Of course she'd been off TV for ten years since committing the sin of turning forty.

"Stein?" she said, deliberately very out loud, "is that you lurking under the partial cover of overhanging foliage?"

"Luckily, I wasn't trying to go unnoticed. How ya doing, Mol?"

Molly Marberry and Stein had passed cordially through each other's lives one pretty summer's evening a year or two back. "I like the new hairstyle," he said as he sauntered toward her. "Is it called a pixie cut?"

"Only you would remember when things were called pixie cuts."

"You're still cute as a button."

"Last time we spoke, you were going to find out exactly how cute a button was, and get back to me later that day. Shall I check my service?"

"I guess I owe you a call."

"Worry not. I cancelled that debt long ago."

"What's going on up there?" he asked as if he had just noticed.

"Log on, sign in, and find out with the rest of my followers."

"No residual privileges?"

"Middle of the road sex only gets you so far." She loaded the last of her gear onto the truck and offered him a bone. "It looks like a domestic accident."

"Anybody hurt?"

"Your interest goes suspiciously beyond curiosity, Stein. What the hell are you doing here?"

"Just trying to earn a day's pay."

She considered the possibility of that for half a second. "No you're not."

She cranked the diesel engine and ground the gears manually into first, stuck her head out the window. "Call me."

"Really?"

"No."

She slid into second and was gone.

It was pointless to try to get any closer to the scene without credentials. He scuffled back to where he had left his car and tried to put together what he knew, which was very little: There had been an explosion, possibly accidental. No injuries were reported so he had to deduce that Goodpasture had not been home at the time of the blast. Nor, obviously, had he returned. If it had been an accident, he or someone he knew would have to have seen the news by now. He surely would have come home to survey the damage. But he had not. And that was why Stein's heart was racing.

He did not have to be there to know this was not just an innocent accident, that Nicholette's fears had been founded. Just how valuable was that stolen crop of his? Could the thieves have wanted something more? Had they come here to get it? Had Goodpasture resisted, been taken? Or was it a signal to the absent horticulturalist that they—whoever *they* were—meant business?

The darker thought kept beating at his brain to be let in. It was what Penelope Kim had said about her fictional detective, about his daughter being his kryptonite. He realized that Goodpasture had a kryptonite, too. If somebody had come here wanting something from Goodpasture, and if that person wanted leverage over him, there was one obvious and beautiful place to exert that leverage. Stein took Nicholette's card from the shirt pocket where Michael Esposito had so recently reinserted it. There, in her perfect handwriting that looked like typescript, Nicholette had written her address under Brian's. It was right here in the canyon.

The fog became denser as he followed Old Topanga up above the two-thousand-foot level. It was far less developed up here. There were still bats and owls and every few years a bobcat. There was still an old lean-to perched haphazardly across the stream. And the smell of the air was the way God had intended it.

Stein arrived at a cul de sac that was barely longer than a driveway, called Lilac Elevation. Wisps of fog hung like a lace mantle over the swaying elm trees that framed the only house. It was all French doors and windows, a magical, windchimey, gingerbread cottage. An unpaved semicircular driveway led toward the garage on the side of the house that faced out into the canyon, but Stein decided to park on the street. He turned the car around to face back downhill. He didn't exactly know why. Perhaps to delay going inside.

It was quiet. No stereo. No TVs. Just the breeze and the night birds twittering across the distance. He walked briskly up the inclined drive to the front door. He knocked lightly and called out Nicholette's name, unsure whether he'd be seen as a savior or an intruder. He waited for a reply and then knocked again. The door was unlocked. He opened it just wide enough to lean through, and called out her name a second time and added, "It's Stein."

Ambient light entering through a skylight made the room seem like a fantastical forest. Potted palm fronds reached to the top of the twelve-foot ceiling. Stein experienced the sensation of running water, heard and felt more than seen. A stream to feed the plants, he reckoned. But no, he saw it running across the hardwood floor in a rivulet onto the porch step, between his feet. He opened the door wider.

His heart quickened as he saw the moonlight reflecting off a long stream of water running the entire length of the hall. Light came from a room beyond the vestibule. He walked silently toward its source. The sound of dripping water became more distinct. He passed through the living room and into the dining room. The kitchen was framed in its archway. He spoke her name again, an announcement of his presence, a request for permission to proceed. There was no reply.

The hallway turned and opened through an archway into a circular room that looked like a gazebo. This was her bedroom. It was slightly elevated, open on three full sides to a sylvan glade. Though it was lighted only by the moon and stars, Stein could see that he was not the first stranger to enter Nicholette's boudoir tonight. Cushions were uprooted from their place. Clothes were laid out on the floor and all the emptied hangers in the walk-in cedar closet were pushed to one side. Her shoes were out of their boxes, arranged ten deep in five long, neat rows. The floorboards of the closet had been pried up.

The flow of water was not coming from the bathroom as he had thought, but toward it. He followed the water back through the main room and toward the back side of the house. The kitchen was airy and open, designed in Tuscan farmhouse style. Frying pans and utensils hung from ceiling hooks. Broad hardwood counters ran along both sides of the double sink. The floor was red Italian tile.

Nicholette's tall, naked body was arched backward against the sink. Her skin was bathed in moonlight. Her feet were bound together by rope at the ankles. Her wrists were pulled back above her head and tied to the cornice that framed the window. Her neck was thrown back in an air of Dionysian ecstasy, so that at first glance she could have been dancing or crucified.

The faucet of a beautifully carved brass tube rose elegantly like a swan's neck from the sink and then down into Nicholette's beautiful mouth. Water flowed from the tap in a slow steady stream; just slow enough so that one could keep swallowing. For a while. The porcelain sink underneath her head was filled with water. Her hair was splayed out in the water behind her. One eye was open and one closed. Stein wrapped a handkerchief around his fingers and turned off the faucet. Water continued to gurgle down her chin from those exhausted red lips.

The faucet was embedded so deeply down her throat that in order to extract it Stein had to lower her neck down into the sink so that her face was several inches below the water level. He stood her up straight. Her spine was still supple. Rigor had not yet begun. Her skin felt almost alive. He cut her arms loose from their bindings. Her ear was alongside his lips. He apologized to her from the depths of his soul and promised that he would find whoever had done this to her and make them pay. Freed of its tresses, her body fell against him in a swoon. Her arms draped around his neck in a belated gesture of gratitude.

SEVEN

By the time Stein emerged from Nicholette's the fog had lifted and the sky was bright enough for wise men to read the stars. But Stein felt neither wise nor bright. He had already made a dozen amateur mistakes obvious to anyone who had watched even a single episode of a television crime show. He had moved the body. He knew that he shouldn't have cut her down but he could not bear to leave her in that tortuous position. Partly for her but yes, more for himself. Her body was a finger pointing at him, indicting his cowardice, his hypocrisy. "*Give 'till it feels good.*" What a joke. He heard John Lennon's voice in his head. *Instant karma's gonna get you. Gonna knock you right on your head. You better get yourself together. Pretty soon you're gonna be dead. What in the world you thinking of…Laughing in the face of love. What on earth you tryin to do? It's up to you.*

He wanted to die or to turn the clock back six hours and say yes to Nicholette instead of being the sticky, smarmy piece of condescending crap he had been. After he cut her down he had held her at the waist with the small of her back braced against the sink. This could not have happened long ago. Her skin was pliant to the touch. The possibility entered his mind that the killer might still be in the house or crouching under the grape arbor, watching him. Nicholette's weight shifted against his chest, and for one ecstatic instant Stein thought he had brought her back to life by wishing. But it was only the settling of all those gallons of water in her stomach. He seated her gently on the floor and went in search of a blanket or a robe.

He repaired her rampaged bedroom, gathered up scarves, blouses, dresses, shoes, strewn undergarments and carefully folded and replaced them in her drawers. He recognized a familiar scent bearing from under the vanity table underneath her mirror. Her scent. He avoided looking at his reflection. He did not want witnesses. Inside the drawer was a long, bounteous, full-length wig, mesh skullcap woven inside it. He wondered why Nicholette would need such a thing with that amazing head of hair she owned. He replaced the hairpiece into the drawer and closed it. Her portfolio of modeling pictures had been tossed contemptuously aside. He sat on the floor alongside her day bed and opened the book of enlarged 11x14 color and black-and-white photographs across his lap. He understood in a moment why Penelope Kim had chided him for not knowing Nicholette's face. She had been on dozens, maybe hundreds, of magazine covers. There was something different about her in every picture, and yet they were all her.

A tan manila envelope was tucked into the back flap of her portfolio with the names "NIKKI & ALEX" written in grease pencil. The envelope was imprinted with the photographer's logo—a camera lens with its aperture open like a flower petal. His name was in the center, David Hart. The envelope contained a cluster of proof sheets and prints stamped "TEST". Two models were cavorting on the beach, kicking sand at each other and splashing in the waves. "Nikki" was Nicholette. "Alex" was a dark-eyed waif with her head shorn like Sinead O'Connor.

There was a note pad on her night table. The top page was blank but he could see the subtle imprint of messages written on previous pages. He tore the first few pages off and rubbed the top page lightly with the side of a pencil. He held it up to the table lamp and was able to make out impressions written in Nicholette's calligraphic hand. But too many levels of intersecting words had left their mark for him to make out anything. A metaphor of the information age where the profusion of data creates the illusion of wisdom to the misinformed. He folded the paper carefully between two blank sheets and placed it in his pocket. He returned to Nicholette's body and draped a red and white kimono over her shoulders.

His second colossal mistake was using the telephone. How stupid would he have to be to call his own home? But in the overwhelming presence of death, he had an irresistible urge to make sure Angie was all right. Of course, yes he knew he should have had a cell phone. It was absurd that he didn't. Angie had chided him. Penelope Kim had chided him. Once again, it was all vanity. He liked his image of the low-tech throwback in the high-tech world. Eschewing air conditioning and microwaves and driving a car with crank windows.

Angie and Hillary would be back from *The Nutcracker* by now and no doubt miffed at his absence. Hillary would want to get going, but he knew she wouldn't leave Angie at Stein's alone. It had something to do with setting an exemplary standard of responsible behavior. With each passing minute she had to wait

Stein could hear Hillary cataloging to Angie her father's deficiencies of character. But he knew he could not risk calling. The number would imprint on Nicholette's phone log and when the police made their routine investigation there would be questions. Not to mention the prospect of trying to explain to Hillary what he was doing at a murder scene in the middle of the night.

He was struck with the brilliant idea to call Lila. He'd tell her to call his house on *her* cell phone and say that they'd stopped somewhere for a birthday drink and had a flat or engine trouble and that he'd be home soon. He couldn't think of one at this very moment, but he was confident he could concoct for Lila a vaguely plausible reason for her number to have been called. He held the receiver carefully in his handkerchief and used a pencil eraser to tap the numbers on the keypad. Lila's phone rang four times and then her voicemail picked up.

He debated for a moment leaving a message and decided not to. He pressed the eraser against the disconnect button and contemplated his next move. There was nothing more he could do here. He knew that the perpetrators had come in search of something that they had not found. (Yes, plural. It seemed incontrovertible that this had been the work of two.) Surely it had to do with the full crop Goodpasture's orchids. In all the news reports around the explosion, there had been no mention of a stash of marijuana being discovered. If they had not found what they were looking for at Goodpasture's, their Plan B was evidently to extract the information from Nicholette by force: Where the stash was or the stasher. Her death told Stein that she had been more loyal and stubborn than smart.

Stein knew he needed to return to Goodpasture's. But he could not leave Nicholette's exquisite corpse here to rot. He carefully lifted the receiver in his handkerchief again and tapped in 9-1-1. When the operator answered, Stein gave her minimal information: the address he was calling from and the circumstances of the crime. He did not identify himself when asked to, nor did he stay on the line as requested. He depressed the disconnect key with the eraser. In the very next moment, while the key was still being held down and while the receiver was clutched in his hand, the telephone rang. Stein stared down at the instrument in horror as if he were holding a live hand grenade.

It rang again. His anxiety caused the pencil eraser to slip off the disconnect button, in effect completing the connection, answering the call. Stein's breath caught in his throat. His first instinct was to hang it up and run like hell. But what if it was Goodpasture calling Nicholette after hearing all of her phone messages? He would be alarmed at the hang-up. He'd call again. Getting no answer he could drive over here, just in time for the police to find him and arrest him as the prime suspect. Stein could not do that to him. He needed to break the news to the young man himself. He owed him at least that much.

He remained absolutely silent, except for his heartbeat, which felt like a hollow oil drum rolling down a flight of metal stairs. He hoped that the caller would speak first and give him the advantage. After a few moments he tapped the mouthpiece with a pencil, as if that would approximate some vague mechanical difficulty. But the ploy had no effect. His next idea was to say hello using a Chinese accent. Which is what he actually did.

A police dispatcher was on the other end. She asked if a 9-1-1 call had been made from this number. Stein muttered an indistinct response. She said that a patrol car had been dispatched and for him to remain where he was until the police arrived. Stein hung up without speaking. The phone rang back immediately, but he did not answer it. It rang incessantly as he knelt alongside Nicholette, adjusted her kimono for modesty, and swore to her again that he would find her killers and punish them. Stein drove quickly away from Lilac Elevation.

The canyon road passed through a section of uninhabited land. 12:03. It was tomorrow, no longer his birthday. He was on the downward slide from fifty now. The amusement park hammer had propelled the little disc as far up the pole as it would go. Probably up to NICE TRY, SUCKER. It would hover here for a moment and then begin its long slow descent to plaid pants, ear hair and "pop, you're drooling." He dreaded the recessional. If the next fifty years were a repetition in reverse of the first fifty? Looking backward, what would he have to look forward to? Seven years of divorce followed by fourteen years of marriage during which Hillary and he would become closer every day, more in love, more optimistic, accumulating acts of good will and good faith, refilling his soul each day with that forgotten sense of pure fun, leading up to the first moment he saw her, which would be the last moment, which was the best moment, at the peak of her beauty emerging topless out of the surf on the Greek island of Ios. And then his other life, which would not be bad at all to re-live, when Stein and his subversive cronies were the disturbers of the peaceful, vanquishers of the vain. When he fantasized traveling back in time and never getting together with Hillary, he always got stopped at the realization that it would mean that Angie would not exist, and that ended all rewriting of history.

Driving alone down Topanga, Stein was filled with an urge to blend into the darkness. He switched off his headlights, put the car in neutral and surrendered completely to the forces of gravity and centrifugal force. Freed of the engine's drag, the car picked up speed through the downhill slalom. Stein whipped the car through its turns by the light of the moon. Only able to see yards ahead, the thrill of possible disaster excited him. The road swung to the leeward side of the mountain. The moon was eclipsed from view. He sped downhill in total darkness. The blast of a horn and the glare of oncoming headlights catapulted him back into reality. He glided to a stop at the side of the road. His shirt was still damp from where Nicholette had fallen against him. Her scent still seemed to emanate from it. Was he inhaling particles of Nicholette?

The street sign for Eden Rock Road was carved into the shape of an oaken arrow and almost completely obscured by foliage. The fire engines and news trucks were long gone, since the suspicion of foul play had been downgraded to foolish accident. Thus Stein was able to drive unimpeded into the cul de sac. There was no point in going home anymore. By now Hillary would have to have taken Angie back to her place and he'd have to deal with that unpleasantness tomorrow. Tonight he had work to do.

He parked under an overhang of cypress boughs. His gaze went up, up, up the hill until he saw Goodpasture's house. Adrenaline lubricated Stein's knee joints as he climbed the stone staircase. He reached the first landing without losing his breath and stopped for a moment to look over the parapet. Galaxies of electric lights cut mystical patterns through the San Fernando Valley below. Civilization's accomplishment in ten thousand years had been bringing the stars down to earth.

The pathway alongside the retaining wall took him around to the back of the house where the explosion had occurred. Broken plaster and glass gave the patio a newsworthy look of disaster, but the structure of the house wasn't as badly devastated as the reports had made it seem. The celebrated barbecue grill was built into the red brick patio wall, ten feet long and four feet wide. There was a pile of dirt alongside that had given the experts all the evidence they needed for their faulty conclusions. But as Stein had correctly intuited, nobody had been throwing any shrimps onto this bar-bee. It was all laid out in Stein's book: In the controlled environment of indoor marijuana cultivation, there are no natural predators. No bird to eat a fly, to eat a spore. So even one unnoticed white fly egg, one mold spore could multiply into the equivalent of a locust swarm and infest an entire harvest. Goodpasture had been using the fire to sterilize his soil.

Stein knelt low to the ground and circled his open palm along the base of the retaining wall. He knew what he was searching for and his fingers found the subtle crease under the ivy that concealed the doorway tucked unobtrusively into the concrete wall. It did not look disturbed. He was satisfied that no one else had found it. The hinges were well oiled and the door opened silently. Stein ducked inside. The door shut behind him and the catch snapped crisply into place. A staircase descended into a cavern dug into the granite bedrock of the hillside. Low-wattage light bulbs were screwed into sockets at five-step intervals. They cast wavering shadows the way wax tapers would in the dungeon of a castle. Grotesquely shaped white ginsengy globs protruded into the staircase through the outer walls. The ivy's roots. As the staircase spiraled downward, the lights behind Stein went out and those below him turned on. He resisted the desire to stop, for fear that he would become out of synch with the timer and be left in the dark.

Suddenly the entire staircase shuddered. The words, "Earthquake. Trapped!" spun up into his brain and he clutched the wall for support. After a few moments the vibration steadied into a subtle hum and so did his heart rate. Yes, it was the compressor for the air conditioner. He liked Goodpasture's style. The boy was meticulous. The stair ended fifteen feet down into the canyon at a low door. Stein ducked his head and entered.

The shock of glaring brightness made him cover his eyes until they could adjust. Even then it seemed like he must be hallucinating. He was in a room twenty feet square with an eight-foot-high ceiling. High-powered fluorescent lights were suspended by adjustable chains above four long rows of cafeteria tables. On each table were three neatly spaced rows of sprouting pots, twenty-four to a row. And in each pot there was a marijuana seedling, three inches tall. By rudimentary guess, Stein calculated roughly a thousand little sproutlings in the nursery.

A valve hissed and a large green metal tank in the center of the nursery blew out a long breath of carbon dioxide over the two thousand cribs. At each end of the room a large oscillating fan had been placed on the floor to circulate the air and dissipate the heat generated by the grow lights. The air was vented out the chimney by periodic bursts of this fan. There was another door at the opposite end. It conducted him into another dormitory room organized in the same way, with grow lights suspended above four cafeteria tables.

The plants here were in a second stage of development. Standing eighteen inches high, their slender shoots reached out like the limbs of young ballerinas in stage light. They stood on point; their bare roots nestled not in resin or topsoil, but in plastic containers filled with liquid solutions interconnected by a winding intestine of plastic tubing that carried to them all the carefully apportioned nutrients that they would ever need.

Even in his heyday Stein had never envisioned growing-chambers of this scope. And he hadn't yet reached the grownups' bedroom. A door at the end of the room opened into yet a larger chamber. Plants stood four feet tall with leaves as large as palm fronds. There were occasional breaks in the ranks; and empty pots. These, he knew, had housed plants that had become male and had been uprooted lest they satisfy their insatiable thirst to procreate, to fertilize the females and create seeds. The beauty of sinsemilla is that all that procreative energy is harnessed within the untouched female colas.

He felt another rumbling still deeper below him. He descended into the final chamber, and he knew how the first human being must have felt upon beholding a forest of Giant Sequoias. Two hundred mature female plants, five feet tall and Reubenesque, stood before him in full blossom. The air was thick with their perfume. Mint and burnt sugar. It's Paradise, he thought. I'm in the Garden of Weeden.

He realized that breathing this air was giving him a terrific contact high and that he'd better get out of here while he could think straight. Logic told him that a door would be near the four large green canisters of carbon dioxide. He located the door, ingeniously built into the granite wall. It did not lead directly outside as he thought it would, but into a small anteroom equipped with a sink and a refrigerator and a TV that had been left on and was playing a mindless drama in black-and-white. The man on screen was prowling around a parked car. Stein had a vague sense that he had seen this show before. And then he realized it was not a show but a surveillance camera, and that the car looked familiar because it was *his* car. And a man in a brown suit was peering into it.

Stein opened the door cautiously and returned to the outside world. He was night-blind for a few moments until his pupils readjusted. But he was turned around. He expected uphill to be to his right; it was to his left. The road was not where it was supposed to be and his car was gone. When he looked up behind him, Goodpasture's entire house had disappeared. And now he realized that the tunnel had gone underneath the street, and that he had emerged on the other side. His car was parked directly below him. The man in the brown suit was using it as cover, glancing up at Goodpasture's house. But as Stein was now behind him, he had a clear path to the intruder's back. The man had a small build, trim but not athletic—the type who would row sixty miles on a machine but never go near the water.

Stein unconsciously grabbed his own flabby midriff in his hand. He calculated his advantages. He had the higher ground, logistically and morally. He could walk brazenly up to the man and say, "Yes, can I help you?" But that didn't seem like the most prudent idea if this was the man who had killed Nicholette. There was no way to get back into Goodpasture's house and he knew he couldn't stay pressed against this wall very much longer. His leg was getting numb and he had to pee something fierce.

He shook his leg to restart the circulation. This was his third major mistake of the evening. He lost his balance and began to slide down the hillside. He scrambled to regain his footing but his shoes had no traction. He surrendered to gravity and careened wildly down the hill screaming a banshee war cry. The man in the suit was startled and jumped backwards, pivoted awkwardly, stumbled as he started to run and fell on his ass. Stein's plan, if he had one, was to startle the man into running away, then jump into his own car and—after that it got vague. But with the man falling, Stein could hardly delay his charge and wait for him to start running away again and still maintain an effective pretense of threat. So Stein ran at him, screaming. His quarry went into a complete panic. He rolled onto his hands and knees. His feet were so knotted that he couldn't stand up; so he tried to crawl away. Stein veered to the right at full speed to head him off. His left foot caught in a pothole and his torso twisted ninety degrees while his ankle stayed rooted. Sickening pain shot up through Stein's leg into his gut. He fell to the pavement.

Both men lay writhing on the ground five feet apart from each other. Stein's adversary made another wild attempt to flee. Stein pulled himself onto one leg and hopped fiercely after him. With one desperate lunge, Stein barreled his shoulder into the man's back. His momentum carried them forward, pinning him against the side of Stein's car.

"Don't hit me, I'm a doctor," the man screamed.

"Making a house call?"

"I swear it!"

Stein spun the man around. He was thirty-five, balding, wore glasses, and was slightly shorter than Stein had first thought. He wrested his hand out of Stein's grasp and groped in his jacket pocket. Stein feared the man was going for his gun. But what he thrust at him was a laminated photo ID from the Marin County Medical Board. The name on the license made Stein's spirit soar. He released his grip on the man's larynx. He felt like Stanley meeting Livingstone at the mouth of the Nile. "Doctor Alton Schwimmer, I presume. Say hello to ~~Harry Stein~~."

EIGHT

3:00 A.M., and Munowitz's Deli in the Fairfax district was jumping. The line of people waiting for tables stretched past the appetizing section all the way back to the bakery. Young girls with radical hair and multiple piercings were draped over their indolent boyfriends dressed in their open fronted vests and techno-grunge leather pants with codpieces, and who looked at anyone Stein's age with a smirk that said, We are the pieces of shit who are fucking your daughters you spent all that money to raise.

"What's good here?" Schwimmer asked, when they had been led to a booth.

"You don't say a word the whole way in, you don't even look at my broken ankle, and you ask me what's good?"

"I told you, it was a mild sprain."

"How can you tell it's a sprain without looking?"

"I'm a doctor."

"Don't doctors sometimes take X-rays?"

"You want a second opinion? Ask that guy." Schwimmer gestured toward a biker who was tearing at his meat sandwich in staccato bursts like a piranha.

"Fine," Stein sulked. "It's getting better by itself."

"Oh for God's sake, let me see it."

Stein extended his leg under the table onto the opposite banquette. Schwimmer lifted Stein's foot and turned it sharply to the
left. "Does that hurt?"

"Aaaargh."

"You're right. Maybe it's broken."

"Don't you people take some kind of oath?"

The drive in from Topanga had been maddening. Notwith-
standing Schwimmer's reputation for making death a dignified experience, he had the social skills of a doorknob, and that was being
unkind to doorknobs. He had deflected all of Stein's questions:
*What was he doing at Goodpasture's? Was Goodpasture all right? Had
he been there when it happened? Where was he now? I'm on your side.
If you know where he is you have to tell me.*

All Schwimmer would say was if you're not part of the solution
you're part of the problem, and despite Stein's ardent avowal that
things had changed since he originally had declined Goodpasture's
offer, Schwimmer had turned his back to Stein and contorted his
body into an impossible shell, his elbows crossed around his knees,
which were also crossed. He looked like a torso that had been
hastily glued together by somebody new to the job, and he sat that
way until they pulled into the Munowitz parking lot.

Their waitress who came to take their order was a distressed
blonde whose life had taken a wrong turn off Easy Street.

"I need a minute," Schwimmer said.

"Order a roast beef on buttered white bread with a glass of
milk," Stein suggested. "They'll think you're a regular."

Schwimmer ordered the barley bean soup, which pissed Stein
off because he was going to order that himself. "Make it two," Stein
said. "But make mine better."

Once she had departed with their orders, Stein leaned across the table to plead his case. "Do you not grasp that we are on the same side here? I know what was lost. I want to help get it back." Schwimmer made brief expressionless eye contact. "I see why people come to your hospice," Stein said. "You make death a pleasant alternative." But Schwimmer was not the only one stonewalling. Stein had not revealed to him what had happened to Nicholette and was not going to gratuitously volunteer any information while Schwimmer was hoarding his.

Their waitress returned with their soups. "Who gets the barley bean?" she asked.

The rich, deep, thick brown broth with barley and lima beans and ham mellowed Stein's soul. "Just what the doctor ordered," he joked, as a kind of surrender.

"You weren't my first choice." Schwimmer informed him. The air between them turned brittle again and filled with tiny invisible flying shards of glass. "You weren't on my list at all."

"Apparently you were outvoted," Stein shot back. His ego induced another ridiculous display, yanking Goodpasture's check out of his breast pocket and brandishing it into Schwimmer's face. He tucked it back into his shirt and made a final effort to be reasonable. "I was off the bus. I admit that. But I'm back on. Things have happened." He let that final chord play out its overtones. Things have happened.

Schwimmer was tone deaf to whatever cantata Stein was singing. He counted out of his wallet and change purse the exact amount to cover one bowl of soup, the tax and a twelve per cent tip.

"I should let you walk," Stein said as he unlocked the passenger side door. But grudging politeness won out, that and the nagging belief that Schwimmer would have to relent and spill all. He was staying at the hotel near the 405 freeway with the revolving restaurant. A twenty-minute ride with no traffic. Neither said a word the entire trip, except for Stein who was still trying to put the little tile fragments together into a picture he could recognize, who asked, "How did you *get* to Goodpasture's?"

To which Schwimmer replied, "…"

"Thank you. That is so helpful."

When they pulled into the circular driveway Schwimmer engaged him fully for the first time. "Let me draw you a hypothetical. You are in possession of a piece of information that is of great importance to a hostile party. And that hostile party, in order to induce you to reveal that information, manages to place your daughter into a life-threatening situation. In which direction do you suppose your loyalties would bend?"

"That's not going to happen."

"There are the two reasons I don't want you involved. One: Because it can happen. And two: Because you are too stubborn or blind to see that it will."

☙ ☙ ☙

FIRST LIGHT was just starting to show in the eastern sky as Stein drove slowly homeward through the residential streets of Bel Air. The Japanese gardeners were already out tending the immaculate lawns upon which their owners' feet would never tread. They were like perfect narcissistic gym bodies—great to look at but keep off the grass. Stein's eyes burned. He realized he hadn't slept yet since he turned fifty and that condition was not going to be remedied soon. Today was a changeover day when Angie was scheduled to go to Hillary's. That gave him three days, three uninterrupted, non-custodial days, to find Nicholette's killer.

He drove with purpose into the parking lot of The Bank of Henry Kneuer. He would have liked the moment to be more theatrical; to be observed with the appropriate pomp to mark the circumstance. But it was barely seven o'clock and the doors would not open for another hour.

He unfolded Goodpasture's check, endorsed the back "for deposit", and executed his signature in a manner congruent with the occasion. He placed the check into an envelope and sealed it, inserted his ATM card into the slot and entered his PIN number, which was the month and date of Angie's birth. The steel security flap opened. Stein slipped the corner of the envelope into the slot.

Powerful rollers seized it from his hand. He held to it for a moment, considered what it meant if he let go. The choice he was making. The risk and its consequence He released the pressure between his thumb and forefinger. The envelope rolled down into the slot. The steel trap door slammed shut. Stein the hippie was dead. Long live Stein the warrior.

He was back on the bus.

All the cars on Stein's street were still peacefully asleep, wrapped up to their windshields in baby blankets of dew. Only Stein's Camry was overwrought. Its unrested hood was hot to the touch, its windows streaked with worry and grime. Stein parked across the street and tiptoed up the pathway through the courtyard to his front door. The joggers weren't even up yet. Only the bougainvillea looked wide-awake. In the early morning light, the blossoms radiated like the eyes of visionaries hatching psychotic schemes.

He opened his front door and slid inside. At first glance he barely noticed the crepe paper streamers left strewn about the living room. Watson struggled to his feet and slalomed through the debris. His one-syllable exclamation, like the yip of the first prairie dog, aroused the next one in line. That was Lila. She rose up from the couch in a state of total disorientation.

"Stein?"

Her voice roused another female who had been asleep on the futon wrapped in Stein's American flag blanket.

"Harry?"

"Hillary?"

"Daddy?"

"Angie?"

In her pajamas, encamped on the staircase. All three females arose and descended upon Stein, cawing at him with variations of the same question: Namely "Where have you been?" Salient details began to register in Stein's brain. The ceilings and walls were festooned with decorations. There were hats with the number 50 glued to them. His desk was covered with a paper Happy Birthday tablecloth.

"Was there a party?" he asked

"Daaaad." Angie bent the word into three long syllables of dismay. "It was a surprise party. For you! Where were you! Everyone you ever knew was here!"

"Yes, the entire 'Who's Not Who' of Hollywood," Hillary sniped.

"Mom."

"I'm sorry. I've never heard of anyone missing his own party."

"Mom."

Stein was touched that his daughter defended him. "If I knew about a party of course I would have been here." His voice playing an emotional duet, to mollify Hillary's disdain and reweave the cocoon of intimacy around Angie.

"Yes, well, it being a surprise party, there was the element of *surprise.*"

"Mom."

Angie threw open the rectangular cardboard box sitting in the center of the dining room table to reveal a birthday cake with fifty candles arranged around a now deteriorated portrait in icing of John Lennon, Jerry Garcia, Dylan, Janis Joplin and Stein. "Happy birthday."

Stein's heart slid down his chest wall. "I'm really sorry, baby. I thought everyone had forgotten and I felt so sorry for myself that I stayed at the warehouse counting their stupid shampoo bottles all night."

"You're such a loser," she wailed.

Stein hated that Angie so easily believed he would be so pathetic, though not as much as he hated lying to her. Hillary gaveled matters to a close, telling Angie to gather up her things, that they were going.

"I guess I'll go, too," Lila said, acknowledging that no one had noticed or cared that she was there. Stein walked her to the door and whispered in her ear, "thanks for having my back."

"I don't even know what that means."

"You didn't tell them I wasn't at the warehouse."

Angie clomped upstairs to her room and returned, weighed down by two backpacks and her book bag. Stein tried to find a clear place to hug her. "We'll do something special for my birthday when you come back."

"Whatever."

She stooped to nuzzle Watson's face against hers. "Bye, Watsie."

His heart always ached when she left. His little refugee. But today he could not indulge his sentimentality. He wondered if she wouldn't be happier living at one residence, and if the joint custody deal was more to assuage his guilt than for her benefit.

It was amazing how quickly after his daughter's departure that a profound silence settled into the apartment. As if Angie were its soul and Stein were merely some organ kept nominally alive while the body was in coma. Plopped down on the futon, he idly stroked Watson's head as his mind began to shrink itself around the problem of Nicholette's murder.

His mind slogged earthbound at the snail's pace speed of sound instead of soaring at the speed of light. What did he have? He knew that Nicholette was dead and her place had been ransacked. He knew that Goodpasture was missing, or apparently missing, and that Nicholette had had some inkling hours before her death that Goodpasture was in danger. Stein knew, or believed he knew, that someone had stolen a crop of Goodpasture's orchids that had been grown for the terminally ill patients at Dr. Schwimmer's hospice. Was there anything else he *knew?* Or was this little rabbit turd size pellet of information all that he had? Where would he start? What was his plan? Did he even have a plan? Or was it just another promise that he would fail to keep?

He had to take a first step in some direction. What was that going to be? In the days of Watergate, Deep Throat had advised Woodward and Bernstein to "follow the money." Stein had no money to follow but he did have the trail of smoke. Goodpasture's "orchids" were apparently so good that people were killing people to get their hands on them. Weed that tasty had to be going for a tasty price. He had to find out who in town was paying top dollar. In the old days he would have known everybody. Even better—they would have had to know him. But these days were not those days. He had been out of circulation so long he didn't know who the buyers were any more.

But he did know the one person who *would* know. Yes. He grabbed the newspaper and opened to the entertainment section, a sudden move that startled Watson. He settled the old boy down and thumbed through the ads for clubs and concerts and saw that The Ravens Family Four and Friends were playing tonight at McKarus's Folk City. Stein knew that was where he would find mister Vincent Van Goze. And wouldn't that be a tender Hallmark moment for him and Stein to reconnect? Two road dogs who had not spoken for years. Simon and Garfunkel. John and Paul. Stein and Van Goze.

He flicked the TV on to see if the media had gotten the story yet about Nicholette Bradley's murder. And good God, had they! TV news reporters were becoming worse whores than the people they covered. Sticking microphones in peoples' faces. Asking their inane questions. And police were learning from the military how to manage news. They had telegenic spin-doctors delivering carefully prepared statements. "The authorities were *processing information,*" others were "*sifting through clues, formulating directions of investigation.*"

In other words, Stein concluded, they didn't know jack shit about who did it or why.

This thought was confirmed when they showed the head of the operation, Chief Jack Bayliss, who ran the Malibu sub-station assuring the public that a suspect would soon be apprehended. He and Stein had an adversarial history that spanned two decades. Somehow, many of Stein's legendary escapades had come at his expense. Stein flicked the TV off. His eyes burned and his Inner Negotiator cajoled him for just one quick cycle of REM. But he knew if he gave in to weakness the day would be lost. He jumped in for a quick shower, threw the same Levis on and a different blue work shirt and dragged his ass outside. He'd find an open diner and grab some coffee until the banks opened. He'd need to cash out a thousand bucks of his recent deposit for seed money. Then find Vincent. He hoped. Then who knew?

A white limo of astonishing length was idling alongside Stein's parked Camry making it impossible for him to pull out. He recognized the driver—Millicent Pope-Lassiter's always impeccably dressed Chinese secretary.

"Andrew? Is that you?"

"Yes sir, that's right."

Stein wondered why Andrew didn't find the coincidence as amusing as he did. "Are you picking somebody up here?"

"Yes sir I am."

"Did you know that I lived on this street too?"

"Yes sir, I did."

Stein rummaged for his keys. "You'll have to undock that boat."

"No need for you to find your keys, Mister Stein. I'll drive."

It took Stein a few moments to register the obvious. "Are you here to pick *me* up?"

Andrew affirmed that he was.

"I'm not going anywhere with you."

"Sir, I know six different ways to kill a man."

"No, you don't."

"No sir, I don't. Mrs. Pope-Lassiter instructed me to say that."

"What does she want?"

"To be obeyed."

After giving Andrew assurances that he would not try any slick tricks and would drive obediently to the corporate offices in Century

City, and after Andrew assured Stein that the limo had twice the horsepower and maneuverability of Stein's Camry and that he would take any perceived detour from the agreed route as an attempted escape, he allowed Stein to drive there under his own power.

"Ten minutes is all I'm giving her," Stein declared.

"My business is getting you there."

With Andrew in the Class II nuclear destroyer staying a car length behind him, Stein drove west on Little Santa Monica Boulevard and turned into the underground parking lot of one of the Century City office towers. Andrew conducted Stein through the ground floor atrium to the private elevator that rose to the penthouse suite occupied by the product liability firm of Lassiter and Frank. Stein was leery about going to the upper offices of these local skyscrapers. The main occupation of the construction industry in Los Angeles was building facades for movie sets, where an erection only had to *look* like it could stand.

"Ah," Millicent Pope-Lassiter said upon seeing Stein. But it was not a sound of welcome. She bore an expression, which if displayed across a kinder face, would certainly have resulted in a smile. "Take a chair," she suggested. Her voice was an instrument strung more for power than inflection. Stein remained standing. His rebellion.

"Oh Harry. Must we go through this charade of conscience every time? Is that part of the Cost of Doing Business with you? Please do sit down."

He sat. She thanked him with another smile-like substance, then began a conversation which had a single destination. "Every client of Lassiter and Frank has the right to expect the highest level of professionalism from members of this firm. Do you not agree?"

"Is this about shampoo?"

She made the slightest gesture to Andrew, who placed a folder into her hand, which she proffered toward Stein. "Do you know what these are?"

He recognized the documents immediately. "Yes," he said, his voice dripping with dry weary irony, "I've seen the *extortion* notes. And yes, I think the entire military might of the NATO should be deployed to defend this company's inherent right to sell fourteen cents worth of sudsy water for twenty-five dollars. So if you will kindly validate my parking, I will be on my way." He rose from the chair he had recently occupied and wheeled around to the door.

"That's an impressive exit, Harry, but that door leads to my sauna. Follow me."

Stein grudgingly allowed himself to be escorted to another wing of Millicent Pope-Lassiter's office. On the far wall was a billboard-sized presentation of the *Espé New Millennium* shampoo package. The box was ingeniously constructed in the shape of a woman's body, transparent in the center to reveal the translucent viscous product flowing through her abdomen. Her eyes met your eyes full on. They changed color from blue to green to gray as the light changed. The flap of the box was so realistically photographed and reproduced that upon opening it you surely felt like you were putting your fingers through her hair. Her face looked vaguely familiar to Stein but he couldn't place it.

"You are looking at the most highly promoted and eagerly awaited product in marketing history," Mrs. Pope-Lassiter pronounced. "I am not at liberty to reveal the advertising budget, but it exceeds the GNP of several Third World nations."

"Milly. When I met you your hair was down to your ass, you had auctioned off your father's Bentley and you could make grown men whimper watching you eat an ice cream cone. What happened to you?"

"I grew out of it, Harry. It's called being an adult. You should try it."

"You make it look so attractive."

"You have some talents. Don't waste them." She placed the Espé package in his direct line of focus. "At this critical time with the product launch scheduled in two days, the integrity of the product must be unimpeachable. To that end, Espé Cosmetics has taken out a twenty-million-dollar policy with us, insuring against knock-offs and counterfeits."

"Twenty million dollars?"

"Are you starting to get a sense of the scope involved?"

Stein shook his head wearily.

"Yes, we are all impressed with your metaphysical ennui. I'm sorry the world didn't turn out the way you expected, Harry. Still and all, I wish you to drive this afternoon to Paul Vane's hair salon in Palm Springs and to determine whether he is counterfeiting Espé shampoo. Although their divorce decree stipulates that Paul Vane grants the rights to the formula to his former lover, Michael Esposito, there is reason to believe that he may be experiencing some seller's remorse. Paul Vane is thirty years older than his protégé. Perhaps his original strategy was to lure the young man back through a show of largesse. Having failed that, his generosity may have soured. I cannot profess to know all the hidden currents in the sea of love."

She nodded to Andrew, who presented to Stein a slip of paper. "Andrew has made reservations for you at the Mirador. And I think that concludes our business."

"You're right," Stein said. "Our business is concluded. But not the way you imagine." The receipt for his deposit of Goodpasture's twenty thousand dollar check gave resolve to his moral stand. At this late moment in life he was experiencing a stunning epiphany: He had always thought that living a socially conscious life was the thing that set you free from the need for money. But no. He understood now that what set you free from needing money was *having* money. And he had money. He continued on down the elevator, his spirit rising in the inverse direction to his descent, so that when he reached the street he was euphoric.

He drove directly to the Fairfax district, into the parking lot of the Bank of Henry Kneuer. Bank of Hank, as its customers called it, was possibly the last single branch bank in Los Angeles. They had only gone to computers a year ago. As Stein entered, Ben Tagasunta, a round-faced, second generation Japangeleno, always well dressed and overly cordial in the way that some gay people are when they neuter their sex for the business world, was at his desk helping an elderly Jewish couple transfer funds out of their CD account into an annuity. Mister Goldstein was ninety-five and stood straight as an arrow. He wore a perfectly pressed suit, white shirt and tie. His wife wore thick glasses and a bereaved expression that came of trying unsuccessfully for seventy-five years to get him to shush.

"With all the letters in the world, they have to make *two* things a CD," he was grumbling. "One of them couldn't be something else?"

"Leave him alone already," his wife said. "The man has to work."

"What? I'm not work?"

"Believe me, you're work."

Ben escorted them to the door, repeating meticulous instructions about what papers they needed to bring in to be signed, as Stein came in.

"Nice to see you, Mister Stein. What can I do for you today?" Stein slid the deposit slip at him. "Need to cash some out."

"Did somebody hit the Pick Six?"

"I wish it were that legitimate." A few months earlier Stein and Ben had discovered their mutual affinity for the ponies and since then their small talk had been about big payoffs and what horses had done what. Ben returned to his cubby. His manicured fingers tapped with astonishing speed across the keyboard. "You've got to excuse me. It's crazy today. They've got me all *meshugah.*"

"That's cute. You're learning Yiddish."

"*Meshugah* is a Japanese word. It means crazy."

"I stand corrected."

"Hmm," Ben said. It was not a good Hmm. "There seems to be a Stop Payment on this check."

"No."

Ben made his face do what Mary Tyler Moore's did when she was really, really sorry.

"Ben, I need it to be unstopped."

"Only the stopper can do that. Not the stopee."

Stein's mind whirled. If Goodpasture had stopped the check it would mean that Schwimmer had spoken to him, prevailed his negative view upon him. But on the positive side it would mean that Goodpasture was intact. "I need to know who stopped the payment, Ben, and the exact time."

"I can't access that information."

"Golly, Ben I'd hate to tell your manager that you've been diverting bank funds to the race track."

"I've done no such thing!"

"And I'm sure after the long internal investigation they'll come to that same conclusion and you'll get your job back," Stein said with straight-faced cheer.

Ben looked to see where the branch manager was. "This machine is very temperamental," he whispered. "If you ask for the wrong information it gets very protective." He zapped his mouse around the pad. Screens of numbers appeared. Then there was a loud electronic pop and a blip and all the figures swam away. "You see?"

"All right. Just …" Stein gestured impatiently, which meant fix this. Get these numbers back.

Ben shook his head indicating a more serious realm of difficulty. "I need my manager to reboot."

Stein realized what a mistake it had been last night brandishing Goodpasture's check at Alton Schwimmer. Was he ever going to learn anything? He left Ben at the bank, went outside and found a pay phone that worked and called the hotel, where three hours earlier he had delivered his surly passenger. But despite giving the desk clerk and then her supervisor four possible alternate spellings, they could find nobody registered there under the name of Dr. Alton Schwimmer.

NINE

In *The Pictorial Dictionary of Rock and Roll* there's a drawing to illustrate the word ROADIE: open vest, shaggy blond Buffalo Bill hair, droopy moustache, shoulders slumped from hauling amps, personality of an onion soaked in tobacco juice and Drano. The real-life model for that illustration was Stein's long time pal and co-conspirator, Winston Frenneau. High in the mountains in Katmandu in the early seventies and high in a mescaline haze, Winston had allowed some girl to stick a pair of earring studs into his lobes. It turned out they were loaded with mercury. When he got back to civilization the bottom half of both of his ears had to be amputated below the pinna.

Stein had hung out with him for the full month that his head was wrapped in bloody bandages. And since the name Winston sounded so much like Vincent, and he had lost *both* his ears, Stein thought that pluralizing the name Van Gogh and calling him Winston Van Goze was pretty damn witty. Most of life's ironies are horribly cruel, but on rare occasions sweet fruit grows out of bad soil and Winston's story was one of them. After the operation on his ears, once the gauze and dressings were removed, those little stubs on the side of his head could differentiate variations of pitch on a guitar string to a hundredth of a VPS. Where he had not given that much of a shit about music before, he turned his gift into an avocation and then a most lucrative way of life. Every serious acoustic player wanted one man to tune his strings and that man was Winston Frenneau.

McKarus's Folk Emporium was the last surviving acoustic club from back in the day. The Long Timers called it "McFolks." Martini bars and chic clothing stores were lately popping up on all sides as another neighborhood gentrified. With rents going into the stratosphere, McKarus's future was tenuous.

It was just past noon when Stein got there. The box office hadn't opened yet. Posters were up advertising the group that was coming in tonight, The Ravens Family Four. These were five generations of Appalachian fiddle players, ranging from Grandpa Cyrus, who was somewhere between ninety-four and the age of rocks, down to three-year-old Baby Raven, who (as the story goes) pulled her daddy's guitar down off the kitchen table at the age of eleven months and hammer-picked "Shady Grove" in E-flat.

Stein knocked a few times and hallooed but got no answer. He tried the front door, which to his pleasant surprise was unlocked. It was dark inside. The vestibule contained the box office and a display of tapes and CD's. Its musty walls were covered with posters for shows, some dating back twenty years. Unoccupied. Stein continued down the narrow corridor that led to the stage. The interior walls were lined with hundreds of guitars, mandolins and banjos; an acoustic cathedral. Once his eyes acclimated to the dark, he saw Winston sitting on the stage, his back to the door, his hair down to his shoulders, stringing Baby Raven's fiddle.

From twenty feet away, Stein rumbled in the stylized gravelly voice that they used to use with each other. "Van Goze."

Winston didn't look up from the fret he was filing and answered back, "I can hear you man. You don't have to yell." He turned around to face the interruption, affecting an aura of casual annoyance. "Shit, that couldn't be who I think it is. I heard he was dead."

"Reports of his demise have been exaggerated," Stein said as he climbed up the three steps to the stage. Winston appraised his flaccid body. "Not by much, I can see. What the hell happened to you?"

"Fame. Fortune. The love and admiration of my fellow man."

Winston took the long drag of his Marlboro and blew out a voluminous cloud that made its way across the room in shafts of brilliant stage light to engulf Stein.

"They let you smoke in here?"

"They let me do whatever the fuck I please."

Winston tightened the string just so, touched it with his index finger and laid his ear across its sound plane.

"You think you could put the thing down and say hello?"

Winston adjusted the string, touched it again and held it to his ear. Stein got the message and wheeled around to leave. "Swell. Nice seeing you, too."

"Don't be a putz. Have a carrot juice." Winston grabbed a half-pint bottle out of the ice chest and lobbed it underhand across the twenty-foot stage. Stein caught it in one hand. "Sounds like a slogan for the Carrot Advisory Board. *Don't Be A Putz. Have a Carrot Juice.*"

Winston nodded without pleasure. "You got that slick ad-man thing going pretty good."

"Yeah that's me. Mister Madison Avenue." He twisted off the cap and took a swig of the juice. It was surprisingly cold and sweet.

"This is great. Did you make it?"

"Why does everything you say sound like complete bullshit?"

"How about fuck you. Does that sound sincere?"

"Not bad."

"Says the man who's making the world safe for the Beverly Hillbillies."

"It's *music*. What are you doing?"

"Making a living. Just like you, Vincent."

"Not even remotely just like me. And nobody I know calls me Vincent. Or Van Goze." Winston put the guitar down, closed the ice chest, was about to say what had been on his mind for ten years but figured why bother, then said it anyway. "You sold the bus, Harry."

"Only my ex-wife calls me Harry."

"How could you sell the fucking bus?"

"The bus? Are you talking about the 1969 VW—"

"How many goddamn buses did you have?"

"Let me understand this. You're pissed at me for an event that happened how long ago?"

"There's no statute of limitations on suicide of the soul."

"The bus was my soul?"

"The fact that you don't understand is testament to its demise."

"I drive my daughter to school. Ok? As if any of this is your business. It embarrassed her. So, I got rid of it."

"It was an icon, man. You don't sell an icon."

"It leaked oil and poisoned the rose bushes."

"You know who I fucked in that wagon?"

"Yeah. All my overflow."

Winston crunched his empty juice bottle and tossed it into the can, laid his ear across the strings and played another note. "You meant something to people before you died. People bought into your shit. They like to think they can de-pants the president."

"Then people should."

Winston plucked a string. It vibrated full and true and resonated with all the A-strings of the instruments hanging on the walls. The room sang. "You hear that? A over middle C. Four-forty every time. Once you have your note that's your note."

"The fuck are you talking about?"

"You changed your tuning, man. Now I don't know who you are."

"You're talking about strings, not people."

"No difference."

"I would have *given* you the goddamn wagon if I knew you wanted it."

Winston still refused to make conciliatory eye contact. "I wouldn't drive that weak piece of shit. You know that beast Arnold drives in the movies?"

"The Hum something?"

"Word is they're coming out with them for civilians. That's my ride."

"Where do you hear this shit?"

"I hear things?"

"Speaking of hearing things." Stein sensed there weren't going to be many openings so he jumped in. "I came here for a reason."

"You *want* something. Let me get over my shock?"

"Can we stop farting up each other's assholes for a second?"

"You looking to score tickets for the Raven Family Five?"

"To score, yeah." Stein tried to pluck the string just right. "But not tickets."

Winston lit up another smoke. "I wouldn't know what that means coming from you."

"Same as it means coming from anybody."

"Nah. Everybody knows a certain ex has got your nuts in a sack."

"Not everybody seems quite as delighted about it as you are."

"Trust me, they are. *Activities deleterious to the well being of the child?* How do you let that shit happen to you?" He did a pantomime of a testicle sac being snipped off.

"Listen to me."

"Ears, man." He shielded his stubs.

"Sorry." Stein modulated his tone.

Winston slapped his attaché case down on the stage and unzipped the inner compartment. Seven sandwich baggies were pinned to the inside wall, each housing a distinct variety of bud. "You want to look at some shit? Here is the basic winter catalogue. Humboldt Sense. Maui Wowie. Jack Herer. Some sweet hydroponic from that dope fiend capital of the world, Minneapolis."

Stein smiled at the buds.

"Enjoying your vicarious window shopping?"

"That shit's fine for the tourists and civilians. If I wanted to buy off the rack I'd go to Macy's. I'm looking for something special."

"Something special, he says."

"I hear there's Goodpasture Orchids around."

Winston gushed out a pillar of Marlboro smoke. "Right. Maybe I can get you a date with Cameron Diaz, too."

Stein unfurled the plastic placenta in which Goodpasture's little embryo was ensconced, and with great care, broke off a small tip of the bud. Unmistakable perfume flooded the room and Winston knew instantly what he was looking at.

"Are you shitting me?"

Stein enjoyed the change in tone from derision to respect. "Would I bother a busy man like yourself, who doesn't have time in five years to call his best bud, with anything but the best bud?" He tamped the fine grains into the bowl of Winston's pipe with meticulous care.

Winston was like a boy leaning toward the bowl where his mother was mixing chocolate pudding "I've never smoked genuine orchid." Pipe now in hand, Winston closed his eyes, folded down and lit a match one-handed, and took a long, luxurious lungful. "Oh man! This is the shit! I take back nearly half of the bad stuff I ever said about you." Van Goze offered the pipe to Stein, who held up both hands in the international gesture of no thanks. "Good. More for me." Winston vacuumed up another bellowsworth. "You know what's beautiful about this shit? You can think clearly and be fucked up at the same time."

"There may be a person or persons advertising to have quantities of this for sale. I'd appreciate a heads up."

"Rather than telling them you're looking."

"You got the idea."

"You're working?"

"Just keep an eye open, will you?"

They made a feeble attempt at an embrace that neither of them was into. Winston conceded an inch. "Look. I've been out in the fucking Ozarks for a month with these crazy crackers. But if you're really interested in Great Smokies you should reach out to my ex-old lady. She's working with her new husband, *Maw-Reece,* in his antique shop."

"Right. She's with the antique dude. I heard that."

Van Goze took a long last dredging hit on the pipe and sucked the smoke down to Australia. Stein narrated to an invisible TV camera. "Don't try this at home, kids. This man is a professional." Van Goze laughed so hard he coughed up chunks of the Outback.

"You're still a putz."

Stein was nearly out the door when Winston called after him, "It's too bad you didn't turn out like your kid. She's a trip."

Stein's face reappeared. "What the hell do you know about my kid?"

"I was at your surprise party, man."

"THE BEST OF TIMES" antique store was packed to a critical mass with chairs, desks, tables, cabinets, armoires: each of them in turn crammed with hats, bowls, glasses, mirrors, jewelry, scarves, cameos. The air was left from a previous century. Stein called a hello, but his voice was absorbed two inches in front of him by material goods. He slithered through the maze, pinching his love handles on an old metal stove, banging his forehead into the edge of a Monopoly board held together by a petrified rubber band. He followed the sound of a power tool into a back open courtyard. Somebody who looked like a Maurice—short, bald, wiry—was sanding down a cherry wood night table that its former owner had slathered in white enamel.

"Howdy," Stein ventured.

Maurice turned around and took the sawdust mask off his face. "Help you?"

"Are you Maurice?"

Maurice nodded that he was.

"Winston's old lady here?" Stein caught himself and apologized. "Sorry, I guess you probably think of her as Maurice's old lady."

"I think of her as Vanessa," said Maurice. "And if she's not inside, she's probably down at the community center changing the world for the better. Do you know where that is?"

Stein indicated that he didn't.

"You're lucky."

Maurice made a little map, directing him to walk a few blocks east then walk a block or two south.

"I notice you keep using the verb 'walk' instead of 'drive.' Is that just a figure of speech?"

"Not if you're married to Vanessa."

The DeLongpre Community Center was a large, rambling one-story house built in the 1920s. A plethora of signs on the bulletin boards would have you think this was international headquarters for the Abolishment of Domestic Violence, Saving the Whales, Saving the Ozone Layer, Free Choice, Free Condoms, Free Spaying and Neutering of Pets and a few other causes whose notices were thumb tacked over by newer ones. The person who met Stein at the door had unruly manes of black hair and beard that left only a small bit of unplanted acreage on his face. He looked like a short, squat version of Allen Ginsberg, and was one of the throng of seven people assembled for this afternoon's lecture and book signing by the famed anti-automobile activist, Brianna Chisolm.

Stein understood why Maurice had told him to walk. A hierarchy of purity existed. People greeted each other not with hellos but by inquiring how they got here. A female in dark framed glasses and overalls who had come here on three buses from Pasadena was dissed for being "too internally combustive" by a geek who had pedaled his Schwinn from El Monte. The winners were brothers originally from Siberia who had pogo-sticked from Santa Monica the previous night for the talk on herbal colon cleansing and had just stayed on.

Winston's now Maurice's ex-old lady, Vanessa, was a striking woman, over six-feet tall with a great shock of wild, electric gray hair. Her eyes were gigantic and a little sad, which made you sad too, because her melancholy was so beyond hiding. When she greeted her old friend Stein her voice still had a bit of the aristocratic British accent she picked up while living in Tanzania. "Look who's here. The man who misses his own surprise party."

"Is that how I'm going to be known in history now? My identifying phrase?"

"You don't look nearly as rotten as everyone says," she smiled.

"Hillary being everyone?"

"Have you come to hear Brianna's lecture?"

"Maybe not exactly. More to see you."

"I know," she smiled. "Winston called."

Word came that Brianna had just called from her car phone to say she was stuck in airport traffic and she'd be late. Stein waited to hear a burst of irony that she was *driving* here in a stretch limo to give a talk on. But zealots are short on perspective. "You see?" squat Alan Ginsberg said with a ferocious shudder of his raid forest head. "Too damn many cars."

She guided him through the assembly room and out the French doors to the community garden. It was beautifully planned and well tended. Healthy vines of winter squash crawled like infantry across the hillocks. There were clusters of late corn, pole beans and delicate tendrils of Chinese snow peas climbing wire trellises.

"Did Winston tell you why I wanted to see you?"

"He told me you might be carrying something."

"He said *I* was carrying?"

"Don't be coy. I've never tasted real Goodpasture."

"God, you people are like the Russian mafia. Graft. Bribe. " He nipped off a little taste for her. "Tell me. Don't you think it's at all ironic that you sustain a low end community center by selling high end weed?"

"Life is a carousel old chum." She took an approving whiff of the bud.

"Did he tell you what else?

She started to say something, held back.

"What?"

"Are you really back in the world?"

"You read about that model up in Topanga?"

"Tragic."

"I owe her a favor."

"Really."

"Really."

She appraised his response. Decided he was on the ups. "There are these two guys. I don't like them much. One called Wylie, one called Phibbs. Do you know them?"

Stein gestured that he didn't.

"One is like a lawyer-rock promoter-wannabe mogul. Wears cartoon character t-shirts. His friend looks like a marine or a CIA pilot. Buzzcut. Lethal empty expression. I occasionally deal with them if I need generic run-of-the-mill smoke."

"That's not what I'm talking about."

"Let a girl finish. You know how you get a sense when people are showing off for you? A week or so ago these guys were talking about bringing home some end-of the-world weed from Amsterdam."

"No, this would be local."

"Sorry. She took another whiff of the bud "I look forward to this."

"So how's it like living in the antique world?"

"All men are merely weak surrogates for him, Stein." She made him almost think she really meant it.

A TV was playing as Stein made his way back through the house to the exit. The "Supermodel Slaying" was all over the news. Local reporters were buttonholing anyone who might have known or worked with Nicholette Bradley, shoving mikes in their faces, asking their imbecilic questions. "How does it make you feel…?" The one person in the whole circus who looked like he truly loved and missed the girl was a hairdresser who said he had known her for years and, according to the crawl, had done her hair for all the Espé ads. He was gay and bald and had eyes that even in grief danced like hummingbirds. His name flashed on the screen. Paul Vane. Stein had heard that name before. It took just a few moments for it to roll into the right pachinko hole in Stein's brain to start the bells ringing.

Paul Vane.

The former lover/mentor of Michael Esposito. The man accused of stealing the Espé bottles. The man Mrs. Pope Lassiter wanted him to talk to. Stein could not imagine what a soulful, compassionate person like Vane had in common with a furtive little tramp like Miss Espé, Michael Esposito. Maybe the thirty-year age difference had something to do with it. Groucho's line about a man being as old as the woman he feels, transcended gender preference.

With Goodpasture gone AWOL, Paul Vane was Stein's only direct link to Nicholette Bradley. He had reason now to drive out to Palm Springs and it had nothing to do with shampoo. It registered somewhere on the spectrum of his hard drive how curious it was that Nicholette was a focal point in both of his current preoccupations. He called his answering machine from the phone booth outside the center. He winced when the mechanized voice informed him he had eight messages. He skipped past the five from Mrs. Higgit without listening. There was a message from Ben at the bank that was so cryptic he had to play it twice to understand. Ben had traced the Stop Payment to a name that sounded so phony he was sure it was bogus. One Alton Schwimmer. The confirmation of Stein's suspicion made him growl and with he had left the doctor to fend for himself last night instead of driving him back to his hotel.

The last message was from a woman with a perky voice that Stein did not recognize, telling a rambling tale about a dress that she had sent to the dry cleaners. It was the longest, wackiest wrong number in telephonic history, but she finally circled back to the point of her story, which was that she and Stein had met two months ago in the produce section looking at a vegetable that was half cauliflower and half broccoli, and that Stein had called *her* Broccolflower and given her his phone number, but she had stuck the napkin in the bra strap of the lining of the dress that she had just now gotten back from the dry cleaners which was why she hadn't called him until now, but if he remembered her and if he had not met the woman of his dreams yet, she hoped he would call her back.

Stein absolutely remembered her. Redhead. Flaky as filo dough. Just as she began to give her phone number, there was a horrible squeak, and the tape went dead. Stein gasped, "Oh no!" But a moment later her voice came back laughing. "Can you believe I can actually make the sound of a tape disintegrating? One of the joys of having eight huge protective brothers. Just kidding about the huge protective part. And the eight. Anyway, call me. I thought you were cute."

He called her back immediately.

"Broccolflower. It's Stein."

"Yes?" Her voice contained no glow of recognition.

"Stein."

"Yes. Hello?"

"You just left a message for me?" He waited for the exultant, *oh of course*, but there was nothing. "Broccolflower?"

"I don't think this is going to work," she said, and hung up.

When he called Millicent Pope-Lassiter to say that he would go to Palm Springs after all, it pissed him off that she was not at all surprised. She had apparently brushed off Stein's entire act of rebellion as a non-event. The trip, she thought, would be an excellent second prong in the attack, in conjunction with the warrant that had been issued for the arrest of the inside man at the warehouse. She rummaged through her papers for the name, "A Mister Duluth Greene." Stein roared from someplace deep in his digestive tract and was still volcanic when he called Mattingly's office and Mrs. Higgit put him through.

"I told you not to do that. Didn't I specifically tell you not to do that? Do you people fucking listen? I'm going out to Palm Springs in an hour. You call the dogs off Morty Greene until you get further notice. Do you understand that?"

His blood pressure was ripping at his eyeballs. He needed Lila's sane, calming influence to take the ride out there with him. Plus she'd love getting her hair done by Paul Vane. He heard the water lapping in the backyard pool of her Beverly Hills home when she picked up her cell phone. He pictured her basking on the chair float listening to her Italian lesson on earphones.

"Do you feel like going to Palm Springs?" he asked.

He heard her sit up and adjust the halter-top of her bikini. "But Stein, you hate Palm Springs."

"That's why I need you to go with me. Something good to compensate for something I hate."

"My God, that was almost sweet. When were you thinking of going?"

"Fairly soon."

"You mean sometime in the next month?"

"More in the nowish area."

"You mean this week?"

"A little more nowishly."

"You don't mean today?"

"In an hour?"

"Stein! Is the last minute the only minute you ever function in?"

He could hear her clambering out of the raft and patting herself dry with her fluffy white bath towel that sat on the redwood lounge chair. "I just have that charity cocktail thing at the Beverly Wilshire tonight but I can blow it off."

"Isn't that where you get to meet the governor's wife?"

"Since when do you care about those things?"

"I don't. But you live for them."

"We'll take my car. You must be the last man in America not to have air conditioning. I have a hair and nail appointment. Give me an hour-and-a-half."

"Lila, it's just a ride to Palm Springs. Don't get all—" But she had already clicked off.

Ninety minutes would give him time to ride out and warn Morty Greene. He didn't know why he was so sure Morty had nothing to do with the missing bottles. No doubt some wishful longing that important parental qualities found their way into their children's DNA. Morty's red pickup truck was not in the driveway. In its place was a zippy new Mini Cooper convertible.

Stein rang the doorbell to Morty's apartment and practically burst through the door when Morty opened it.

"Man, you must have a death wish," Morty said. "You bust in here like John Wayne? You're not even Wayne Newton."

"There may be an arrest warrant out for you."

Edna Greene quietly entered from the room beyond. Her hair was up in a bun and she was wearing a red Jamaican robe. She looked at Stein with grave severity. "No suggestion of crime, you said?"

"I'm sorry. This isn't my doing."

"You're going to be sorry in motion." Morty moved threateningly to Stein.

"Duluth!"

"Why did you quit your job?" Stein demanded.

"How is that your business?"

"You practicing for what you're going to tell the SWAT team?"

"Do you remember the seven horse?" He rubbed his fingers together. "Would you go back to a loading dock?"

"That's a fair point. So once again I present you with this document." Stein offered the bill of lading in Morty's proximity. He glared down at it and breathed fire.

"Duluth, this man did not get you in trouble. Tell him what he wants to know about that piece of paper."

Stein was suddenly apprehensive that once again all his instincts had been wrong. "Is there something I should know about this piece of paper?"

Morty surrendered. "Hell, I guess you already know. I suppose you talked to Delores Brown."

"Why would you think I did that?" Stein asked.

"I'm being straight with you, man. Don't treat me like a boy."

"Let's talk about you and Delores, then."

Edna Greene retreated to the back room and Morty nodded for Stein to take a seat. "You ever work on a loading dock? I'm guessing probably not."

"Is this going to be one of those long stories with poignant sociological implications?"

"The job sucks, all right?"

"That I can relate to."

"So they make me a supervisor. For an extra buck-thirty an hour I keep records on everything that comes in and goes out and bring all the records down to Accounting."

"I'm on a bit of a time crunch."

"In accounting there is a particular fox they just hired who wears pants so tight you can see her smile."

"Downtown Delores Brown?"

"So we have this little rap going and one afternoon she sashays up to the dock. She says she locked her keys inside her car, and did anyone know how to, you know, open a door with—"

"I get the idea."

"As it turns out, I possess a little experience in that area, so I volunteered to help."

"Anyone could tell at first glance you were an altruist."

"Only trouble was, a shipment of bottles was due in the next twenty minutes and it's my responsibility to sign them in."

"I'm beginning to get a bad feeling about this, Morty."

"It gets good before it gets bad."

"You went with Delores and helped her gain entry."

"In a manner of speaking."

"You found her ignition key?"

"All right, Mister Stein," Edna called in from the next room. "The point is made."

The sexual innuendos made Stein gloomy, not eroticized. "Just so I can feel as horrible as possible, Morty, are you telling me you weren't there when the shipment arrived? That you had somebody else sign the manifest with your name?"

"No, man. I signed the paper. But ..."

"But what?"

"But before the truck ever got there."

"So you never actually saw the merchandise?"

"Oh, I saw the merchandise." Morty grinned.

"I'm talking about the bottles."

"You wouldn't be if you saw Delores."

"Duluth!"

His mother's scolding voice straightened him up. "I never saw the bottles," Morty admitted. "But I'm sure they were there. Why wouldn't they be?"

"And how many bottles were in this shipment?"

"A hundred cases. Times 24 in each case."

Stein perked up. "Did you say a hundred cases?"

"That's right."

"Not a thousand?"

"A thousand? Hell, no!"

"Swear on your life that it was only a hundred."

"It was a hundred cases, man."

Stein was inwardly relieved. This brought it back down again to the trivial.

"That time," Morty added.

"Excuse me?"

"There were a hundred cases that time."

"There were other times?"

"Delores would come down there every now and again."

"Let me take a wild stab. When there were shipments of Espé shampoo bottles?"

"I didn't think about it at the time."

"Morty, damn it. Have you and your little partner from the track been scamming up Espé shampoo bottles? Trucking them out to Palm Springs?"

"Naw."

"I noticed a sharp little Mini Cooper down in the driveway. What happened to your Ford?"

"I traded up."

"You could wear that thing on your foot."

"It's surprisingly roomy."

Edna Greene came in from the back bedroom. "That's Roland's car. He borrowed Duluth's truck. How much trouble is my son in?"

"Him? Nothing. He'll do twenty years in state prison and then get on with his life. Me, I have to tell Mattingly he was right."

She pulled her son's collar down so he was at her eye level. "Duluth Greene, did you have anything to do with moving those bottles?"

"No, Mama, I didn't."

She released him and turned to Stein as though she had proven the irrefutable existence of gravity. "He had nothing to do with moving any bottles, Mister Stein. He stepped aside with that woman. That was all. Can you trust that I'm telling you the truth?"

"What court of law could argue with the *my mama says I'm innocent* defense?"

"We'll deal with court when we have to," Edna Greene said. "Right now I want to know if you believe us."

"Against my better instincts, I do."

"Then you can call me Edna."

Stein pushed a couple of bills into Morty's hand. "I want you to stay in a motel for a couple of days 'til I get this straightened out."

Morty pushed the money back at him. "Hey man. I don't need your damn twenty dollars. I hit the seven horse."

Before Stein could insist, the LAPD patrol car pulled into the driveway. Moments later Stein watched dolefully as Morty was read his rights and taken down the steps in handcuffs. "I told them not to do this, Edna. I'm going to fix it. Don't worry."

"That's Mrs. Greene to you."

TEN

"STEIN!"

Penelope Kim's voice sang out his name in a parabola of delight. Stein had knocked on her door to see if she'd walk and feed Watson in case he didn't get back from Palm Springs in time that night. There was something different about her: her long black hair was brushed to a sheen and the clear outline of her breasts delineated themselves beneath her silk blouse. There was a touch of color on her lips and a line that accentuated the depth of her eyes.

Stein apologized. "This appears to be an inopportune time."

"Come in," she chided. "You look so forlorn standing out there in the rain."

"It's not raining."

"You make it look like it is. Come in."

"I get the feeling you're expecting someone."

"I am. He's here. It's you."

"What's me?"

She pulled him inside. The room vibrated with the heady aroma of smoldering sage and the pure tones of koto and flute from her stereo.

"Penelope, I don't want to get in the way of whatever ceremony you're performing here. Can I ask you to do a favor for me?"

She smiled at him as though she were privy to all his past lives. "I know where you were last night," she intoned. "I know why you missed your party."

Last night seemed ages ago. Stein tried to remember where he had been and where he had said he had been.

"You weren't counting shampoo bottles, my sweet mendacious mentor." Penelope undulated the newspaper in front of him. Its front page carried lurid pictures of Nicholette Bradley's murder scene. "Stein, you covered her body! You preserved her modesty. You're like a knight of the Round Table."

"What are you talking about?" It was a weak denial. He enjoyed the praise.

"I never would have thought of that for Klein. I've underestimated your depth."

"Why would you think I was there?"

She engulfed him under a silken, feathery aura of affection. "You can't hide from me, Stein. You know that I see the events outside the bands of visible light. You were there with her. I *smell* her on you!"

"Look, you're in a weird kind of mood and I have to—"

She stood in his way. "You made love with her, didn't you? You had sex with her right on the floor."

"Somebody here has a rich fantasy life."

"You held her in your arms. You pressed your fingers into the spaces between each vertebra."

She pressed Stein's fingers into her hand. "You've never come on to me. Do you know how incredibly sexy that is?" She tugged on the sleeves of his blue work shirt. "Lift your arms."

He bowed obediently, not sure if he was about to be stroked or beheaded.

"What are we doing?" he whispered.

Her fingertips pressed so gently against his temples that he was not sure whether he was being touched or merely wishing to be touched. "This is called *L'ang Pao Tong*. It means 'Caress of Butterfly Wings.'" Sensation shot through all of his nerve endings. She pinched his earlobes between her fingernails. He cried out in surprise. "There are no barriers between our thoughts, Klein. You had her right on the floor, didn't you? Tell me what she looked like naked. Put me there with you alongside her."

"Did you just call me Klein?"

She unwrapped the fabric tied round her waist, and her skirt was no more. She wore nothing underneath. Her legs were long and slender. She had a small tuft that looked like the brow over one modestly averted eye.

"Tell me how it felt to be inside her," she breathed. "Was she soft like dandelions?" She laced her fingers behind Stein's neck and brought him closer to her.

"You're using me as your sexual surrogate."

"And what would be the downside of that?"

"You want to use my body as a vehicle to have virtual sex through a character you invented with a woman you think I had intercourse with after she was dead."

"Too intimate?"

"I wouldn't know who I was making love to."

"It's never who we think it is anyway."

Her soft, supple skin, her desire for him, the scent of the sage, his exhaustion all wove an erotic blanket that snuffed out the fire of reason. He brought her to him. He felt a jolt of electricity as her nipples pressed into the flesh of his chest. From across the court-

yard Watson began barking like a hoarse, frail lunatic. Stein catapulted himself from the embrace and ran outside, tucking his shirt
into his pants as he stumbled out of her apartment.

Which is what Lila saw from Stein's front steps.

IT WAS HOT as a Gila in heat in the desert, but it was frigid in
Lila's Acura even without the air conditioning. She had stared
straight ahead for seventy-seven miles without speaking, without
needing to pee, without yielding to Stein's repertoire of annoying
pranks, which in the past had succeeded in extracting her from the
periodic funks into which she was prone to fall.

Earlier that day, fearful that Stein might leave for the desert
without her if she were late, Lila had gotten a quick trim and set
but had foregone her manicure, had dressed with what for her was
wild haste, had the gas tank filled, the oil level and air pressure
checked, and arrived at Stein's apartment fifteen minutes early. On
the way over she had telephoned from the car and gotten his machine, which intensified her anxiety. She was overwrought when
she arrived and did not notice that his car was parked across the
street. She had knocked and rung the bell and gotten no response
but for Watson's disoriented barking.

She did not knock at Penelope Kim's door. Lila had made clear
to Stein that she was not as big a fan of Penelope as he was. What
Stein perceived as Penelope's loopy mysticism, Lila viewed as lazy,
magical thinking. Where Stein saw non-judgmental, all-accept-
ing youthful exuberance, Lila saw an immature lack of awareness.
And Lila also thought that Stein's tacit approval of Penelope's he-

donistic lifestyle sent the wrong message to Angie at an impressionable age.

Stein had to laugh when he saw the look on Lila's face as he stumbled across the courtyard pulling his pants on. "I almost wish it were what you're thinking," Stein said. She had slapped her car keys into his hand without looking at him, uttered her only two words for the next hundred miles. "You drive." Ninety minutes later he pulled into a rest area that contained a string of twenty luxury clothing outlet stores, cut the engine and reached for her hand. "We're not married, Lyle. I don't want you to be miserable. We don't have to prove we can endure an ordeal. Let's just go back. Or you can leave me here. I'll get a cab."

Lila refused to respond. He backed up to turn the car around.

"I thought you had to see somebody."

"It's really not worth your being so unhappy."

"You can fuck whoever you want to," she snapped.

"That's not entirely true in practice, but I appreciate the sentiment."

"I don't hear you denying it."

"I would, if I thought it would help."

"It would, if I thought you were being honest."

He turned the engine on so the air conditioner would work. "She's working on a script and she likes to pick my brain."

"Well, that makes more sense than her being physically attracted to you."

Stein felt that she was mollified and that the siege had lightened. "I'm just speaking hypothetically," he said, "but some young women do like older men."

"Older *rich* men, Stein."

"You think money is the only attraction?"

"No, I'm sure that flaccid skin, diminished sex drive, and increased risk of prostate cancer are all major turn-ons."

Stein extended his arms to her and she allowed her head to be coaxed onto his shoulder.

"Just explain what our relationship *is*," she lamented. "We're not lovers anymore. We're not colleagues. We're not business associates. We're not related. We're not clients. What the hell are we?"

"What about *flovers?*" Stein offered.

"Flovers?"

"Friends-Who-Used-To-Be-Lovers."

"Are we not the two most pathetic beings on the planet?"

"We're up there."

🌿 🌿 🌿

"THERE IT IS." He looked down and sighed. Palm Springs lay before them, wedged into the mountain pass like a tracheal tumor. It represented to Stein everything that was wrong with America. Conspicuous consumption. Privilege and entitlement. Start with the name. *Palm Springs.* You had to say it in Italics. Like everything else liquid and verdant sounding around Los Angeles, it was a lie. The *Palms* were imported from Florida. And the *Springs?* Without the trillions of gallons of water it plundered from the Colorado River it would rank among the six most inhospitable climates on the planet. The theoretical temperature/misery index stayed consistently above one-seventy for eight months out of the year, and with an annual rainfall of less than an inch, its natural ecology supported but two indigenous creatures: the red-rimmed scorpion and a leafless, rootless, anaerobic cousin of sagebrush. Yet the median value of a home was upwards of three million dollars and it boasted more banks, more large American cars, and more golf courses per capita than any other metropolis in the world save that other bastion of democratic ideals, Kuwait City.

Lila's mood had vastly improved. "I like it," she smiled. They drove slowly through the commercial main strip of town, passing a succession of restaurants, pottery shops and real estate offices. "Don't take this as a criticism," she said, "but you never actually told me why we're here."

"It's a surprise. I'm going to make up for all the times I've ever disappointed you."

"We're staying all month?"

He slowed down as they approached a beauty shop where a crowd was waiting to get in. But it wasn't the name he remembered. "I'm looking for a beauty shop called Pavanne," he said. "Have you heard of it?"

"Have I *heard* of it? Is that some kind of joke? Stein, I have told *you* about it a hundred times. It's where all of my pampered, trust fund girlfriends go."

"Good, then you're really going to like this. Using all of my influence, and cashing in a shitload of important favors, I have arranged for you to have your hair cut and styled by Mister Paul Vane himself." Stein waited for the round of applause. Instead, her eyebrows caved down in the center.

"Stein, this hits an all-time low."

Truly he did not understand her reaction at all.

"Did I not tell you that I just this afternoon had my hair done?"

"Yes? So?"

"So? I cannot have my hair done twice on the same day!"

"Why not?

"Just tell me you're not being serious and I'll play along with you."

"I really don't get it."

"You don't get it? You don't get why you cannot have hair—I'm not even going to talk to you about this. Just drive." She folded her arms across her Givenchy blouse.

"I think you think I'm doing something bad to you on purpose … Suppose I said Wolfgang Puck was going to cook for you, would you tell him you'd already eaten?"

"I'd puke if I had to, and if you knew in advance we were going to Puck's and let me eat anyway, I'd puke on *you.*"

"So I should have told you."

"YES. So I could have cancelled my appointment with Rene."

"Ok. All I'm just saying is, since Paul Vane has never seen you, what difference does it make if his starting point is your hair the way it is now, or the way it was this morning?"

Lila blanched. "Is there something wrong with it?"

"No! That's not at all what I was saying!"

She flipped the vanity mirror open and obsessively scrutinized her coif. "What aren't you telling me?"

"I'm not not telling you anything."

"I get frightened when you use double negatives."

"Fine. I admit I have ulterior motives for bringing you here."

"Thank God. At last!"

Every time she made Stein laugh it reminded him how much he loved that she could surprise him.

"This is the actual truth of why I'm here: The people who hired me think Paul Vane stole some of their shampoo bottles. I have to ask him about it and I thought he'd be more easily diverted if he were working."

"So you brought me along as a decoy?"

"That and your air conditioning. And of course your scintillating company."

"Nice afterthought."

He mistook her irony for compliance.

"So you'll do it?"

"Absolutely not."

"Really?"

"I'll change my life for you, but not my hair."

The green art deco awning had been a landmark on the corner of Indian Wells and Sirkont for twenty-six years. Some people thought its name, Pavanne, derived from the courtly French dance. Those in the know understood it was a contraction of its proprietor's name, Paul Vane. At its peak of popularity in the Reagan-Bush decade, Pavanne employed eight full-time cutters, two colorists, a facial practitioner, an herbal nutritionist, a receptionist, a bookkeeper and two custodian-stockperson-intern-trainees. One of whom, Michael Esposito, had become Paul Vane's inamorata.

Stein and Lila were greeted at the door by the proprietor himself. Stein guessed that Vane was close to sixty, though he was very elfin. His skin was pulled taut across his delicate facial bone structure. His eyes were without guile and looked reverent when he looked up, which was almost always, since Vane was barely five foot four. He wore a maroon shirt that clung to his meticulously trim body. Even at rest he seemed to be constantly in motion, like a hummingbird whose wings flap at 4,000 beats per second just to hover. When Stein introduced Lila to him he threw his arms around her and squeezed hard. "It's so good to finally meet you," he exulted. "You are all that Charlotte and Rita ever talk about."

Vane released Lila and alighted in front of Stein. "I've heard nothing at all about you," he swooned, "but it's all been fabulous. Come in!"

The décor of the salon had the decadent feeling of faded French elegance. Pictures of Southern California's blue-blooded ladies graced prominent spots on the walls. Vane enthralled Lila with tidbits of gossip about the Presidential First Ladies he had done: Nancy Reagan ("Ronnie's mom"), Barbara Bush ("A political breeding machine"), Roslyn Carter ("The only woman who ever came out of here looking exactly the way she looked coming in"). He ran his finger lightly along the perimeter of Lila's hair. "I see you've been to Rene Douglas."

"Really? Can you tell?"

"It fits your face perfectly. The man should be knighted."

"Maybe you can give her a little trim," Stein suggested. "Like an autograph signature."

"We're not here to have my hair done," Lila abruptly announced. "We've come under false pretenses."

"False pretenses. My favorite kind," Vane exulted. Then he shrunk in mock horror and grabbed Stein's forearm as if to forestall a faint. "Am I being audited?"

"I'd like to speak to you about Michael Esposito," Stein said quietly.

He looked around wildly. "Michael? Do I know a Michael? Doesn't ring a bell."

"Your former business partner and intimate companion?"

"Oh, you mean *Miss Espé*," Vane exclaimed with an exquisite mixture of self-deprecation and world-weariness. And for the first time he sounded like what he was—a man at the end of middle age who had suffered one more disappointment than he could endure.

Stein looked down directly into Vane's troubled eyes. Gay or straight, pain is pain. "Is there a place where we can talk privately?"

Vane's private retreat was part gymnasium, part French kitchen. Giddy laughter accompanied the pop of the cork as Vane cracked open the second bottle of chilled Fumé. He kept a mini refrigerator alongside his Pilates machine, and Stein noted that both appliances had been well used. He had lived through the worst of everything, seen death often enough and at close enough range to clear his eyes of bullshit, and it had made him a reliable barometer. His only problem was the same as everybody else's. He fell in love with the wrong people.

He had been fooled at first by Paul Vane's Scarlet O'Hara excesses. But Vane was a solid citizen.

In the preceding forty-five minutes Stein had had all his prejudgments about Vane dispelled and all those about marketing confirmed. It was about making people feel horrible about themselves and offering the product to save them.

"Let me see if I've retained any of this," said Stein. "Manufacturers of designer products like Espé distribute only to exclusive salons. They don't want discount drug chains to sell their goods at a cheaper price—God forbid the public should benefit."

"Amazing," Vane praised him. "The man has perfect retention."

"I knew that, too." Lila pouted.

"Of course you know it," said Paul. "But we expect it of you."

Lila was sitting on the pommel horse. The first glass of musky amber liquid had gone straight to her head. The second had whetted the warm spot between her legs and put her censor to sleep. "You should see his closet," she giggled. "Three pairs of jeans that he still calls *dungarees*. Two sport jackets, previously owned. And no air-conditioning. How can you marry a man who doesn't believe in air conditioning?"

Vane refilled their empty glasses. "That's just what she needs," Stein said.

"Do you think I'm smashed?"

Stein leaned over and kissed her on the forehead.

"Thank you. I'm sober enough to recognize the most patronizing kiss I've ever received."

"I love this woman," Vane exulted. He went on to outline the marketing plan that had been devised to create the maximum buzz around the release of Espé New Millennium. Only one salon in every area would be granted the license to market the product.

"Luckily you're connected," Stein said.

"One would think." The sigh that Paul Vane let out could have changed the atmosphere of Jupiter.

Stein perked up, catching a glimmer of the unspoken truth. "Are you saying he didn't choose you?"

"*C'est la guerre. C'est l'amour.*"

"The dirty little rat," Lila shot.

"I bet it was that other place we passed," Stein remembered the long lines. "They seemed to be doing a land office business."

"Not all of us are in land," said Vane.

"It must have hurt you not getting the franchise."

"Why would I be hurt? Just because I took the little trollop in? Gave him a home, gave him love, made him a reasonably civilized human being, taught him the business, taught him all of my secrets, and as a reward he left me and marketed the things I gave him freely? Why would that hurt?"

"I only meant financially," Stein murmured.

"Of course. I forget that straight men can make the distinction."

Time had worn thin some of the zeal that Vane had once possessed in defending his lover's transgressions. Only a frayed inner grace still remained. "Young men don't know what love is," Vane said. "If any of us ever do. Yes, he hurt me, but that's what people do who are inexperienced in the world. It's up to those of us who know better not to hurt back."

"That's very evolved of you."

"When you've lived as long as I have, you're lucky if the worst thing that happens to you is that a lover leaves. At least the little shit is enjoying himself."

"I'd make him suffer," said Lila.

"I love this woman."

Stein declined having his glass topped off. Lila accepted. "You knew Nicholette Bradley pretty well," Stein ventured.

"God yes. The poor angel. Can you imagine?"

Vane nodded toward the gallery of photographs on his wall of celebrity clients. Prominent among them were several of her *Vogue* covers and layouts for the old New Radiance shampoo ads.

"Do you have any idea who could have done it?" Stein asked.

"It's too ghastly to think."

"No enemies? No rivals?"

"You couldn't do anything but love her."

Stein nodded ruefully. "True."

"You didn't know her," Lila scolded.

It was a long shot that Vane would supply something helpful.

He was just a bystander, like Stein, a victim of collateral damage. Stein felt the irrational desire to hug him. "We'll be out of your hair in a minute he said. No pun intended. I just need to hear you say, so I can tell my boss, that you are not hijacking any shampoo."

Lila had become Vane's staunch defender. "Stein, that's rude and ridiculous."

Vane was feeling wicked himself, or flirting, or showing off. "Why would I steal what I can make right here in my sink?"

Stein had a bad premonition. "What are you saying?"

Vane extended his arms to them both like an ambidextrous courtier. "Would you like to see the plant?" He conducted them into a smaller room that was painted white and furnished with laboratory sinks and copper tubing. Shelves and cabinets were lined with retort jars containing all manner of exotic ingredients: dried and freshly preserved orchids, berries, buds and small twigs.

"Anybody can make what is essentially Espé New Millennium shampoo. It's not the *formula* that's copyrighted; it's the *name* and the packaging. Ninety per cent of the products on the market have the same ingredients."

Stein marveled when reality outflanked irony. "Are you saying that anyone could brew up a vat of Espé shampoo but they couldn't *call* it Espé because Espé doesn't exist outside its packaging?"

"That is the million dollar secret."

"More like twenty million," Stein observed.

"Probably closer to four hundred million worldwide. But I just make the bare necessity to satisfy my regulars."

Moments earlier Stein had thought he was done with shampoo but now it looked like Mattingly and Michael Esposito had been right, that Paul Vane had been knocking them off. But why was Vane showing him? His shell cracked with barely a tap. Lila was crashing off the high and getting cranky. "Stein, can we go? I'm hungry."

An 11"x14" photo hung on the wall above one of the sinks that struck Stein with a vague sense of familiarity. It was Nicholette Bradley cavorting on a beach with another girl. Stein noticed the photographer's logo under the photo—an aperture opening like a flower petal. He remembered the envelope he had found in Nicholette's bedroom with that same logo. Weird things began to snap together.

"Is David Hart an acquaintance of yours?" Stein asked.

It was Paul Vane's turn to be surprised. "How would you have known that?"

And then a voice emanated from the recesses of the room that said, "I was waiting for someone to introduce us." A figure materialized. Stein thought at first it was a hallucination. The person standing in the doorway was the image of young Michael Esposito. Punk-blond hair, snakelike curl of the lips.

"Speak of the devil," Vane said. Meet David Hart in person."

"I've been listening to the conversation," David said. "We are not amused." On that, he abruptly strode from the room. And Paul Vane did what any man would do who feared that he had lost the last person on earth allotted for him to love.

He gave chase.

ELEVEN

ARGUMENTATIVE VOICES rose up through the grates of the elevator cage that carried the spatting couple to the lower level. Even a foreigner who didn't speak the language could follow the story of the opera. The timbre of one voice was strident and unyielding, designed to hurt without remorse. The other was tinged with a depth of sadness that comes of knowing that more is about to be lost than merely an argument. Still on the floor above them, Stein looked rapidly around for a staircase.

"Leave them alone," Lila said. "They have enough problems."

"I wish I could."

In her reluctantly assumed role as helpmate, Lila pointed out the stairway door. Stein yanked it open and raced down ahead of her. "Don't wait for me, or anything," she admonished, and began a careful, wobbly, banister holding descent

Vane and Hart were so deep in their argument that they did not immediately step out of the elevator when it reached the basement. Only in the ghastly aftermath of a particularly savage comment was there a moment's silence, during which David Hart emerged from the elevator, with his suppliant in futile pursuit. Both were surprised to see Stein already there, taking in the sight.

The walls were well stocked with Espé New Millennium shampoo bottles. Perhaps a thousand of them. Stein hated being lied to by people he liked and he liked Paul Vane. "So this is 'just barely enough' to satisfy your few loyal customers?"

Vane dropped his countenance in shame. Hart did not. He turned upon Stein the full unleashed power of the Post-Reagan disdain for anyone who thought that guilty executives should face consequences. "Whose lackey are you?" he spat. "That bitch cunt Espé?"

"Please, David. You're being rude," Vane said quietly.

"I'm being rude? That little whore stole your life's work. I'd think you'd care, if not for your own sad self then for *me*. You'd think I'd count for *something*."

"You count," Vane said, his voice disappearing into the stale canyons of old arguments. "David has nothing to do with this," he confessed to Stein. "It was all my doing."

"And of course I believe you, since you've never lied to me."

"Come," Paul Vane beckoned them. "All will be revealed."

He led them back up the flight of stairs to the main level where Lila was still waiting, then through the double door that opened into a large, sunny white-walled room with high windows and a beautifully redone blond wood floor. There were rolled backdrops and reflective umbrellas. Stationary lights were mounted on aluminum poles and a 35mm camera on a tripod. A pair of handcuffs and a silk top hat were left on the sofa, props from a recent photo shoot. At least Stein hoped they were props. But what arrested his attention was the life-size, three-dimensional cutout of the Espé bottle; the same icon he had seen that morning in Millicent Pope-Lassiter's office.

"You're David Hart, the photographer," Stein declared. "I've seen your work."

Hart replied a suspicious but flattered, "Really?"

"You shot the Espé box?"

"Yes," David replied, puffing up.

"And no," Vane added.

"But mostly yes," David insisted. "Uncredited and unheralded. And of course unpaid."

Lila poked Stein in the neck. "I'm still here by the way. In case you were wondering."

Paul Vane told an extraordinary tale, the gist of it being that marketing strategy for "New Millennium" would feature a new face, one who would replace Nicholette Bradley. Of course that created a tremendous buzz. Thousands of girls were interviewed. And finally—

"Don't tell me," Stein interjected. "Is her name Alex?"

Lila hooted at him, "Stein, you don't know anything about that."

"How did you know?" Vane marveled.

"You mean he's *right?*" Lila spent the next ten minutes wondering how that could possibly be.

Vane went on. "They tried to keep it hush hush. They began shooting the national ad campaign last summer. Print ads. Billboards. TV spots. But of course no secret is safe in the ad business. Once it leaked that Alex was the next big thing, clients were lining up to hire her after her exclusive with Espé expired. Twin Peaks, the sports bra company, won the bidding. They paid her a million dollars, and the deal was she had to shave her head."

Stein remembered he had seen those pictures. His mind, which did strange things like this, presented the proof sheet he had seen in Nicholette's bedroom. "So she must have known she was being replaced.

"Nikki's a darling. She helped find Alex."

"She wasn't irked about being replaced?"

"It's show biz. Everyone replaces somebody."

"Do you think you can get to the part about me before the dinner break?" David Hart pouted.

Vane smiled at his lover, who did not smile back. "Alex's last contractual obligation to Espé was for the shoot that would create the package. Ray Ramos was the photographer. It was there that I set eyes on Ray Ramos's magnificent, young, overworked, *underappreciated* assistant for the first time.*" Here Vane bowed in David Hart's direction.

"At last." Hart fumed.

"It was the assistant's job to do everything. Make coffee. Load cameras. Set the lights. Process the film. After the last shot was done, Alex came to my salon. She had agreed to the deal with Twin Peaks and wanted her head shaved immediately because if she let herself think about it too long she knew she'd back out. I had just finished doing her when my darling David (of course he wasn't my darling yet!) came bursting in. His face was the color of blanched mushrooms. He had screwed up all fifteen rolls of film that Ray Ramos had shot. The negatives were ruined. There was no shot for the box, nor for the billboard. It was a disaster of global proportion.

"David's plan was that *he* would reshoot the Ray Ramos session and substitute his film for Ramos's without anyone knowing. He knew the entire lighting setup and all the lenses and angles that Ramos had used. He had never shot before but he was sure he could do it. All I had to do was to get the world's new top model to agree to work with an unknown photographer when all that was at stake was her entire career and the success of a ten million dollar ad campaign.

"He swore he would do *anything* for me in return which was a very tempting offer. And then he saw my wicker basket filled with her shorn auburn hair. I thought he was going to stroke out on the spot. His jaw froze. His eyes fluttered. He lost the power of speech. He grabbed me around the neck and begged me to perform a miracle, to make a wig out of Alex's hair."

"Don't embellish," David complained. "You always embellish."

"My darling, I am nothing *but* embellishment."

Stein stepped in to short-circuit the domestic spat. "So you made a wig for Alex out of her own hair that you had just cut off her? Is that what happened?"

"It's technically called a *fall*, not a wig, because it's her own hair, but yes. And David did the reshoot and it came out brilliantly." Vane bowed to his protégé. "More brilliantly than the original, I'm sure."

"And then everyone started proclaiming Ray Ramos a photographic genius," David sulked.

"Yes," Paul Vane commiserated. "The injustice."

The picture began to coalesce in Stein's mind. "So you gents decided to start your own underground distribution arm? You whipped up your own private batch? You enlisted the girl at the warehouse to distract Morty Greene and diverted a few shipments of Espé bottles … How am I doing so far?"

"Stein, all this talk is getting me hungry," Lila pouted.

"We're done here in a second. As soon as they tell me which of them wrote the extortion letters."

"What letters?" Vane blurted before he could stop himself.

It became clear in a flash that the extortion letters had not been part of the plan the two had agreed upon and that David Hart had written them without Vane's approval or knowledge. The *Fall* of the House of Espé. Stein got the joke now. Hart knew that the hair on the label was not real. The truth-in-advertising laws were very clear now that beauty products had to be accurately represented. The notes were thinly veiled threats that Hart would *blow the lid off* the campaign. The lid of the Espé box was where the false hair fell. Of course David Hart knew that. He had shot the damn thing.

"Oh my God," Paul Vane cried. "We're going to jail and I look ghastly in orange."

"Nobody is going to jail," Stein assured him. "If you do exactly what I tell you to do." Stein's patience was losing its patience. "You're going to pay for a truck and return all their bottles along with an apology. And then you are going to leave Espé Shampoo alone. Is that cool with everybody?"

It was so cool with Paul Vane that he practically fell into Stein's arms. Hart was a line drawing of disappointment. "Why don't you just roll me over and fuck me missionary style," he groused. "What do *I* get?"

"How about for openers you get not to go to jail," Stein said, "And your partner gets not to go to jail."

"He promised to take care of me," David wheedled. "In *perpetuity*."

Stein envisioned how he would take care of the little weasel in perpetuity. It involved carpet tacks and his eyeballs. He addressed Paul. "Last question and I'm done with you. How did you get the bottles here?" At that moment the sound of the service elevator

clanged to life. Summoned from above, it began its labored ascent. "Ah. Perhaps this is the answer to my question," Stein observed. He began his own laborious climb to the surface.

"Stein, wait." Lila pulled her shoe on and hurried after him.

In the hour they had spent indoors, winter evening had fallen
and life on the street had undergone a radical transformation. The
main strip through town, which earlier had been about as lively as
a doily, now had become a teeming, volcanic landscape of college
students on winter break. Boys leaned out of their cars, hooting
mating calls at the constellations of girls, whose every movement
of torso and limb released crackling trails of pheromones. The flash
of an incongruous image on the far side of the road caught Stein's
eye—a truck carrying a load of hay. It was only a glimpse but its
afterglow remained printed on his retina as it moved through the
parting crowd of pedestrians, and disappeared. He was certain that
it was Morty Greene's truck or a reasonably close hallucination.
"Wait here," he instructed Lila.

"Stop saying that."

She clutched his arm and together they serpentined through
the moving maze of pedestrian and vehicular traffic. "I hope you
appreciate that I'm *running*," Lila gasped. "The only thing I ever
ran for is secretary of my stock club." They crossed on a long diagonal to the other side. An unbroken protoplasm of humanity
flowed along the sidewalk. Stein stopped for a moment to scan
the terrain. But the red pickup truck was nowhere in sight.

"I see a sign for hot food. Is that what we're looking for?"

The blind alley appeared out of nowhere. The angle at which
it met the street concealed it from view until he came upon it. The
red pickup was parked catty-corner to the side of the brick build-

ing, tailgate open, directly alongside an open elevator shaft. Stein sidled up to the entrance and peered down. He could see the tops of a load of wooden crates descending into the sub-basement. He muttered to himself as he thought of Morty lying to his face. All he'd been trying to do was keep him *out* of trouble.

The elevator's gears clanked, and the car began to ascend. Stein's mind raced through a dozen possible next moves. The one he chose probably wasn't the best of them. He grabbed Lila around the waist and hoisted her up onto the hood of the truck and told her to sit there and look serious.

"It's actually kind of nice. The metal is still warm." She adjusted her legs around the hood ornament.

"A little bit more serious."

"Is something bad about to happen?"

"Define bad."

The wide purple brim of the felt hat first emerged, then the face of Morty Greene's partner dude, Roland Dupuis. He had seemed diminutive alongside Morty Greene, but here alone he looked full-size.

"The fuck?"

Roland thrust the iron gates powerfully aside. The tomato slug on his face seemed to crawl closer to his eye as his expression assumed full battle alert. He was dressed elegantly for driving a truck: a white silk shirt and purple silk trousers. "I know you. The man who doesn't take good advice from his friends."

Stein gestured toward Lila. "She's Federal. You got yourself into some deep shit."

Roland took one cursory glance at her and scoffed. "She's no damn FBI." He came toward Stein, who raised neither his hands nor his voice.

"She could be a crossing guard and you'd still be looking at five years if those bottles cross a state line. You ever hear of the Federal Racketeering act?"

Roland lost a bit of his bravado. "Nobody said anything about state lines."

"Of course nobody said anything. The fall guy is for taking the fall." It was important not to break eye contact with Roland. But Lila, trying to scooch herself down off the truck, caught her heel on the hood ornament and was stuck with her legs splayed apart.

"Stein, would you get me down off this thing? It's toasting my buns."

He removed her shoe and lifted her down. "Thanks that was excellent timing," he whispered.

"My foot got caught."

He set her down and turned back to Roland in time for Roland's fist, traveling toward Stein's body at great velocity, to make impact with the unmuscled pit of his solar plexus. All the air blew out of his system in one huge "OOOF" and he folded like a slab of melting cheese. Roland vaulted into the cab of Morty Greene's truck, proclaiming that he was not taking the fall for anyone. Its eight-cylinder engine roared to a start. Other people nearby gasped and screamed and held their faces the way witnesses do in the aftermath of sudden violence. Most kept doing what they had been doing.

Lila bent over Stein's body and kept repeating, "Are you all right? Is there anything I can do?"

TWELVE

EVERYTHING ABOUT the Hotel Mirador was picture-postcard perfect. The hacienda-style main house was built harmoniously into the rolling rugged desert hills. The landscaping design consisted solely of desert blooms—coral aloe, Natal plum, Chinese lantern—except that the plants were not indigenous, they came from Africa—and the hills never existed in nature. They had been manufactured to fit a computer-generated artist's concept of western/rugged. Six hundred thousand cubic yards of limestone had been shipped in by companies located in Yuma, Arizona from East Meadow, New York and twelve thousand miles away from Yokohama, Japan.

Millicent Pope-Lassiter had been so ecstatic when Stein called her with the news that the bottles had been found and would be returned that she had upgraded Stein's accommodation at the Mirador from a room to a suite. He made sure that she understood that Roland had borrowed Morty Greene's truck without Morty's knowledge of what its purpose would be. All he wanted from her was the assurance that the charges against Morty would be dropped and for this whole horrifically trivial episode to be stamped CLOSED AND DONE. He was not naïve enough to believe Morty had not signed on for a little taste, but Stein was was less interested in criminal justice (that grand oxymoron) than he was in karmic harmony. And if he would make Edna Greene's life a little less complicated, that would be a day worth living.

In one of the two separate bathrooms in their suite at the Mirador, the cascading shower massage bathed Stein in a hot monsoon of melancholy. He had called home and checked his phone messages as soon as he and Lila arrived. There was nothing from Schwimmer, nothing from Goodpasture, nothing from Winston's old lady.

He had called Police Chief Jack Bayliss's office, but they had not called back either. He was exhausted by minutia and wanted to crawl under the covers and wake up thirty years ago.

Lila was blow-drying her hair when Stein came out the shower. He was wearing the boxer shorts he had purchased at the hotel gift shop that were a size too small and decorated with pictorial representations of local attractions. Lila displayed her thoughtfully packed overnight bag that contained a nightgown, slippers, and travel-size portions of nine different items of makeup and toiletries.

"I always keep one packed in the car," she chirped. "Just in case something like this happens."

"And does that happen fairly often?"

"Do you want to hear about the solar plexus?" Lila had purchased a pamphlet on the Chakras from the hotel's New Age bookstore. "The third chakra is your emotional power center that projects love and light into the world. When one is pure and at peace with others all conflicts are stopped, facilitating learning instead of fighting. This is a good part for you. 'If one stands humbly to solve the conflict, love is expressed. A resolution will eventually find itself thus the chakras of both parties remain balanced.'"

"I'm sure that's exactly what he was thinking when he tried to do spinal surgery through my gut."

"Sorry about distracting you out there but I didn't want to have sex with a hood ornament."

A bottle of champagne was on ice alongside a cart appointed with elegant silver dining trays. Lila had tied her bath towel the way women in forties movies did, knotting it just above the cleavage point. She had slender shoulders and a long elegant neck. She had reapplied her makeup and her hair was slicked back with a glossy gel that made her look sexy as Winona Ryder. Stein took the scene in with some bemusement.

"What is all this? Did you call room service?"

"You make it sound like a war crime."

"It's an indulgence."

"It's an *amenity*, Stein. I'm hungry! If we're not going to sleep together, then at least I get to eat. I don't think personal comfort is a crime against nature. I know I live in what a lot of people would call luxury. I've been lucky, and I don't think this makes me heartless. But *I do* believe I'm entitled to eat well. And I sincerely hope I'm not fucking up the ozone layer, but I'm not going to be the only person in Palm Springs not to use air conditioning."

She turned the switch back on that Stein had turned off and patted the cushion of the sofa alongside her for him to sit down. "You look so forlorn. Do you hate being stuck here with me?"

"I just wonder if I'm doing anyone any good," he sighed and plopped himself down

"You just solved a big case."

"It's shampoo. Who gives a shit?" He sighed out one last deep pocket of air that even Roland Dupuis' blow to his guts hadn't dislodged. "Nicholette Bradley, the girl who died. I could have prevented it."

"Stein, how?"

He realized that Lila had no idea what had happened last night after he left her at the warehouse. She listened now to the events unfold like she was hearing *Alice in Wonderland* for the first time. "Is any part of that really true? You know I believe anything you tell me."

He nodded with rueful weariness that it was all true. "I just don't know what to do next." She kneaded his neck and shoulders. "Thanks. That feels good." His chin dropped toward his chest. "Nothing I do changes anything for the better. Nicholette. Angie. You, for that matter."

She resisted the urge to follow up on 'you for that matter,' and asked what the matter was with Angie.

"She's always so angry at me. For things I did. For things I didn't do. For *existing*."

Lila got up onto her knees for better leverage. Her fingers probed deep into his back and knotted shoulder muscles. Her chin was close to his ear. "Listen to me. Number one, your daughter is a bright, sensitive, emotionally mature young woman."

"This is Angie we're talking about?"

"All of my friends have teenagers that are either in rehab or should be in rehab. They drink, they shoplift, they do drugs, they're having sex."

"You're telling me this to make me feel better?"

"I'm saying you have a good kid. At this age, derision is the purest expression of love. And you are its legitimate target. If she thinks she has no effect on you, then later when adolescence is over and she rejoins the human race, she'll always doubt her power. She'll choose the wrong men to test herself. She'll be hurt and disillusioned and she'll blame you for everything that went wrong in her life because you didn't accept her when she was horrid to you."

"So the lesson is to be grateful that she's abusing me?"

"Exactly."

"What would I do without you?"

The bath towel came not quite down to her knees. Her legs were tanned and waxed. The champagne was disabling her inhibitions. "It wouldn't take a Boy Scout to untie this knot."

"Lila, you know we shouldn't."

"What are we saving up for? We die in the end anyway."

"I do love you, you know that."

"Yes," she said with bored indulgence. "You're just not *in love*. As if you had a clue."

"Do you think I'm afraid to fall in love?"

"Stein, you're afraid to fall into giving a shit."

"You know what would happen if we slept together?"

"Yes, I'd be thoroughly addicted and ruined for other men. " With sweet humor she turned him to face the full-length mirror. "Look at yourself! Do you think you're some exotic rodeo boy who has to warn women they may get hurt? You're a balding, paunchy, fifty-year-old, divorced single parent. You drive a Camry. You got a birthday card from AARP. You're from the demographic group called normal. Get over it."

"Maybe I'm just worried I'll disappoint you."

She turned off the light.

"Lila—"

"Don't think, Stein. It takes you to bad places." She let the towel drop.

There was a knock at the door.

Lila yelled through the door. "If it's room service, come back later."

There was another knock. This time more insistent. Stein disengaged from Lila and went to the door. The man who stood in the threshold was definitely not the room service waiter.

"Well, well," said Stein.

"Who is it?" Lila asked.

"Where the hell have you been?" Stein berated the visitor. "I called your hotel half a dozen times. They don't *have* any *Doctor Schwimmer* registered there."

"I've heard from our mutual friend," Schwimmer said.

"Goodpasture?"

Schwimmer looked pointedly at Lila, meaning they shouldn't talk in front of her.

"There's nothing she wouldn't wring out of me in five minutes. You may as well say what you have to say."

"He's in Amsterdam. He needs you to fly there right now."

"Now?" Stein drew his head back and shook it for ironic effect. "Amsterdam, *Holland?*"

"There isn't time for burlesque reaction," Schwimmer said in his annoying, humorless way. "Are you on the bus or off?"

THIRTEEN

THE KLM ROYAL DUTCH PASSENGER JET rose up off the tarmac at LAX, banked over the Pacific, and established its flight plan that would take it across Canada, Newfoundland, the North Atlantic, then down over Western Europe into Amsterdam. The aircraft weighed seven hundred thousand pounds at take off, carried forty-eight thousand gallons of fuel and consumed four gallons per each mile during its eleven-hour flight. There were three hundred eighty-seven pillows and blankets, six tons of food and equipment, three hundred and ninety-one frozen meals. Thirteen liters of hard liquor had been loaded aboard plus two hundred forty-three liters of wine and beer, sixty-seven of tea and eighty-four liters of coffee. The captain was Jan Verheoff. The film was *Jumanji*. Stein did not watch it.

He thought that he had to be insane to be flying a quarter of the way around the world on a whim. At first he had flatly refused. Schwimmer had not begged or cajoled or offered the crown to Caesar a third or second time. He had shrugged his shoulders, as if to acknowledge Stein's response was neither a surprise to him nor a matter of much importance but rather a diplomatic courtesy that had to be observed before putting the real plan into motion.

Stein had to follow him down the hall through the lobby and into the parking lot to get a reaction. "You put a Stop Payment on my check? You disappear? You don't tell me one goddamn thing that you know. Then you expect me to fly across the universe because you say he says he wants me there? This is bullshit!" In the end, with all of Stein's ranting and railing, it was obvious to anyone half-listening that he already knew he was going.

Lila had risen to the occasion like a friend. Like a really good friend. Like— he hated to acknowledge it because it made him feel like he was taking advantage of her or squandering a good thing—like a steady, solid committed long-term life companion. She made the drive back to Los Angeles utterly guilt-free, devoid of complaint, knowing not to ask for any more information than she was given.

Once back at Stein's she had packed a suitcase for him while he tried to find his passport. She had made a list of things she would take care of, which included collecting his mail, taking care of Watson and providing a contingency plan for Angie to stay at her house in case Stein was detained in Holland. She even headed off what appeared from his facial expression—tilted head, soft smile of wonderment—was going to be a sentimental declaration from Stein. "In moments like this," she said, "love is better than being in love." Stein agreed and loved her more for knowing that any declaration he made would have come out of a moment of weakness, and would be enforceable maybe legally but not in any way that really mattered. The practical side of her added, "Of course how many moments like this are there?"

Dr. Alton Schwimmer's social affect had undergone no miraculous conversion now that he and Stein were officially allies. He remained dour and irascible. He had dispensed information in the tiniest doses, as if it were a precious commodity that needed to be husbanded over a long winter. Stein had still been unable to pry a gramsworth of new information from him—just that everything would be made clear when he arrived. He had given Stein two envelopes containing small quantities of Dutch currency and the telephone number of a taxi whose driver would be expecting Stein's call and who would know where to take him.

"You're still acting like I'm the enemy," Stein groused. Schwimmer looked for a moment like he was going to respond but dismissed the thought.

Six hours after take-off with the plane racing over the Atlantic at five-hundred miles per hour in pursuit of tomorrow, most of the passengers were asleep, their bodies Salvidor Dali'd into surreal fluid shapes dangling over the armrests or contorted against a shaded window. Stein's shade was up. He couldn't sleep. He watched an earlobe of moon that hung outside the window nestled between underlit clouds.

Stein hadn't anticipated the strength of the feelings his returning to Amsterdam would engender. He had found something there that had defined his life. The sixties had happened to him there. In Amsterdam. When migrating hippies were shunned by most European cities as deterrents to tourism Amsterdam welcomed them. The Dutch were cool people. While they shared the Germans' Teutonic love for order and cleanliness, they possessed a rogue chromosome in the deep end of their gene pool that gave them a goofy sense of humor in place of the need to exterminate people. Living below sea level must have taught them the futility of legislating against nature. Every night in Dam Square, sleeping bags opened out from the center fountain to the edge of the square like a giant mandala. The police were not concerned by the sounds of singing and guitars, the commingling bodies or the wafting aromas of Acapulco Gold, or the soft, sweet, orange hash from Lebanon, or the hard black, bricks from Afghanistan. It was there that he became Stein. All the goofy antics of the time, which for most people was a costume they put on for a while and then, after Stein went back to being their real selves. For Stein it was his life.

In the Autumn of '69, after Woodstock, after the moon walk, after Chappaquiddick, after Helter Skelter, either by coincidence or through a preordained Harmonic Convergence, Stein and Winston and five or six of their buddies had found themselves in Amsterdam, each of them happening to have with him a bud of the best weed they had smoked that year. Sitting in lofty judgment like the World Court of Cannabis, they awarded each other prizes for best in show. The following year without any of them mentioning it, leaving it in the hands of the universe to decide if it would become a tradition, they all convened again. Plus a few friends.

The year after that a hundred people showed up. This was no Woodstock II. There was no promotion. No hype. The people who knew just knew. They came with buds of the best weed they had found. People stayed high for record amounts of time. Prodigious quantities of Dutch chocolates were consumed. Contests evolved with gonzo prizes. An emperor was crowned. The crown was smoked. They knew with absolute certainty that the changes they were making in the world would last forever, that this was merely the dawn of the Age of Aquarius and that they were the first generation that would never grow old.

Thirty years later, now at the dawn of the false millennium, the festival had become so corrupted and commercialized, so mainstream and institutional it was like Disney Times Square. According to the brochure in the airline seat pocket, forty coffee houses were entered in this year's competition. There were more than six hundred judges. Morley Safer, for God's sake, was doing a segment on it for *60 Minutes*.

He pictured Hillary in those days, dressed in her peasant blouse and perpetual smile. They were uncorrupted embryos, cells in the hippie jet stream that wafted down over Spain to Morocco, cast across the Greek islands and Turkey through the Hindu Kush to Katmandu. "A long way to go for a shortcut to Enlightenment," the people who did not go had scoffed. Stein and Hillary had been inseparable, revolving around each other like twin stars. It bewildered Stein now to wonder where all that heat and fire between them had gone.

He had tried several times to explain to Angie why he and her mother had gotten divorced, what had gone wrong. But he could describe it only in metaphors about adjacent raindrops on opposite side of the Continental Divide or comets whose orbits just touched for a brief moment on their ways to opposite sides of the Galaxy. But none of this explained to her why people married, had children, and then broke each other's hearts.

Stein hadn't slept in days but his mind was too wired to surrender now. Lila had told him it was good for his circulation to walk while flying. So he took an excursion up the aisle to the back end of the plane. A cute, dark-haired flight attendant had taken her shoes off and was curled up in a window seat. Her lapel button said

"Jana." She patted the seat alongside her and invited him to sit down. "You are coming to Amsterdam for the Cannabis Cup?" she asked, though it was more of a friendly presumption of fact than a question.

"Why would you think that?" he flirted. "I'm a respectable citizen." He waited for her to laugh at the word 'respectable,' as an acknowledgment of how anti-establishment he was sure he looked. "I'm kidding," he had to say, and attributed her gaffe to the language barrier

"You American lawyers like to pretend to be radicals," she said

"You think I'm a *lawyer*? Oh, man! That hurts." He played up the pouting.

"So you are not a lawyer."

"The exact opposite of a lawyer." Whatever in the hell that meant. He took his shoes off and brazenly pulled some of her blanket over his feet.

"Are you high already?" she scolded. "And you don't offer me any?"

"After we land that might be arranged."

She rubbed the ball of her foot against his leg and Stein began thinking of the mile-high club and converting feet to meters but the movement came in response to an announcment in Dutch over the intercom.

"That means me," Jana said. She extracted those lithe limbs from the blanket. She nodded that she'd be back soon but Stein doubted it. His thoughts became more focused as preparations began for their descent into Schipol Airport. He knew that a long delayed, long avoided moment of truth was approaching that would define what kind of a man he had grown into. In protesting the Vietnam War he had risked the bite of tear gas and Billy club. Yes, he had led protests. Yes, he had hunger-struck, yes, he had draft-resisted, Yes he had bedeviled authority, exposed hypocrisy; all of which were admirable. But he had not fought. He had not faced the possibility of death. He had been, for all of his bravado, for all of his audacious demonstrations, as safe and immune to the infliction of real harm as any pentagon general.

He had no idea now what awaited him on the ground; whether Goodpasture had tracked Nicholette's killers to Amsterdam or fled here from them. If her killers were here and meant to do danger to Brian, it meant that Stein would be in their crosshairs as well. But he couldn't think of it that way. He had to think that they would be in his. That he was the hunter and they were the prey. He wondered how he would perform under life-and-death pressure. He pictured himself as a high diver wondering as he peered down at the distant water from the top of the cliff, whether he was still as good as he once had been, and thinking, perhaps foolishly, that yes, yes he just might be.

Captain Verheoff set the 747 down on runway number three. The passengers were thanked for flying KLM and informed that the local time was some number of hundred hours and that there were very, very few degrees Celsius outside. Stein looked at his watch but it was a meaningless gesture. After an eleven-hour flight across nine time zones and not having slept in God knows how long, his biorhythms were so askew he could have laid eggs. In the arrival terminal he telephoned the number for the taxi that Schwimmer had given him. Rather he had someone do it for him.

He sailed through Customs. The inattention to him by authority was becoming irksome. Didn't they know who he once was, for God's sake? Jana, the stewardess, waved a cheery goodbye

as she strode across the lobby, linked at the elbow to Captain Verheoff. The pilot looked just like his voice: tall, grey and surgeonly
in his uniform, but with a slightly odd walk like he was trying to
shake something out of his undershorts.

Stein potted a taxi driver in the lobby holding a handwritten
sign bearing his name transliterated into Shtejne but close enough.
He pushed through the revolving door and was hit by a blast of air
so cold it had to be a mistake. He batted his chest with his crossed
arms as he ran to the car and got inside. "No coat?" the driver said.

"I live in L.A. We forget that the rest of the world has weather."

The road layout into town followed the route of the concentric
circles of century-old canals. Trams and bicycles were the primary
vehicles. Cars had to create their own lanes, which they did with
kaleidoscopic mayhem. It was hard to tell in the diffused, weak
winter light but Stein guessed it was probably around noon. They
chugged along the banks of the Singelgracht Canal passing the
Rijksmuseum, which held nearly all of Van Gogh's paintings. They
took a hard right across the bridge at Nieuwe Speigelstraat, which
ran smack into the one-way Prinsengracht and turned into the
flow of traffic that proceeded onto the broad Leidseplein, pene-
trating into the inner circle of the city.

A throng of young people was gathered in the Dam Square
making music. They were not the hippies of Stein's day, rather well
heeled nouveau Euroscuff. The whole feel of the city had changed.
Young money had found it. Across the park facing the Palais
Royale was the venerable Grand Hotel Krasnapolsky. The cabbie
drove up to the front door and stopped.

"This is it."

"This is what?"

The driver showed Stein the written address.

"I can't be staying here—I do battle with the people who stay in places like this."

"You have an envelope for me."

It was too cold to argue and Stein handed the driver the packet of cash. A doorman led him inside and looked down his nose at Stein's hemp rucksack. Stein was pleased to note that at last he was being seen as a disturbance. Entering the lobby of the Grand Hotel Krasnapolsky was like being transported into a lost world. The place had been built when the empire of Austria-Hungary dominated Europe. The legendary Winter Garden restaurant, with its high-glassed roof, looked like the waiting room of the Vienna Train Station. James Joyce had stayed here in the 1920's and fifty years later, Mick and Bianca. It wasn't the Youth Hostel, that was for damn sure.

"It's YOU!" Goodpasture sailed into the lobby on a zephyr of glee. He clapped Stein around the shoulder and spun him around. "Would you look at this place! Can you believe something like this still exists? Judging by Goodpasture's ebullient mood Stein reckoned that poor boy must not have heard about Nicholette and that he would be charged with the sad duty of telling him. He waited for Goodpasture to settle down for a moment, then placed his hand on his arm.

"There's something you need to know about and it's not good."

Goodpasture sobered. "You mean Nikki. Yeah. I know. That's horrible."

Yeah, that's horrible? Stein thought. Is this the way a person reacts to his girlfriend being murdered? But before he could say anything the bellman was there, pushing before him an elegant cart built to accommodate the trunks and footlockers that accompanied traveling aristocracy. He lifted Stein's hemp rucksack by a shoulder strap, using two fingers the way one might hold a rat, and then wheeled the cart to one of the sixteen elevators.

Goodpasture was excited again. "Wait till you see these rooms."

The glitz of the suite that Goodpasture had booked offended Stein nearly as much as the young man's cavalier attitude about Nicholette. The bathtub was the size of a lap pool. There were two four-poster beds. Persian rugs. It commanded a view over the square and the royal palace. Once the bellman had shown Stein all the amenities (towel warmers, all three TVs) and had departed (well-tipped), Goodpasture accelerated again into a whirlwind of energy.

"Dig this. I've got you set up as 'The High Exalted Cannabis Cup Magistrate,' which means you will have access to every bud in competition! If my orchids are here, and I know they are, those suckers are going to be so busted!" He draped a ribbon around Stein's neck with a judge's gold credential dangling at the bottom. "Anyone who pays the hundred bucks can be a regular judge. But there's only one High Exalted Magistrate."

Stein took him seriously to task. If the kid was saying Stein was his role model, that gave him the right to interfere. "I don't get it. Your girlfriend gets murdered and your prime thoughts are with your missing weed? You fly off to Amsterdam, and then you fly *me* to Amsterdam to help you find it? Don't you find that behavior just the slightest bit…disproportional? She died trying to protect you."

Stein's diatribe left Goodpasture perplexed. It took him a few moments to sort it out. "Were you under the impression that Nikki and I were a couple?"

It irked Stein that Goodpasture would try to conceal that. "Brian. She made it pretty obvious."

"We were great friends," Goodpasture said, "but not that way."

Stein drilled through the sincere geology of Goodpasture's expression for the topographical error. He was sure Nicholette had referred to Brian as her boyfriend. But now as he replayed the conversation in his mind he realized that the words she actually used were, "I believe you know a *friend* of mine." Friend. But surely in that coy, italicized way she said it she had meant to convey boyfriend. Or had he presumed just that? But no. No no no. There were the hourly phone calls she had made to him. The knowing where he was. The unconcealed concern. The very act of seeking help when she feared he was in danger. Who else would do such a thing but a lover? Stein's thoughts played across his face before he even spoke.

"I know," Goodpasture said. "Everybody says we're perfect together. I just wasn't attracted to her in that way."

Stein looked rightfully dubious.

"Of course. She's beautiful. I can see that. But you can only love who you can love. I'm sure women have loved you where you didn't feel the same even if you wished you could."

Stein's mind drifted to the person in his life who fit that description. "I guess it's possible," he conceded.

"We tried, but…" Goodpasture let the thought drop away. It's still hard for me to believe it happened." His cool exterior cracked for the first time and gave Stein a glimpse inside. "And the way it happened. Who would do such a thing?"

"That's what I'm here to find out"

Goodpasture poured a glass of water from the delicate Oriental pitcher that sat glistening with condensation on the oak side table. He passed the glass to Stein and poured another for himself. He sat on armrest of the sofa. Now it was he probing fault lines. "I thought you came here to find my weed."

"Brian. Whoever killed Nicholette was trying to extract your secrets from her. We both know that."

"What secrets?"

"They stole the golden egg. Now they want the goose that laid it."

"Why would they need that?"

"Don't be deliberately dense, Brian. It offends me. They want you for the same reason America wanted Werner Van Braun. You have the product. You have the know-how."

"Werner Van Braun? Who are you talking about?"

"Oh Jesus, are you that young? There was something called World War II? There were these German rocket scientists. Never mind. The point is she died being loyal to you. You owe her that much."

Goodpasture gave up the pretense and surrendered to honesty. "All right, Harry. May I please call you Harry? I don't mean it as disrespect."

"Call me what the hell you want. Stop bullshitting with me."

"I just thought if you saw the connection between Nikki and my weed it would be outside the NO DANGER zone and you wouldn't come. Forgive me for underestimating you."

"You don't get it. She came to me for help, Brian. When I said no, I violated every principle I ever believed in. I fucked up. Nothing I can do will ever unfuck me. But I'm going to keep trying until it starts to feel a little bit better."

Goodpasture nodded like he had seen this sort of thing before. "People fall in love with her quickly," he said.

"I'm not talking about love, Brian. I'm talking about principle!"

"Yes, that's definitely what you're talking about." Goodpasture reached into the leather pouch slung over his shoulder. "I want you to see that I have principles too." He handed Stein a chunk of hundred dollar bills.

"I owe you this for bringing you here under false pretenses. And also for underestimating you."

Stein fanned it and guessed there were fifty. He put it in his pocket with no pretense of declining the offer. "Not to mention the little matter of a stopped check."

Goodpasture winced. "Sorry about that. It was somebody else's idea."

"What's the deal on that guy anyway? He's got the sense of humor of turpentine."

"He does have his social liabilities. But, you know, what he does. You've seen those people. The government makes 'life' a holy grail until people get old or sick. Then they're dumped into the same crap heap as old refrigerators. Do you know what they spend on law enforcement trying to stop us from bringing in a little weed? Wouldn't it be better to spend that same money on life enhancement?"

"You don't need to sell me on the cause. I'm just saying about your doctor friend. Get him a colonoscopy, man. Unclog his sorry ass." Goodpasture smiled and tipped his water glass to Stein as a toast. And then Stein was all business. "I have two days here before I'm back on daddy duty. There are forty some-odd cafes with buds entered for the Cannabis Cup. We can split the work. You go to half, I go to half? We find the one that matches yours and—no, wait. You're right. I have to go to them all. They'd know who you are and hide the stuff if they saw you waltz in. All right." He girded himself to go into action. His legs didn't quite get the message and buckled. He had to brace himself from tipping over.

Goodpasture guided him to the bed. "Plan A is for you to take a nap. Your eyes are falling out of your face. It's probably yesterday or tomorrow for you."

The mention of a nap brought the exiled thought of sleep tumbling back into Stein's consciousness and he instantly craved it. Goodpasture stood and massaged the tight ligaments alongside Stein's neck. "I'll be back for you in a couple of hours."

"Just one question. Why didn't you tell Nicholette where you were going? Why make her worry like that?"

"She knew."

"She knew?"

"Of course she knew."

Goodpasture smiled at how blindly in love with Nicholette Stein was.

"She was an exceptional woman," Stein said.

Goodpasture agreed. "She was."

The door closed behind Goodpasture's departure. Stein's body dissolved down onto the luxurious feather bed. The pillow looked wide as the Appalachians. It beckoned him and he swooned. The wall mirror above the bureau reflected somebody's elderly uncle. Only it was Stein. He had to look away. His rucksack was still hanging on the inside door handle. It had caught in the door jamb when Goodpasture left and air currents in the hallway had left the door partly ajar.

There was a rustling of motion passing the open door and perhaps that was what had caught his attention. But there was something else, more persuasive and more subtle. It was a smell, wafting in from the hallway. It had not been there before. Whoever had caused the sound of motion had left that scent in her wake. It made Stein's entire body tingle from toe to scalp. He had smelled that scent on only one person in his life and there was no mistaking who that person was.

It was Nicholette.

FOURTEEN

A JOLT OF ADRENALINE propelled Stein into the hall. At the same time that his brain knew it could not possibly be Nicholette, every other system in his body ordered Go. Find. See. Get. The corridor was deserted, but the scent hung keenly in the air. Stein felt a peripheral sense of motion to his left. The impression of a trailing garment disappearing down an adjoining corridor. He broke into a trot down the carpeted hallway. The plush pile felt firm and resilient. To his pleasant surprise, so did his calf muscles. He felt no sharp, crumbling pain. No ache of rust and gravity. No shock of protest from the shallow cavity of his chest. He imagined himself a Lakota brave running tirelessly through woods and plains, his body its own vehicle.

That feeling lasted about fifteen feet.

As he approached the T-shaped intersection he heard the elevator door slide open in the corridor to his left. He tried to accelerate but his breath was now wheezing through constricted passageways and his legs had taken on weight. He latched onto the edge of the wall and used it to whip himself around the blind corner. The elevator doors were closing. "Hold it, please," he called out but to no avail..

Brushing aside the internal voice that repeated "what are you doing?" at each new escalation of the insanity, Stein pulled open the heavy metal door to the fire stair and vaulted into the passageway. The stair went straight down then hooked a hundred and eighty degrees to the left. He grabbed the guardrail and yanked himself hard into each turn. He was wearing only his jeans and a flannel shirt over his 1969 Mets T-shirt, but he broke a sweat as he hit the seventh floor landing. Air was not plentiful. He wanted to stop at each floor and run into the corridor in hopes of having gotten there before the elevator. But the thought of just missing it again and losing those precious seconds kept him going. He staked everything on the hope that it would stop at enough floors for him to beat it down to the lobby. He thought of himself as John Henry battling the steel-driving machine. Then he remembered that John Henry dies at the end of that song.

He reached the mezzanine and jumped down the last three steps and pushed forcefully through the door into the lobby. In other cities people might have looked askance at a wild, disheveled creature bursting out of the catacombs. But Amsterdamers during Cannabis Cup season took such occurrences as matter-of-fact. He heard an elevator bell ping. The sound came from his left, which puzzled him because his inner compass told him it should be to his right. But he followed his ears. The light for floor #2 was illuminated in the bank above the elevator door, and Stein positioned himself in front of the doors that would open in a moment. But instead, the light indicating floor #3 went on. It was going up, not coming down. In a panic he spun around and saw that another elevator car had preceded him down and its passengers were dispersed into the lobby.

He had not won the race with the machine after all. There was kaleidoscopic motion all over the lobby, a universe of particles simultaneously expanding and contracting. He didn't know what he was looking for. But amidst the sea of scents and pipe tobacco and shoe leather and artificial heat, Stein sniffed out that floating Jet Stream of aroma that had guided him. His neck swiveled until he locked in on the source. The glimpse of a woman hurrying out the front door, a trailing arm, the back of a leg.

Stein hastened across the voluminous lobby, trying not to be too conspicuous The front door opened before him. He barely noticed the frigid street air. He saw the woman scurrying across the street in the brief lull of oncoming traffic, and getting into a taxi. Her profile was framed for an instant in the passenger-side window. A jaunty fur cap and her drawn up collar covered most of her features. It wasn't much past noon but the sun was already at a low angle and shone directly into the window. The taxi eased into the flow of traffic. Stein ran into the street and waved his arms like discouraged semaphore flags. He looked desperately for another taxi but they were all engaged.

A delivery boy of about nineteen stopped in front of the hotel and braced his bicycle into the rack. Stein grabbed him. "Do you speak English?" Stein demanded.

"Yes."

"Do you want a hundred dollars?"

"Yes."

A moment later Stein was pedaling the thin-wheeled bicycle in pursuit of the taxicab and the kid was putting Stein's money into his pocket, probably wondering why somebody would pay a hundred dollars for a free city bike. Traffic was heavy and the taxi could not get far ahead. Nor could Stein quite catch up to it. Clusters of cyclists trailed behind the buses and trams like pilot fish. He ducked his head to try to avoid the wind. The moisture in his eyes was freezing over. His nostrils crackled. He pulled his flannel shirt tight around his body. Frostbite seemed inevitable but just then the cab got stopped at a red light at the next intersection. Stein pedaled madly between lines of traffic and nearly caught up. But the light turned green before he reached them, and the cab turned parallel to the frozen Herengracht Canal.

Stein's hands and his crotch were completely numb. A cold steel ingot was expanding through his rib cage. He couldn't feel the handlebars or his ass on the seat and was on the verge of turning back. But he caught sight of the taxi again. It was turning around and heading up the hill toward him. But its flag was up and its passenger seat was vacant. She must just have gotten out where the cab made the U-turn. Stein pedaled down the ramp into the lower roadway.

A stone staircase led to the bridge that crossed the canal. Young and old skaters were gliding across the canal's frozen surface using the ice as a means of travel. He compared this to pampered Angelenos driving their cars to their expensive gyms and fighting to get the closest parking spot to save walking a few extra steps.

He saw her coat first, trailing out behind her. Her hands were clutched to the small of her back. She skated out toward the center of the canal, then folded her full-length camel coat into a square and placed it on the ice. Underneath it she was wearing a gold jacket and gold pants. She began to skate figures using the coat as the axis of her circles. Her movements were precise. Her arms maintained elongated positions; her eyes followed her fingertips.

She skated backwards on one long egret leg, the elevated limb reaching straight back at ninety degrees, then arching higher as her back bowed and the blade of her skate bisected the sky.

Stein was not the only spectator mesmerized. Other skaters stopped to watch her display. Spewing flumes of shaved ice, she spun to an abrupt stop in front of her folded coat, picked it up and tucked it under her arm, and, the cadenza over, skated with sublime ease of purpose upstream.

The medicinal power of lust restored circulation to Stein's extremities. He noticed for the first time that a saddlebag was draped across the back tire frame of his newly purchased bicycle. He unfastened the Velcro fasteners and reached inside. There was a green lightweight Israeli army jacket tucked away, which he immediately put on. A pair of gloves was in the pocket; a scarf and wool hat stuffed into the sleeve. How nice to have noticed these items before, he thought.

He set off along the narrow footpath that ran adjacent to the canal. It was frozen hard, bounded on the left by the canal and on the right by a waist-high stone wall. He ran a few strides but the air hit his lungs like spikes of liquid Freon. A trio of aldermen clad in long black coats and friars' hats skated past. He pushed himself onward into the wind for another two hundred yards until his legs became sodden pilings and his will dissolved. The skater had long since disappeared around the bend in the canal. Stein was going so slowly that even the power of reason had caught up with him. What the hell was he doing? Chasing an apparition? Exorcising his guilt through ordeal? It wasn't going to change anything.

He walked slowly back in the direction he had come. In the concave curve of his spine, an interpreter of body language would read defeat and resignation. The wind was at his back and the return trip seemed to take almost no time. His profound relief at finding his way was quickly replaced with the feeling indoctrinated at a young age to Jewish males: If getting back was this easy, he had not gone far enough. And what would he have said to the skater even if he had caught up? *Oh hello, do you speak English, you smell good?* It was absurd.

The bicycle that he had left carelessly unlocked was standing unmolested. Traffic on this side of the canal flowed one-way, and he carried his bike across a footbridge to the opposite side. There, his inner guidance system told him the road was heading in the general direction of the hotel. He pedaled over cobblestones that rattled his kidneys and sent pains up through his knees. He recognized no landmarks, but he felt he could intuit his way back through the winding concentric byways. Twenty minutes later he knew he was hopelessly lost.

He found himself at a glass front triangular building that bore an unpretentious sign reading 'Sensi Seed Bank'. As a matter of principal, Stein avoided places that other people thought of as shrines, and The Sensi Seed Bank was one of those places. But he had to check it out, even if it was just to get directions and out of the cold for five minutes.

Like most conventional nurseries, it had a section containing fertilizers, soil enhancers, weed killers and the like, another with equipment—shovels, hoes and watering apparatus. The one minor exception was that all the seeds and plants for sale were strains of cannabis, and all the apparatus was designed specifically for its cultivation. An entire section was devoted to hydroponic cultivation. On display were low-amperage lighting fixtures, carbon dioxide fans, thermometers, pH testers, products for control of aphid, fungus and mildew. Stein recognized highly sophisticated extensions of the gadgets he and his boys had improvised thirty years ago. Amidst the proliferation of books and pamphlets on the subject, every back issue of *High Times* and all Ed Rosenthal's books were on display, plus Stein's own protean work, *Smoke This Book*. His opinion of them softened. He took off his gloves and warmed his hands under a grow light.

Right out in the open, casual as if they were drinking coffee, people of all ages and hues were sampling the buds that constituted the Sensi Seed Bank's official entry into this year's Cannabis Cup competition. There was the perennial favorite, "Northern Lights," winner in three successive years in the pure Indica division. They also had entered "Early Girl," a potent medium yield with a hashy taste and aroma, an ideal choice for balcony growing, and the crowd pleasing "Super Skunk," a more aromatic descendent of the popular Mendocino "Skunk #1."

Stein could not stop his mind from working even though he professed disinterest. It was an intellectual exercise now, nothing more, but even a superficial glance told Stein that none of these buds were Goodpasture's. The conformations of his orchids were so distinctive; the tight weave of the flower, the long, graceful, conical shape, and of course its aroma of spice and honey and sea air. He was sure these people ran too classy an enterprise to rely on theft. But you have to confirm the legitimate before you can pursue the suspicious.

There were piles of glossy color brochures and annotated maps to all the other forty-eight coffeehouses whose goods were entered in the competition. Stein got his bearings and saw that his pedaling had taken him neither closer nor farther from the hotel, but in tandem. He mapped out a bike route that would take him past a dozen of these shops on the way back to the hotel. At every stop, groups of people were sampling and discussing the philosophical merits of each strain: the taste going down, the feeling in the lungs, the properties of the high. There was nothing furtive or paranoid about it like there'd be in the States.

"Whoa! Sorry man, I didn't know." He practically genuflected. "There's only one of those badges."

He pedaled from café to café. Nothing resembling Goodpasture's weed was among the selections offered by the Siberie Coffee Shop. Nor was it at Lucky Mothers, the Sisterhood Coffee Shop, nor at Boven Kamer, which sported a psychedelic painting of the cosmos on its ceiling and a huge Afghanistani hookah. It was not at de Dampkring nor at cozy Picasso's nor at spacious Free City, whose walls were a collage of found objects—boxing gloves, a sled, a birdcage.

The shortened northern winter light began to wane. Stein was cold and weary and dispirited. He had somehow thought that by placing himself into the equation, some inner magnetism would have led him to stumble on success. It had always been that way. In all of his past capers he had just put himself into the flow of events with the faith that good things would happen to good people, and they nearly always did.

Then, anyway.

Now continued to be another story.

He made one last stop before pedaling the final leg back to the hotel. The vestibule of the Open Doors Coffeehouse rubbed Stein the wrong way. The art was too self-consciously artsy. A trophy case displaying previously won Cannabis Cups from the mid-nineties was too prominently situated. It would have been like going to Raquel Welch's house and seeing awards for best tits displayed on her mantle. Stein ordered a hot chocolate and made a superficial examination of the buds on display. They were overwrought overgrown, overproduced overpriced and overpackaged. Tourist stuff.

The waitress who brought him his cocoa asked if he'd like to try one of their house specialties. She was a tall, slender nineteen year-old Susan Sarandon type wearing a silk blouse and no bra. Her English was slightly accented, incredibly sexy. "We have many interesting varieties," she said. "You won't be disappointed."

He didn't know why he needed to lecture her, it just came out. "Actually you don't have any interesting varieties here. They're all bred for show. Your Indica has fat leaves but less cannabinoids. Your Early Girl was harvested a week early. Quick lick, no stick. You're skimping on phosphorus and nitrogen in your hydroponics, going for height at the expense of depth." He took a sip of his drink. "And your hot chocolate is from a mix."

He reached into his pocket for money to pay the check. His fingers were still thick from the cold and the bill slipped through them. He bent to pick it up from behind his bar stool. When he came back to upright he was flanked by two men who had been standing nearby and overheard his diatribe. One of them said to the waitress, "We'll take care of this," and glided up to Stein, smooth as shaving gel. He sported a '50s style buzz cut and wore a '70s Nehru jacket. "You sound quite knowledgeable," he said.

Stein already regretted the whole ridiculous demonstration. "I didn't mean to hurt her feelings."

"I wouldn't worry about it," the other one said. He wore a Yosemite Sam sweatshirt that had been ironed. His hair was carefully messed. He introduced himself as Dan Wylie. His partner with the buzzcut and Nehru jacket was Ray Phibbs. Where had Stein heard those names? Wylie and Phibbs? His mind felt sluggish. Phibbs was distracted momentarily by a statuesque black African girl walking a long diagonal across the room with her equally tall, icy blue-eyed Danish model girlfriend. "There goes twelve feet of wasted leg," he sighed.

Yosemite Sam tugged on the sleeve of his partner's Nehru jacket. "I think we know what he's looking for, don't you?" Without much subtlety he tried to guide his partner's gaze away from the blips of every attractive woman who crossed his radar screen to the badge around Stein's neck, which for his own amusement Stein had decided to flaunt instead of hide. Then it hit him. Yosemite Sam. Wylie and Phibbs. Winston's old lady at the community center had told him they were selling overseas superweed. All his circuitry came to Red Alert.

"What makes you think I'm looking for anything?" Stein vamped.

"I've generally found that everyone is looking for something." Despite the Yosemite Sam shirt, Wylie seemed to be the brains of the duo. He nodded to the waitress, who had stationed herself the perfectly discreet distance away. "Alysha, please take a silver box down for this gentleman." Stein was escorted to their office. They seemed to be going for a look somewhere between a New Orleans whorehouse and a college frat house, though it may have been the unintentional product of their two personalities. There were plush, silk divans and ergonomic office chairs, 1880s oil lamp replicas and a wide screen TV.

"Nice," said Stein.

"We like to treat special people in a special way."

There was a soft knock on the door and Alysha was admitted. She looked less sure of herself here in the power chamber. She placed a small silver box in Wylie's hand, then withdrew. Once the door had closed behind her, Wylie opened the box and proffered its contents. Stein half expected an engagement ring. But nestled in a bed of plush velvet was a beautifully manicured, identical twin sister of the bud that Goodpasture had given him.

"We call it the 'Holy Grail'," Yosemite Sam smiled.

Stein felt his heartbeat rev with the thought that he might be sitting between Nicholette's killers. His mental projectionist threw up a reel of the two of them astride Nicholette's bound, naked body, forcing her head under the faucet. He remembered the mental exercise his old pal Shmooie the Buddhist had taught him to modulate his pulse and he brought himself under its control. He mustn't leap to conclusions. He must go from one stepping-stone to the next. What did he actually *know?*

They had a bud of Goodpasture's weed. No—they had a bud that *looked* like Goodpasture's weed. And even if it *was* an authentic Goodpasture orchid, and even if they *were* the two lawyer types Winston's Old Lady had described, it did not mean that they were the pair who had stolen it. They could easily be the unsuspecting victims of the original thieves. Or the second or third or fourth parties down the line of distribution. But none of that was probable. Not given the time frame of events.

"Holy Grail," Stein repeated without missing a beat. "Good name."

"The vessel of truth," Phibbs advertised. "In cannabis veritas."

Stein lobbed them a softball to see if they were for real. "Tell me about its genealogy."

"We've told the story so many times," said, Yosemite Sam, with an air of world-weariness.

"It's all in the brochure," said Crewcut.

It took Stein four seconds to eliminate the possible-though-unlikely chance that Wylie and Phibbs had independently evolved, designed, cultivated, and hybridized a strain of cannabis identical to Goodpasture's. Growers were like fishermen. They loved to tell their stories. These guys had their thumbs in a lot of places, but topsoil wasn't one of them.

"Did you have any trouble getting it out from L.A.?" Stein casually asked.

"Why would you think it came from L.A.?" Yosemite Sam said.

Stein smiled enigmatically.

"What's with all the questions?" steamed Phibbs. "Just smoke the shit and you'll know everything you need to know."

Wylie apologized for his partner. "He's still annoyed at the two lesbians."

Stein hinted that there might be some profitable enterprise in the near future. "Provided there was sufficient quality and quantity to justify the venture."

"I doubt that would be an impediment," Wylie assured him.

Stein stood to leave and carefully closed the silver box. "I trust you won't object to my sharing this with my associates."

"You mean you want to take it?" Phibbs blurted.

"We'd be delighted," said Wylie, who had seen the badge and knew what it meant.

Early northern winter dusk had descended upon the city as

Stein pedaled back to the Krasnapolsky. He left the bicycle with the doorman and stumbled gratefully into the warmth of the lobby, beating his sides with his arms like a distressed penguin. He took the elevator to his room and locked the door behind him. He had to be sure about this.

He took Goodpasture's birthday bud out of its nest in his rucksack and placed it on the smooth, polished surface of the ebony coffee table. He then unclasped the silver box he had taken from Crewcut and Yosemite Sam and placed their bud alongside. Their color was identical, their shape and configuration as well. Their leaf structure and the veining of their resins reinforced the superficial evidence. He carefully clipped away from theirs the same amount he had sampled out of the original. He held the buds in either hand and then reversed them. They registered the same heft, the same density. Their aroma, a fingerprint as specific as the signature fragrance of any wine, was identical.

His mind began to churn again. Getting Wylie and Phibbs to return the stolen booty under the threat of exposure and complete loss of face was the easy part. Goodpasture would be happy. Schwimmer's patients in the AIDS hospice would be happy. But how to connect them to Nicholette's murder? That was the question. He called Goodpasture's room but voicemail kicked in, so he left a cryptic message to the effect that, "On the matter of authorship of a certain property, I have acquired evidence which supports your contention. I'll be in if you wish to discuss it."

Stein was still half-frozen from the bike ride. He stripped down and turned the hot shower on full blast. Just before he stepped in he heard a boisterous knock. He wrapped himself in a towel and padded back into the living room and opened the door. Goodpasture stood alongside a woman in her early twenties. She was wearing black silk pants and an off-the-shoulder top that gave the imagination a terrific starting point.

"Harry, this is Alex. Alex, I want you to meet my hero and mentor, Harry Stein, who I'm hoping from the phone message I just heard is no longer cheesed at me."

She glanced down toward the towel tied precariously around Stein's waist. "It looks like we're about to meet him at any moment," she quipped.

Stein had inhaled a breath of her the moment the door opened. It was the scent he had been chasing all afternoon.

"Harry? You're embarrassing her." Stein realized he had been staring at the girl for several seconds.

"You didn't happen to be skating today on the Prinengracht?" he asked.

Her eyes opened wide. "How would you know that?"

"I told you he was amazing," Goodpasture beamed.

The scent of Nicholette was all over her. But there was more, some tenuous connection. Something in the way she moved her head? The natural ease with which her body compensated for the change in weight. A movement of light crossed the plane of her cheekbones and in that snap of the shutter he saw it. The proof sheet he had found at Nicholette's. "Nikki and Alex." Alexandra. Alex.

"You shot a layout with Nicholette Bradley for David Hart."

Her eyes blinked. "How would you know that?"

"You're the Espé New Millennium girl."

"How do you know *that*?" She was freaking. "It's supposed to be secret."

"Is that your real hair?"

The girl flared. "Who sent you?"

"I did." Goodpasture was delighted as a child with a new piece of Mylar at Stein's display.

Stein was engulfed in Alex's tantalizing fragrance. "You smell just like she did." Alexandra did not draw back. She was not a woman intimidated by men, Stein touched her hair and sniffed her hand, recognizing what had arrested him. "Oh yes," she said. "It's haunting, isn't it?"

"They gave you a few bottles in advance for doing the shoot?"

She nodded. That was what Stein had smelled on Nicholette. It was not her inherent scent, it was Paul Vane's intoxicating creation, being marketed as Espé New Millennium shampoo. It disquieted him to understand that his strongest memory of Nicholette wasn't Nicholette at all. It left him with nothing tangible of her to hold.

"I'm sorry about Nicholette. You were close friends?"

"She was like a big older step sister."

"Don't get all choked up about it."

"What I reveal to the camera is for me to decide."

"Am I the camera?"

"Aren't you?"

Goodpasture was not used to waiting in the background. "Harry. Your message said you found something."

Stein's mind zigged away from Wylie and Phibbs and zagged to the pair of beautiful people standing before him. Who knew what went on in the souls of the privileged? The lives of beautiful people were so different from the rest of the world. They were always the sought after, never knowing the pain of the supplicant. They held an instinctive proprietary right to everything they saw. No barriers for them between want and have. And if they wanted something Nicholette had? They had access, they had Nicholette's trust. Maybe the missing weed was a smoke screen for the oldest story in the book—two women in love with the same man. Alex, the new young thing, ousting Nicholette, the old young thing, not only as the Espé girl, but also as Goodpasture's number one gal pal? Steam billowed out from the open bathroom door. Stein used it as a distraction to get time alone. He had to hide these thoughts.

"Look," he said, "I'm half naked here. The sight of it is probably destroying this poor girl's sex drive for life. Let me take a quick shower and I'll pop by to your room and we'll talk."

He escorted them to the door and once they were gone, enclosed himself inside the bathroom and held onto the sink while the horrendous scenario resumed its display in his mind. What if Nicholette did not surrender the New Millennium crown as easily as Paul Vane said she did? Maybe it had to be wrested from her grasp. Not to mention losing her friend-boy to her ambitious little younger figure-skating protégé?

If Alex and Goodpasture had come to Nicholette's late at night, she would certainly have let them in. Stein recalled seeing no broken windows or kicked-in doors, no forced entry of any kind on his way to discovering her lifeless body. But what motive could there have been? What was he missing? If there had been any ill feeling it would have emanated from Nikki, not from Alex. She was the only one losing anything. Ditto the boy friend. Stein could possibly visualize Alex, with her model's detachment, watching Nicholette squirm and die. But not Brian. Whatever shortcomings of youth his character possessed, murder was not one of them. He refused to believe he could be that wrong about a person. And if he was, if he was misjudging Goodpasture's character so profoundly, then he deserved whatever consequences came to him.

No. He ruled them out. It had to be Wylie and Phibbs. Stein could see them doing those awful things to her. It made him sick to his stomach to visualize that scene, and he forced it to be projected on his mental screen from a distance.

In the shower, he let the torrent of hot water permeate his bones and felt his own weariness. He soaped himself down with the hotel's complimentary lotion. He lathered his hair and rinsed as per the directions on the shampoo tube. Wet hair thoroughly. Lather. Rinse. Repeat if desired. Should he repeat, he mused? Was he desired? He was sleeping standing up. His mind was going into dream mode. He girded himself and cut the hot water, letting a blast of cold shock him back into linear.

A nagging thought tugged at him. How would Wylie and Phibbs have gained access to Nicholette's home? She didn't know them. He'd return to that thought in a moment. The phone was ringing as he came back into the bedroom.

"Is she there with you," the female voice demanded. It was a familiar voice but he couldn't quite place it out of context. "Harry, I swear if she is there I will castrate and kill you."

He felt his blood chill.

"Hillary. What's happened? Tell me. What's happened?"

FIFTEEN

HILLARY WAS ON TILT. Stein tried to calm himself enough to be able to calm Hillary enough to get enough accurate information.

"You're just loving this, aren't you Harry? It must give you such a sense of validation that your daughter hates me as much as she hates you."

"Oh yes. I'm adoring that our daughter is missing."

"And whose fault is that?" Hillary snapped.

"No one is assigning blame."

"I am. I blame *you*."

"Me?" He invoked Shmooie the Buddhist's trick of moving one finger at a time as though he were practicing a scale on the piano.

"Where have you looked? Who have you called?"

"If she ran away from me, she's not going to advertise where she is!"

"Are you telling me she ran away from you?"

"Yes. Do you want me to say it? Yes, she ran away from me."

"Damn it, Hillary. I'm trying to find out what happened so I can help!"

"That's how you *help*. You go to Amsterdam to get high with your pathetic loser friends."

He played "Moonlight Sonata" on his scalp in a slow tempo. "Which of her friends have you called, Hillary?"

"I'm calling you. You're her father."

"Are you saying you haven't called anybody else?" He tried hard to mask his astonishment, not make it sound like an indictment, make it feel like he was petting her. "When was the last time you saw her?"

"I was moving her things out of your apartment. She said I was a controlling bitch and took off."

"You were doing what?" "Moonlight Sonata" was playing at the speed of the Minute Waltz. "Hillary. Listen to me. I'm going to get on the first flight out of here and I will be home as soon as humanly possible. I'm sure she's fine. "

Stein cradled the receiver and expelled a long geyser of breath. He was sure she was fine. Where had he heard himself say that before? If it was the 1950's and they were living in some sweet wholesome Norman Rockwell suburbia, sure it would be fine for Angie to run off. Blow off some steam. Hide from your parents. But the Los Angeles night scene chewed up kids like Angie for breakfast. Every demonic creature that Stein had tried to implant into Angie's imagination as a warning, Angie had imbued with her father's traits so that she could easily outwit him; and thus she thought herself far too clever and ruthless for any danger to befall her.

He instinctively called Lila. He didn't bother trying to wrangle his brain enough to attempt the time zone conversion. It picked on the fifth ring. "I'm glad you're there," Stein said, when her groggy voice said hello.

"Where did you think I'd be at five in the morning?"

"I really need a favor." He waited for a reply and panicked when he got none. He was sure that she had dropped the receiver into her quilt and faded off back so sleep. "Lila?"

"I just went to turn on the lights."

"I assume Hillary called you to find out my whereabouts."

"I'm sorry. She's Angie's mother. I couldn't not tell her."

"No. You did the right thing."

Lila assured Stein that Angie was probably perfectly fine. He heard echoes of his own voice making the same assurances.

"Lyle. You've got to do something very important for me. You know in that packet I gave you that has my will and everything? There's an address book. On the back page I have the phone numbers of Angie's friends. I need you to call them. Tell them to pass the word to Angie to call me, just to say she's ok. Give them this number. Tell her to call collect."

There was a short silence where Stein could hear the sounds of a drawer and a metal box opening. Then Lila's voice. "Yes," she said. "It's all here."

"I can't tell you how much I appreciate this."

"You know," Lila said, "there's a word for something that a woman usually *gets* before she helps raise a man's children."

"You have my house key."

"I was referring to *engaged*."

He smiled at the phone. "You're one-in-a million," Stein said.

"I'm sure once I look through your phonebook, I'll know that's true."

Stein dressed and went down to the concierge's desk. There he peeled off a few bills from Goodpasture's wad and told him to get him on the first flight back to Los Angeles. "Get me anywhere close to Los Angeles." He suddenly felt very ugly American, and added quietly, "Please. It's my kid."

As he came off the elevator he heard the phone ringing in his room and dashed in. "Yes! What do you have?"

The voice on the other end was far more belligerent than the concierge. "Where the hell are you?" it demanded.

"Angie?"

Relief and gratitude filled those two syllables.

"I'm not going back to her. I'll live on the street."

She felt as unstable as moonlight on water. "Where are you, Sweetie?"

"What are you doing in *Amsterdam?* Did you go to that hippie pot festival?"

A little anger, he thought. That was good. She wasn't hurt. She wasn't drunk. She wasn't high. She wasn't kidnapped.

"I came to score a lid for you," he deadpanned.

"That's ok. I have plenty."

Ok. Humor. That was a good sign. "I appreciate your calling me. That's very mature of you." He thought he heard a male voice in the background. He was relieved that she was not alone. He didn't want to ask directly yet. "If you tell me where you are I can call you back. I don't want this costing somebody a lot of money."

"It's not. I called on your credit card."

He heard a rustling on Angie's end and a muffled conversation.

"Are you at a friend's house?"

"I'm fine."

"I don't want you running around unsupervised."

"Un-*supervised?* What am I, eleven?"

"You don't know how dangerous Los Angeles is."

"*You* don't know how dangerous Los Angeles is."

He feared that they both were right.

"What happened today? What—?"

"First she pillages your apartment. Then she throws a fit and tries to ground me, pretending she thought I was *expelled*, when she knows very well I was only *suspended.*"

"Are you talking about *school?*"

"No, the Air National Guard."

"Why were you suspended from school, Angie?" He heard his voice getting shrill.

"Because they're a bunch of morons."

"But specifically."

"I answered a question on my civics test about what kind of government we had, and I said a Mediocracy. And they marked it wrong. And I said that proved that I was right. So they sent me home."

"You called it a Mediocracy?" In spite of everything, he couldn't help smiling. She was his daughter. Stein heard a familiar-sounding dog bark. "Was that Watson? Angie, are you at our place?"

The phone was covered again. There was muffled struggle or horseplay. "Stop it," Stein heard Angie whisper. Though not to Stein.

"Who's there? Angie, I want you to go to Lila's."

"Don't you trust me?"

"Just go there, will you please?"

There was an interminable silence. "Fine," she said at last. He felt his body relax. "But not tonight." The line went dead in his hand.

His first impulse was to call her back. Angie was obviously there with a boy, but what could he do about it? He had never demanded the *obedience* from her that a lot parents did. It didn't seem like a trait, that if well learned, would serve her as an adult. Instead, he had encouraged her to question authority, and foolishly presumed he'd be granted immunity. Another responsible choice would be to call Hillary. That tactic might preserve Angie's virginity for one more night, if indeed it still existed to be spared. But it would be at the cost of losing Angie's trust permanently.

When Angie was first born, Stein had harbored so many romantic projections of the way they would share all of her milestones, how he would have a knack for saying the exact right thing at the occasion. Instead, he'd always been two turns of the road behind what she had already done, trying to play catch-up. Edna Greene had said it right: Children make us strangers to our own lives. He thought about calling Penelope. But the concepts of Penelope and Chaperone did not quite merge. She'd more likely go over and make it a threesome.

He felt an irresistible tug on his male umbilical to get home. To be there. To fix what was wrong. To plug the leak. But there was nothing he could do. He could not Mighty Mouse himself there at the speed of light. That umbilical was cut. Maybe it had been cut for a long time and he was just now accepting it. She was there. He was here. And he had to do finish what he came to do.

He placed both buds out on the coffee table and studied them one last time. Stein had not gotten high for six years three months and a few days, give or take. Men hate to break streaks. Men like to elongate. One of the countless numbers of women he had met in his excursion through the Single Scene—her name might have been Brenda—who had called herself a Feminist Behavioralist, attributed the male linear orientation to the absence of a menstrual cycle. The only people who were surprised when Columbus discovered the world was round were men.

He took a bottle of Courvoisier from the minibar and poured it into a snifter. He covered the glass with a piece of aluminum foil from the stem of his complimentary rose and pulled it taut across the rim of the glass. He tapped delicately on the foil with the needle from his sewing kit, making a cluster of tiny holes against the rim of the snifter. Directly opposite, he cut out a small mouth hole. He snipped a small sliver of Goodpasture's orchid and carefully pared it into shards. These he placed over the mesh holes he had tapped into his improvised bong. He had the sensation that he was watching himself from above.

He lit a match and placed his lips on the opening he had cut in the foil. The sweet smoke billowed down into the snifter, met resistance at the level of the brandy, and was drawn up and out of the glass into the wind tunnel down into Stein's alveoli. Clusters of nearly atrophied neuro-receptors in Stein's cerebellum sprang to life. The last crescent of sun radiated a shaft of orange light that shot across the room from the window to the sofa and Stein was astonished to see that it was filled with atoms. Trillions of them. Jumping and dancing through the air like a hatching of mayflies.

He smiled as he visualized the indulgent looks on people's faces if he told them he could see atoms. They would explain that he was seeing particles of dust in suspension being carried about by tiny vectors of air currents. What a laugh, Stein thought. As though atoms and dust particles were remotely alike. Dust flecks were clunky, sluggish dirigibles; fish tank diving bells that could rise or sink slowly. Stein was seeing clouds of minnows, sunlit quicksilver darts of energy.

The shaft of light passing through the vase of flowers and the fruit bowl cast a perfect shadow profile of John Lennon onto the middle section of the sofa. His thin wire frame glasses. The long shoulder-length billow of his hair. The beard. Stein reckoned that John had come to impart a secret to him. People of John's status did not make unannounced appearances without reason. Stein rose from the bed to come closer, but in doing so his own corporeal body broke the plane of light and the effigy disappeared. Was that the message the cosmos was sending to him—don't get too close to people, they'll die? Don't stand in people's light?

But John was leaving. Not fading, but morphing slowly into less of a likeness of himself. Now Stein saw a cow grazing in a grassy field. He flashed on that summer on Crete when the tour guide had explained how archaeologists had put together the few fragments they had unearthed of two thousand year old Minoan tiles, and had extrapolated from them what the full mosaic would have been. Art books carried pictures of those extrapolated Priest King frescoes for decades. Lately more fragments had been found which demonstrated that the experts' projection of the whole picture had been completely wrong. The figures in the mosaic weren't priests at all, they were monkeys.

He grokked in its fullness that the angle between earth and sun was changing and that to keep John here, he simply had to move the vase and the bowl of fruit. But no, they were so perfectly set. He would move the sofa to catch the day's last afterglow. Ah, but to move that he would first have to move the end table. Wisdom revealed itself in layers. The truth that the lamp sitting atop the end table was plugged into the socket under the armoire was not revealed to him until he tugged the table to the left, yanking the support out from underneath the lamp.

The truth of galvanic response was next revealed to Stein as his torso instinctively lunged forward and made a shoe top catch of the bulb and saved it from shattering. The truth of the lamp cord next revealed itself, as it had pulled taut around his ankle like a bolos. The wire went under the armoire. The electric socket was centered on the wall behind it. To reach it, he would have to pull the huge mahogany closet away from the wall. He braced his body, placed his open palms on the side of the armoire and pushed. His muscles strained. Ligaments exerted to their breaking point. But nothing budged. He had reached the crossroads of The Truth of Healthy Retreat and The Truth of Never Quitting.

He tried an alternate approach. He lay on the floor and reached his arm as far as it would go under the armoire. His extended fingers could just reach the plug. He tugged on the wire. It pulled free from the wall. Or more accurately, the ancient wire pulled free of its own *plug*; the plug remained embedded in the socket. He sat with a live electric wire in his hand.

In his enlightened sagacity, he knew this was not a good thing. He would have to slide the frayed wire carefully out from under the three inch high clearance without the two exposed ends making contact with each other or the underside of the armoire. He imagined himself one of those steel-nerved British explosive specialists who did the delicate work of defusing unexploded German ordinance. Slowly he drew the wires out toward his chest. What a savage bouquet, he thought.

His elbow was drawn fully in to his chest, but the hand at the end of that arm, the hand that was holding the wire, was still under the frame of the armoire. To pull it completely out he had to scoot his body backwards. However, in doing so, Newton's third law of motion took effect, dislodging the throw rug upon which the lamp table was now precariously balanced. The lamp teetered. On impulse Stein lunged for it. As he did, the pair of uninsulated bare copper wires in his right hand made contact.

The inevitable arc of electric current did not shoot across the gap. Stein looked intently at the wires and wondered why they were disobeying the laws of physics, when he had the immense revelation that he must be *seeing* at faster than the speed of light. What other explanation could there be for the thing that must have happened not yet reaching his eyes?

Or, as he held the wires for a few more moments, he realized to his immense amusement that there was another, less grandiose explanation for why he had not received an electric shock. As he had pulled the wires out of the socket, there was *no* current running through it. He threw himself back on the easy chair, still holding the lamp. This would be a funny cartoon of God, he thought. God holding a busted lamp in one hand and a frayed wire in the other, saying "Let There Be Light." And there being no light. He wondered for a moment what kind of easy chair God might sit on. That was certainly a provocative question. He wondered if any of the great philosophers had ever pondered that same thought or had he just framed a completely original metaphysical question.

What qualities of a chair would give God pleasure? Would God even need to experience pleasure? Could he imagine it and create it without having the experience himself? Did he even need to sit? To take a load off? Did he get lower back pain? Did he have pain at all? Or does omnipotence make him immune to the very thing he made the center point of human life? Is that why he seems indifferent to human suffering? Was Jesus his effort to try to experience pain? What did God do on his day of rest? Come to think of it, Stein thought, why would God need to rest at all? If God *needed* to rest, didn't that imply weakening? Depletion? Good God, Stein thought, he had just disproved God's omnipotence! *The Doctrine of Depletion!* He had to remember that.

He rummaged for something to write on. He found scraps of paper in his pocket. He breathed in the last remnants of Nicholette's scent. It was practically gone now, and even though he knew that it was not purely Nicholette, he felt the loss of something irreplaceable. Nicholette's card was still in his breast pocket. The scent had faded from there, too. But he vividly recalled Michael Esposito plucking that card from his pocket, certain that it had been Paul Vane's. He heard his whiney voice in his mind: *Mea culpa, mea culpa, mea maxima culpa.*

That moment had been so weird and Halloweeny that Stein had jettisoned it overboard. But now he hoisted it back in, dried it off and looked at it more carefully. Stein understood now why "Miss Espé" had been so certain the card had been Vane's. It carried the scent that he would have known so well, his New Millennium shampoo. It would have confirmed his suspicion that Vane was concocting a rip-off batch of his own.

But! Uh oh. A mental light bulb way down at the far end of a tunnel snapped on. *Mea culpa, mea culpa, mea maxima culpa.* When Esposito saw that the card was Nicholette's, it had shocked him. It had not registered to Stein at the time that it happened, but now in the backlight of Nicholette's death, that strong reaction was significant. He would have known that there was no reason for

Nicholette to have the scent of his new shampoo upon her. She was no longer the Espé girl and would have no access to it.

Stein put himself into the dark corkscrew mind of Michael Esposito. He would have come to the irrefutable conclusion that Nicholette had formed an alliance with his former lover/mentor, Paul Vane. Vane and Nicholette were linked by what they had lost. She had lost her identity as the Espé girl and possibly lost Goodpasture. Vane had lost the product he had created and his protégé-lover.

Stein's other inner voice elbowed his way through the waves of verbiage and met the errant train of thought head-on: *All of this is marginally interesting but it has nothing to do with Nicholette's being killed.*

There was a moment of empty air. Then. His other internal voice answered. What about the extortion notes? "Blow the lid off." "Fall of the house of Espé." Somebody was threatening to bring Espé down.

That's all been settled. Morty Green and his partner dude and Paul Vane and David Hart...

Let's just go slow here. Maybe there's something we didn't notice. We know that only three people knew that the original Espé box had been re-shot after David Hart screwed up the negatives. David, because he shot it. Alex because she was in it. Paul Vane, because he made the hairpiece, the fall, out of Alex's hair that he had just shaved to the skull. Mattingly never knew. Of course he never knows anything except for how many squares of toilet paper are missing. Who else? Even Ray Ramos, the photographer who had shot the layout, didn't know.

Who cares about the fucking shampoo?

We may have a priests/monkeys thing here. We made the wrong

picture out of the fragments. We thought she died for smoke. But maybe it was lather.

What are you saying?

Listen, Espé and Mattingly are getting extortion notes. They figure it's from Paul Vane. We go there. Confront him. He's cool about confiding that he's making the product for his regular clients. We find all the missing bottles. Turns out he's making a little bit more than he let on. Ok, maybe a lot more. He and his new partner have their own private little distribution company going on. David Hart wants to be taken care of "in perpetuity." But you saw Vane's reaction to the extortion notes. He knew nothing about them. This was David's side deal off the side deal. Why stop at one little golden egg when you get the whole goose?

You just want it to be Paul Vane.

His voices were getting quite roiled at each other.

You won't let it be Paul Vane and it's making you blind. Here's the scenario: Michael Esposito finds Nikki's card in our shirt pocket. He sees that she is Vane's ally. He goes to her place to confront her. He's known her for years, so she'd certainly let him in with no struggle. He wants her to confess to the notes. She refuses. Maybe she wrote them, maybe she didn't. Maybe she got the shampoo from Paul Vane, maybe she got it from her friend Alex. But "Miss Espé" drowns her before he finds out.

No! It's about the weed. Look at the note pad from her night table. Something about a "lid of."

What if it's "lid *off*"? Blow the lid off!

Oh, fuck! Oh Shit. You might be right.

This is what I'm saying.

All right, but. Wait a minute.

Stein's heart raced. Trouble breathing. "Moonlight Sonata."

Espé couldn't have killed her alone. He had to have help.

Mattingly?

Mattingly would never be that daring. Think. Who would do anything in the world for him? Who is more vulnerable but a discarded lover who sees the last person put on this earth who might ever love him leaving his solar system forever.

Not Paul Vane.

Yes, Paul Vane.

No. Why was her place ransacked? They were looking for something.

Or maybe planting something they wanted to be sure was found. Like the fall. The fall of the house of Espé.

We could have prevented it.

It's worse than that. Her card in our shirt pocket put them on her trail. We killed her. We killed the thing we loved.

Stein threw his head back against the mattress in despair. The trouble with searching for the truth is that we sometimes find it. We're hoping for priests, and get monkeys. He pictured a beach with smooth wet sand and wrote in it with a pointed stick the solution to the murder.

The one force that had been sustaining him was now abruptly gone. Sleep beckoned him to escape once again, caressed his eyelids, massaged his forehead. And as there was nothing left to discover, he yielded without struggle. Ocean waves rolled over the shore. Now the waves filled in the crevasses, smoothed away every indentation, left the surface shiny and with no hint anyone had ever walked there. He should've written it down.

Hours later there was a soft knock on the door and a voice

spoke his name. When there was no response, a passkey was inserted into the lock. The door opened slowly. A figure advanced furtively toward the bed where Stein lay. A hand reached down and grasped the phone cord leading to the receiver under the pillow beneath Stein's head.

"Mr. Stein," the voice uttered.

Stein awoke with a start. A man in hotel livery was standing above him telling him they had gotten the plane flight he requested. That they had been calling all morning to tell him but his receiver was off the hook.

Object by object, Stein began to reorient himself. He saw the bong with the residue of weed on the nightstand, the sofa rearranged, the lamp wire pulled apart. He remembered now that he had gotten high. He had the impression that he had entertained some interesting thoughts. Something about the nature of God … Something about who might have killed Nicholette … But if someone had asked him what any of those thoughts were, he could not have remembered if his life depended on it.

SIXTEEN

FROM HIS WINDOW SEAT at three thousand feet Stein watched the speedboats cut tic-tac-toe figures across the Santa Monica Bay. Trim and tanned men and women played beach volleyball, rode bicycles, roller bladed, all with a perverse joy and myopic disregard for the world outside of this Wizard Ozian bubble of make believe. Winter was not supposed to be this easy. Its Darwinian purpose was to weed out the infirm, kill the weak, cull the herd. But the winters in Los Angeles were like a joke. Four drops of rain, or even the threat of rain, was enough to dispatch breathless teams of "*Storm Watch*" TV news crews to street corners if there had been rumors of some wind.

In nature, if a wild pig gets eaten by a crocodile while trying to cross the Orinoco, he doesn't get the yams on the other side. In L.A. everything survived. There were too many crosswalks. It softened resolve, forgave indolence, rewarded mediocrity, created the need to explain Natural Selection by false exaggeration. Stein had always favored New York street rules, the continuation rule applied and taxi drivers trying to knock down a pedestrian were allowed to pursue him up to the third floor.

And yet. Stein could not quash the feeling that he was glad— maybe 'glad' was too strong a word—but certainly not displeased, to be home. Home. That was the weird word. For all these twenty years he always thought of himself as just happening to be here, not living here. The thought made him cringe that he was becoming one of them, an Angeleno.

The Stewardess reminded him with a bored smile to bring his seatback to its upright position in preparation for landing. He mirrored her smile with just enough exaggeration to make it ironic, which she either ignored or didn't get. Or maybe did get and thought he was a prick but didn't give enough of a crap about to bother telling him. The bottom line was that he was coming home a failure. Not even a failure. Worse. A minor success, the equivalent of winning Miss Iowa High Fructose Corn Syrup Second Runner-up.

Before he had boarded the retirn flight from Amstgerdam he had swooped down like an angry pterodactyl upon Crewcut and Yosemite Sam, accusing and exposing the two frauds for what they were. How theatrically he demonstrated with all his old eloquence and panache the congruence between the weed they were alleging to be theirs and the sample of the stolen crop of Goodpasture's Orchids, and exposed their crooked business plan to commercialize their success, by selling the seeds they would derive for thousands of dollars, and reproducing the strain for their financial aggrandizement. The guilty parties were shamed and shunned and exiled from the Garden, banned for life by the Cannabis Cup authorities (if that wasn't a gigantic enough oxymoron).

But what he had not done was solve Nicholette's murder. For when he had them indicted and bound and pilloried in the public spotlight and then accused them of the more serious crime, they were able to slide easily from his grasp. Their passport stamps proved without equivocation that they had left the country five days before the night of his murder. Goodpasture had only discovered that his crop was missing on the day he came to Stein. The pilferage had occurred a week prior.

Stein took a certain small pleasure in returning Goodpasture's pilfered orchids to their intended destiny, restoring Schwimmer's people appetite and remission from some of their pain. But he was no closer to keeping his pledge to Nicholette than he had been before he left. His accomplishment was on a par with England defeating Argentina over the Falklands. There would be very little kissing in the streets.

The whole episode had left him with a sour taste. Amsterdam had changed along with the rest of the world. Stein could never think of that city again as a place he'd wish to return. The repository of his youth had aged. He felt very much alone in the world. He knew that feeling was in large part generated by the prospect of losing custody of Angie. It was hard to gauge how far Hillary would go to punish him. The question was not so much about her sense of fairness or equilibrium but whether she'd get enough short-term pleasure in hurting him to mitigate the long term inconvenience of taking on the extra responsibility.

He felt a compulsion to write Angie a letter so she'd know who her father really was. Or at least who he hoped he was. He rummaged through his pockets for a pen and some paper. The slips of Hotel Krasnapolsky memo paper that he found folded in his pocket were already written on. He had to laugh. They looked like they had been written blindfolded. Words were scribbled on top of other words, and disappeared off the paper. He could kind of make out: *God … Deplete*. That sounded provocative but he had no idea what it meant. It swam just outside the orbit of his memory and each time he reached in for it, it darted away like moonbeams on water.

The writing on the second piece was slightly more legible. He recognized his own handwriting. It said: *You must remember this. Life depends on it.* Once deplaned and herded into the cavernous, third-worldish Customs Lobby, Stein again was waved through without a second glance but he was too engrossed in trying to remember what the heck that note meant to be offended that he did not set off alarms.

Outside, he searched for an unoccupied phone. American money looked unfamiliar in his hand. He had been gone only two days but he felt like a Time Traveler returning after a millennium. As it always did, Lila's voice grounded him in the familiar. "Did Angie get in touch with you?" Stein asked without saying hello.

"Stein, don't you check your voicemail? I left messages for you at the hotel, at home. She's fine. She's here."

His body sagged and rose in relief. "You're really the best. Put her on, ok?"

"I think she's in the shower. Hold on."

Stein glanced again at the memo paper. *You must remember this.* What did he want himself to remember? Lila came back a moment later. "Her head's full of lather. Can she call you right back?"

"I'd really like to talk to her now."

"All right. Come with me. I'll take you upstairs." Stein visualized Lila walking up her spiral staircase with the cordless phone, passing her bedroom, where he could so easily be lord of the domain. He allowed himself a moment to think of Lila as his domestic mate, barbecuing out by the pool, squiring her to black-tie charity events, Angie rooted in a stable home life. Before he got to the scenes where she would drive him batty, her voice bubbled through.

"Stein, guess what *brand* of shampoo she's lathering up in? Thank you for telling everyone I was the brains behind the operation. They sent over a case of Espé New Millennium. Do you know how many *bottles* there are in a case?"

"Unfortunately I do."

"I hate when you do something nice and make me take back all the bad things I've ever thought. Even Angie has upped her opinion of you."

"When have you thought anything bad about me?"

"We'll discuss that another time. Today I know you love me. It was so amazingly sweet of you to tell Michael Esposito that I helped you get all his shampoo bottles back. I'm having lunch with him today at the Ivy. I'm wearing my black Vera Wang. I look fabulous. Then he's going to bring me back to the Espé headquarters to take pictures. Angie had her friends over all day for a shampoo party. She was the complete star, of course. I mean, the very first person in her crowd to have it! I'm taking her with me. Of course she's pretending not to be excited, but she's psyched out of her mind. Here she is."

Stein heard the sound of streaming water and the shower door opening. "Hi, Dad." Her voice resonated in the tiled echo chamber. She sounded so adult.

"I hear you're going out to see how the pampered bourgeoisie live."

"Cool, huh?"

"Don't get used to it."

Maybe it was jet lag but Angie's unbridled enthusiasm made

Stein profoundly sad. He had never taken her to The Ivy. She never had her friends over to his place for a shampoo party. Or for anything. His place was never home for her. It was joint custody.

Traffic from the airport was horrible. Stein had drawn the one law-abiding cabbie in America. He stopped at yellows. He looked carefully before changing lanes. Another annoying sensation kept biting at the fringes of Stein's consciousness like minnows nipping at a crust of bread. *You must remember this.* The conversation with Lila kept jumping in on channel two. She could be so unintentionally hilarious. She sounded like a teenager herself, all excited about being taken to The Ivy with a celebrity, if that's what Michael Esposito was.

The slight irritation that Stein felt came from his not being able to reconstruct the bridge of events by which Michael Esposito would have known that Lila had been with Stein in Palm Springs the night he had busted Roland Dupuis delivering the pilfered Espé bottles to Paul Vane and David Hart. It was great that Lila was getting to star in the moment. But how had Michael known she was there? That was where the canker gnawed.

Stein played slowly back through the archival mental footage of that night at the Hotel Mirador. The only person he had told about terminating the operation was Millicent Pope-Lassiter. He was unequivocally positive he had not said anything to her about Lila's being with him.

Who else would have known?

Alton Schwimmer had seen her there when he had arrived at just the moment before hanky would have become panky. But Stein could not imagine a sequence of events that would have brought Schwimmer and Michael Esposito into proximity. Who else knew? Roland Dupuis? Stein caressed his rib cage where

Roland had scored. He too had *seen* Lila, and whether he had or hadn't believed she was a Federal Marshall, he'd have no idea who she was and less reason or access to report that information to Michael Esposito. So how could Michael have known and been grateful enough to invite Lila to the plant?

You must remember this.

What must he remember? He held the slips of paper up against the back window of the cab. The translucency let the writing on both sides intermingle. His own handwriting looked large and deranged to him. The cab turned onto Stein's block. He paid the driver and went inside.

There were thirteen messages on his machine. The first was from Hillary before she had found him in Amsterdam. Angry and frantic at Angie having gone missing. How long ago was that? He jumped ahead to the second and third. Hillary, Hillary. After the fourth he stopped listening. The apartment was a pentimento of his recent domestic catastrophes. Debris from his missed fiftieth birthday party was still lying about intermingled with discarded remnants from Angie's bedroom that Hillary had been removing. Her bulletin board sat propped on the living room floor against her stereo and TV. Sweaters and notebooks were scattered on the staircase, left there when Angie had bolted and Hillary had given brief, futile chase.

He wondered why he didn't hear any barking.

"Wats?"

He checked the kitchen, the hall. His heart sank out of its cavity.

"Watson?"

He slowly climbed the stairs. Angie's bedroom door was ajar. Stein had never entered Angie's room without permission even when she wasn't with him. He knocked now out of habit before stepping across the rubicon uninvited. He felt like he was entering the royal chamber of the queen. This was not the room of a child. Sexy rock and roll posters were tacked and taped to the walls. Her shelves were cluttered with beauty products: lip gloss, eyeshades, skin exfoliants, hair tints, hair conditioners. Her bed frame was taken apart. The mattress stripped and turned half on its side. He remembered carrying all of it up these stairs, assembling the frame and headboard, a routine job for someone with minimal mechanical abilities, for him a sixteen-hour epic.

"Wats?"

He tiptoed into his own bedroom. He whistled softly and clapped his hands and called his dog's name again. A whimper began to form itself in his throat at the prospect of finding his soulmate lying lifeless and small under a piece furniture. Then Penelope Kim's wind chime voice sang out across the courtyard. "Stein. You're back! Come see your dog dance the tarantella."

Stein looked out the window to see Penelope standing on her front steps wearing a silk jacket zippered half way up and a haltertop underneath. Watson was alongside her, and when she hopped down the steps, so did Watson. Stein gaped like one of those people at a religious revival.

"What did you DO?" He lumbered down his own stairs into the living room and out the front door.

"I knew you'd be happy. My friend Lin Pei does canine acupressure. His energy was way too yin."

Stein embraced Watson's frail body and nuzzled his cold wet nose. "I owe you gigantically for this, and I'll tell you everything about Amsterdam for Klein."

"Klein?" Penelope giggled as if he had brought something up from the 1920's.

"Your detective. Or did you change his name again?"

"Oh, I dropped the whole thing."

"You dropped it?"

"Too linear."

A pink-and-orange-haired Asian woman wearing a sarong and a brocade songket waddled out of the back room. She carried a cluster of smoldering blue sage in her right hand waving it before her priestess style.

"If you're Lin Pei, thank you," Stein gushed.

"Cool dog. Have many more years."

"You know this?"

"Believe me, if she says it she knows it." Penelope chimed in.

Lin Pei looked closely at Stein. He waited a beat for her to extend the polite prophecy of long life to him.

"Hmm," she said.

"Hmmm?"

"Could go either way," she said, as though she had seen the outcomes of both amusing possibilities.

It truly was a miracle that Watson's arthritis was gone. They trotted across the courtyard to Stein's apartment. Watson stopped to raise his leg to pee, then bounded to the top step in one Jordanesque elevation. Stein flipped on the TV. All of the local channels were carrying live feeds from the Mortuary of the Eternal Flame where Nicholette Bradley was going to be cremated, intercutting with clips of celebrity friends expressing their shock and grief and recounting beautiful memories of her.

It occurred to Stein that Hillary might not know Angie was

safe. Angie most likely had not called her. Stein had punched in the first six digits of Hillary's cell phone when he saw Paul Vane in an interview "RECORDED EARLIER" being interviewed on TV. Stein believed the pain behind his soulful eyes. He had truly loved Nicholette. The figure lurking behind him was David Hart. At least that was how it first registered to Stein because he expected it to be David Hart. But as he looked more closely Stein was bewildered to realize that it was not David Hart, it was Michael Esposito. How in the hell could that be? How could Paul Vane and the lover who had jilted him be in the same frame together?

In that moment of not trying, the sealed membrane of his Amsterdam vision popped open into his conscious mind. He remembered the two buds. And getting high. And the Doctrine of Depletion, which did not sound as profound in daylight. He remembered priests and monkeys and smoke and lather. And he remembered that Michael Esposito had killed Nicholette Bradley. And that he had done it with Paul Vane's help. In the moment of stunning revelation, in the bittersweet thrill of having solved the mystery of Nicholette's murder, came the ghastly realization that the pair of killers had lured Lila to have lunch with her today.

And that Lila had said she was taking Angie.

Holy Kryptonite.

SEVENTEEN

STEIN NEVER WANTED to hear anyone's voice as much as he wanted to hear Lila answer her phone. It rang two, three, four times before her recorded OGM meticulously described the possible contingencies (not home or on another call) followed by a detailed litany of information describing how to wait for a beep and leave a message and what would happen next, as if nobody had ever done this before.

Finally the beep came and Stein yelled loudly into the phone so that his voice would resonate through her home and that if she and Angie had not yet left he could head them off. But no one picked up. There was no screech of electronic feedback that came when someone tried to talk with the recording still going. He would have welcomed the sound like the sweetest chorale. But the waiting was in vain. He had to move. "Call me if you hear this. I'm going to look for you at the restaurant."

He dashed out of the house, with the revitalized Watson at his heels. He opened the driver's side door and Watson vaulted in, skittered across the seats and found his rickety equilibrium. It was just like the old days. Zooming down the highway with Watson's face stuck outside the window Except that Watson's fur was gray and the VW bus was history and he wished he had listened to Angie and gotten a cell phone.

He sped through a red light at the corner of La Brea, and cut wildly between cars driving west on Beverly. He would have been frightened of himself if he had seen the expression on his face. It was not until he reached the intersection at La Cienega, where he had to decide whether to go straight or take the left turn arrow, that rational thought penetrated into the control center of his brain. He had no idea where The Ivy was.

He pulled over into a pod mall and looked for a public phone. He called 411 and got the bad news that there were two The Ivys; one in town, one at the beach. He got no help at all from the hostess who answered the phone at the city location. He could picture her perfectly from her voice. Tall, classy looking. Mid maybe late twenties. Suntan. Something slightly wolfen in her gray predatory eyes. She would neither confirm nor deny that a reservation had been made under the name Michael Esposito. Privacy issues, she explained, to protect their high-profile clientele from unwanted attention. "What about protecting a murderer," Stein blurted, "Does that fit into your privacy issues?" He heard the word whacko either directed to him or about him and then the connection ended.

He took a deep Buddhist breath before calling The Ivy at the beach. Smooth as an oil slick, Stein gave his name and apologized that he was running late for his lunch with Michael Esposito, and could she please page him, or if he had not yet arrived, to deliver the message as soon as he did. Apparently Stein had not been the first person to try that ploy, for it was easily deflected. He did at least manage to get the restaurants' addresses.

He hit the joint in town first. He expected something large and mirrored like the Krasnapolsky. He was surprised at the white picket fence and the open patio and country cottage look of the place. The eight-dollar valet parking was more what he expected. He gave the valet five to hold it and said he be back in a second. Leaving Watson to guard the car, he sailed past the maitre d' into the dining room. He ignored an anxious progression of, "Sir, excuse me sir, can I help you?" and scanned the hoi polloi of Hollywood elite, lunching on their thirty dollar spaghetti bowls, forty dollar salads and fifty dollar glasses of port wine.

There was no sign of Angie or Lila, and he was confident he'd made enough of a scene that they would have noticed him if they were there. He strode back through the gauntlet of the maitre d's disapproving eyes, his expression announcing very clearly that Stein would never be seated on his watch. Stein reached into his pocket and pulled out the first bill his fingers found. A Goodpasture hundred. Nice. He had forgotten Goodpasture had wadded him with cash. He was also amused at the change of expression the host's face underwent when he saw the money in Stein's hand coming closer. So it gave him even more pleasure when he slipped the Ben Franklin right past his greedy face and instead pressed it into the parking dude's hand. There wouldn't be a lot more pleasure coming his way for a while.

He headed out toward the ocean and Ivy by the Sea. All along the way, workers on cherry pickers were putting new billboards in place, whose content was scrupulously covered except for the message "COMING SOON. ESPÉ NEW MILLENNIUM SHAMPOO." It oppressed Stein's heart to imagine Paul Vane as an accomplice to violence upon anyone, much less upon Nicholette

Bradley, much less Lila. Much less Angie. What could Esposito possibly want with her? It didn't hold together. The pieces of the mosaic still shifted when Stein tried to make a complete picture.

As he headed west he realized he was approaching the Espé warehouse. Somewhere in Lila's excited rant she had mentioned that she was being brought there for pictures. He made an impulsive quick series of right turns and circled down around the rectum of Culver City to the artery that led to the gate. He stuck his card out the window at the electric eye. There was the sound of a faint electronic burp but the gate did not nod and rise. He tried again and got the same result. His access code must have been disabled, he thought. Of all times for a system to run efficiently.

A sixteen-wheeler chugged in behind Stein and air-horned him. Stein made a series of vague gestures meant to communicate something about his card and the gate. The driver jerked his thumb in a return gesture that left no ambiguity. Stein held his hands over his ears to muffle the throbbing diesel, and yelled up to the driver. "I need to follow you in." He waited a moment until he had gotten what he thought was a nod of assent or at least recognition, then got back into his car and backed off the road into the weedy, rutted debris strewn apron that bordered the entry.

The truck's gears ground, the air brakes hissed, the barrier gate rose and the leviathan truck squeezed through the narrow opening with inches to spare on either side. Stein was impressed with the driver's skill. He revved his tinny sounding engine and attempted to ride in after him. The robotic arm came moments after the caboose of the truck had cleared, and Stein was shut out again. He tooted his horn to get the driver's attention, but it made no noticeable impression. He had never realized how similar his horn sounded to a detesticled kazoo.

He abandoned his car and marched past the gate following the truck as it lumbered up to the shipping dock. It found its place in a mandala of other trucks that were already parked, their tail gates open wide, filling their holds with an endless supply of cartons being disgorged from the warehouse. They resembled maggots suckling at a termite queen. Stein was intercepted halfway across the yard by a woman wearing a hardhat and carrying a clipboard stuffed with shipping records. She informed him he had to vacate the premises.

"I'm not trespassing. I used to work here."

Her long, white lab coat was splayed open to reveal a tank top and jeans when she waved her arms at him in the international gesture that meant go no further. He tried to show her his non-functioning card.

"I'm not looking at anything. And I wish you'd do the same."

He had to smile to himself. Morty had described her well. The avodado breasts, the twin eggplant buttocks. Her voice as creamy as sweet ranch dressing. "You're Delores."

"Yes?" She regarded him warily.

"I need to see the boss. Is Mister Esposito in?"

"I wouldn't know any of that. I work supply."

"It's very important. Could you please open the gate so I can drive around to the executive side?"

"How do you know my name?"

"A friend of mine did a favor for you."

"Is that right."

"Yes, Delores, that's right." He felt himself getting stronger. "And neither he nor I have any interest in implicating you in certain disappearances. That's all been put to rest."

She took him a step aside into the shadows. "Are you talking about who I think?"

"I don't have time to dance." He raised his hand a foot above his head to Morty Greene's height.

"Shit. You the police?"

"Much worse."

She became fiercely defensive. "I just brought him around the side like someone told me a coupla times. But I'm not down for killing shit!"

"What are you talking about?"

"I know how you people work. You think everyone he ever talked to had something to do with it."

"With what? Had something to do with what?"

"You telling me you don't know?"

"Look at this fifty year old Jewish face. Does it look like it knows anything?"

She gave him a slow steady scan and agreed with his assessment. "It looks like Morty Greene comes by his name 'The Mortician' legitimately. He got taken in for killing that girl."

"Killing what girl?"

Delores nodded toward the warehouse where at that moment a thirty-by-fifty foot billboard was being carried out proclaiming the arrival of Espé New Millennium shampoo. "That one," she said.

The billboard had not yet been covered. The girl on the bottle and the package was not Alex, as it had been in the prototype. No.

The Espé New Millennium girl was Nicholette.

Bradley. He took a moment to wonder how every thing he was sure of was wrong. And for how long that had been true.

EIGHTEEN

STEIN CAREENED into the Malibu substation and parked in the restricted spot right behind Chief Bayliss's Cutlass Sierra. He left the windows cracked open for Watson and hurried inside. Every police station Stein had ever been inside of—and during his activist days he had been inside quite a few—reeked of the same musty stench of arrogance and petty abuse of power that dispirits everything it touches.

It wasn't the tear gas and truncheons that cops used to break up anti-war demonstrations that turned Stein into an activist. It wasn't for any bleeding heart liberal outrage at their excessive violence against violent criminals. They had a dangerous job. Some of them snap. Ok, so do timing belts on Mercedes. It happens. What ultimately galvanized Stein against them was their attitude toward ordinary citizens. How they made people feel like criminals. How they made inefficiency the rule, taking the greatest number of steps possible to perform the simplest request. As if before they could make a phone call for you they had to first invent electricity.

The desk sergeant was typing a report on a stolen car. After each keystroke that he thumped in with a heavy index finger, he picked up the Driver's License, changed glasses, found the next number, changed glasses, typed it, changed glasses and fumbled to pick up the license for the next letter. All the time ignoring Stein, who stood eighteen inches from him and made several futile efforts to impose himself in the sergeant's line of sight. The name under the ON DUTY sign said Sgt. O'Bladovich.

"Sergeant O'Bladovich. I need to see Chief Bayliss."

"O'Bladovich got transferred downtown."

He continued his ritual, typing another letter, undoing it and correcting it. That was it. Stein strode past his post, barged through the door clearly indicated FOR AUTHORIZED PERSONNEL ONLY into a vestibule outside the private office of Stein's long-time foil and adversary, Deputy Interim Precinct Commander Jack Bayliss.

Bayliss' career in law enforcement began as a seventh grade gym teacher. He had a tight, compact body, piercing gray eyes and a well-earned reputation for the liberal use of lanyard on ass cheek. When Bayliss's uncle, a local hack politician and part owner of a roofing business, got himself elected to the local Civilian Police Review Board, he fast-tracked his ambitious nephew out of the gym and into the penal system. In the wake of the corruption scandal in the mid-90s that involved too many high ranking cops and too many hookers in hot tubs up in Arcadian Fields, Bayliss's appointment to the job of assistant chief was LA politics at its purist. His uncle, by then sitting on the city council, made him a compromise choice over two men and a woman who were far more qualified than he, which is to say qualified at all.

There was a three-seat wooden bench outside the chief's private office. Morty Greene was sitting on that bench, his left wrist in a metal cuff.

"Oh Jesus," Stein sighed. "What the hell is going on?"

"Well look who's here," said Edna Greene. She was sitting beside her boy almost entirely eclipsed at first by his frame. "Mister no suggestion of wrongdoing." Stein felt the sting of her rebuke for trusting him.

"Edna, I'm here to fix this."

"It's Mrs. Greene to you."

Stein pushed open the door to Bayliss's private office and marched in.

"Coach. What the fuck?"

Bayliss glared up at his long-time adversary. Over the years, by design or coincidence, Bayliss had been the victim of Stein's most celebrated pranks. His original "Victory Garden" had been grown behind the parking lot of Bayliss's first precinct; the "Pot in every Chicken" happening was staged at his promotion dinner.

"You don't 'what the fuck' *me*, Howard. I 'what the fuck' *you*!"

The door was ajar and Edna clapped her hands in ironic appreciation of the performance. "Look at the two white boys arguing with each other. Oh, yes. I'm convinced."

Bayliss kicked the door shut. "Don't call me Coach. I will have you in a cell 'till you're ninety." Bayliss was short and cold as the month of February. He prided himself on remembering the full first name of everyone he had ever arrested. Stein wisely withheld correcting him until he had gotten what he had come for.

"I just thought I would tell you, the guy you've got handcuffed out there isn't Nicholette Bradley's killer."

"And you would know this, how?"

"Trust me."

The hoarse gust of wind that wheezed out of Bayliss's throat approximated an ironic laugh. Bayliss glared before speaking. The temperature in his eyes rising to the melting point of tungsten.

"I was up at the victim's house the night she was killed. It was me who made the 9-1-1 call."

"What in hell were you doing in that house, Howard?" Did you kill her?"

"Yes, coach, I did. You've busted this case wide open. Shall we call a press conference?"

"You think you're so goddamn clever. Do you know how long I can put you away and not have to tell anybody why?"

"I'm coming to you as an ally."

"Don't take this the wrong way. But were you always this Jewish?"

"How could I take that the wrong way?"

Bayliss eyes half-lidded into a smile of savage mirth. "I know exactly what kind of athlete you were, Howard. Eleventh man on a nine-man team. Splashing oil on the base paths and thinking it's funny to see other people fall. That's what you are, Howard. You're a disrupter."

"I appreciate where you're coming from. If I were you looking at me I'd think the same thing. But I am sincerely here because I know who killed Nicholette Bradley. She came to me earlier that day. She thought her friend was in danger."

"She thought her friend was in danger and she came to *you?* How did that work out for her?"

Stein took the cheap shot and did not return fire, which quelled some of the chief's animosity, though he remained healthily wary. "If you are fucking with me, Howard, I will have your Sammie's tacked up to that bulletin board."

"I'm here. Why would you think I'm fucking with you?"

"Because a prick can only do two things and you're not pissing."

"Why are you holding Morty Greene? He didn't kill her."

"You're so sure of that?"

"Yes I'm sure of it."

"His truck was stopped under suspicious circumstances."

"Carrying a load of designer shampoo bottles?"

"Yeah. How'd you know that?"

"This is what I'm saying."

"In the course of a legal search, the deceased's name was found written on a piece of paper in the glove compartment of Duluth Greene's truck."

"Give me a fucking break. By that logic I killed Chiquita Banana and Jennie Craig."

"Nobody's charging him with any crime yet. We want to talk to him."

"And that's why he's handcuffed?"

"You see the size of that boy?"

"Coach, I'm going to repay you for every bad thing I ever did. You're going to be a national hero."

Stein gave Bayliss the streamlined version of the connection between Morty and the counterfeit shampoo bottles, and what had happened that gruesome night when Michael Esposito and Paul Vane had killed Nicholette. It choked Stein to mention Paul Vane's name in connection with the event, but in the spirit of full disclosure he did. The only minor detail he omitted was that he had come to his revelation stoned on Goodpasture's orchids.

The funeral cortege played on Bayliss's TV in the background. His office was sparsely furnished with the impersonal essentials, desk, metal chairs, file cabinets, a phone with six buttons, a computer— highlighting the chief's tenuous interim status. Celebrities and common people alike pronounced eulogies for the slain woman. From PETA, from the pope, from parents of children with anorexia. It was a revelation to Stein that she was so much more than just a pretty face.

The desk sergeant who was not O'Bladovich blew into Bayliss's office, all red-faced and puffing. "Chief, there's a civilian loose in the building." Then he noticed Stein standing there before him. He put two and two together at the speed of a battleship trying to change direction. He finally came up with, "Oh," and reckoning that his work had been effectively done, he hitched his pants up over his belly and exited.

Bayliss had never taken his eyes off Stein. "Why are you telling me this, Howard? Maybe to set me up to arrest the wrong people in the biggest case of my life?"

"Not this time, chief."

"What's in it for you?"

"The people who killed Nicholette have my daughter."

Stein saw the two movies running alongside each other in the chief's internal Cineplex. In Theater 1 he is a decorated hero, parades in open cars, fear and respect in the eyes of the world and the interim tag is removed. In Theater 2 Stein is pointing at him and laughing hysterically.

"I swear to God, Howard. If this is you being you I will see you burn."

BAYLISS'S ASSEMBLED TASK FORCE was all in military black, adorned with gas masks and automatic weapons. Stein felt the room begin to shudder. He thought at first it was his heart but it was the police chopper revving up on the helipad. Bayliss strapped his flight helmet in place.

"Where's mine?" Stein asked.

"You're not going anywhere."

"It's my daughter. What about our deal!"

"We had no deal."

"And if she needed an appendectomy would you do it yourself? No, you leave it to the professionals."

Stein hurried along in their wake. Morty Greene was still handcuffed to the bench outside the office. "And let this guy out of his damn cuffs, for chrissake!"

Bayliss nodded subtly to his sergeant and Morty was carefully uncuffed.

"Thanks for nothing," Morty said, and wouldn't look at Stein.

"Hey! I didn't get you into this. I'm getting you out of it."

"Boys," Edna mediated, "Thank you, Mister Stein."

Stein's attention was arrested by the TV at the front desk. Celebrity mourners were being interviewed like it was the red carpet at the Emmy Awards and again there was the aggrieved face of Paul Vane on screen. The pain behind his soulful eyes still looked real. Was he that good an actor to feign such innocent grief? And why wasn't he at the Ivy, which was where he was sending chief Bayliss? Stein tried to peer behind Vane in the camera's shot to see if Angie and Lila were with him in the limo. But its windows were tinted. He yelled to the chief to wait a second, but the cordon of commandos was clattering up the stairs to the roof.

He jumped back into Bayliss's office and used his phone to call Mattingly at the warehouse. He was actually glad to hear the familiar nasal, wheedling tones.

"Mrs. Higgit. This is Harry Stein."

"Why are you calling from the police station?"

The caller ID thing still freaked him out but he brushed past it. "This is very important. I need to know if Michael Esposito is there."

"I have no dealings with that area of the company," she said even more officiously than usual. "I work strictly with Mister Mattingly."

"I know who you work for. But I want—"

She would not yield him conversational right-of-way but plowed straight through the verbal intersection. "Whatever goes on behind closed doors, and I'm not saying anything does, it's not my business."

"Mrs. Higgit."

"I don't judge. What other people choose for themselves—"

"Stop talking!" he commanded.

She allowed herself to be interrupted long enough to hear his question and to reply that although she had neither the time nor inclin-a-shee-on to keep tabs on anyone else's business, she had noticed in passing that Mr. Esposito had two visitors today. She described Lila in fastidious detail and the "wild and unruly" teenage girl with her.

Stein smarted under the indictment of his permissive child-raising. "Listen to me carefully. Your office looks down onto the visitor's parking lot. Is there a white Acura?"

"I don't know brands."

"Look out your window."

"Is there a white *car*? With a sunroof?"

"It would appear to be so, yes."

"Do not let them leave."

Watson was barking excitedly in the car when Stein ran out into the parking lot. A cordon of police had surrounded Stein's Camry. Stein looked with disbelief at his rear tire. It had been booted.

"Real sorry," the fat desk sergeant said looking with ironic concern at the piece of heavy metal machinery locking the wheel in place. "I had no idea it was you." He made a show of examining his key ring, then pronounced with great dole. "Oh I seem to have misplaced the key."

The chopper had lifted off and was vectoring off toward the canyon. Stein was crazed enough to grab non O'Bladovich by the shirtsleeve. "Listen to me. You've got to radio the chief and bring him back." He looked deeply into his face for a sign of intelligent recognition. From the far side of the complex, Morty Greene's red pickup truck had gotten out of impound and was heading down the driveway.

Stein released his hold and unlocked his own car door, grabbed Watson out of the front seat and chased after Morty's truck, which had now driven past. He waved his free arm wildly, trying to put himself into the reflection of his rearview mirror. The truck slowed by degrees, allowing Stein to catch up.

"They booted my car," Stein heaved, out of breath. "We've got to get to the warehouse."

"I don't think so," Morty said and he popped the clutch and began to accelerate.

"Duluth. Where are your manners? You do as the man asks."

"Mama."

Morty slowed the truck down. Edna opened the passenger-side door and slid into the nest between the two front seats to make room for Stein. "No, please. I'll sit there," Stein insisted and climbed over her into the metal crèche alongside Morty so she could have the cushioned seat. "They have my daughter," Stein said looking straight ahead and shrinking the volume of his body so Morty would have room to drive." They tore ass down Topanga Canyon. At Pacific Coast Highway they hit a dead stop. Nicholette's funeral cortege, inching its way up the coast, was endless. Police scrutinized the credentials of every driver and passenger; the Paparazzi long since having learned the trick of turning on their headlights and pretending to be part of a funeral procession.

The tinted window of a silver Mercedes sedan opened. As the glass slid down, the reflection of the helmeted CHP officer yielded to the face of the driver inside the car. Stein leaned forward and wiped away grime from the inside of the Ford's windshield. He could not see the driver but the passenger alongside him was Michael Esposito. That took some brass balls! Coming to the funeral of the person you'd killed. He couldn't see into the back seat and was suddenly possessed by the possibility that Angie and Lila might be tied up there.

The woman in the Escalade directly in front of them was conducting an animated conversation on her cell phone. Stein looked desperately to the right of the Escalade. There was narrow shoulder and to the right of it, a ditch that in winter was a creek.

"Don't even think about it," Morty said, preempting Stein's next thought. "There'd be two funerals."

"You're right."

In the moment Morty relaxed, Stein stamped his left foot down onto Morty's colossal right boot, jamming it down onto the accelerator. The truck lurched forward. Stein yanked the wheel to the right and they darted around the big tank and careened precariously along the shoulder. The grade was too steep to pull back onto the road and the line of cars was unbroken. They could see the horrified looks on people's faces in the other cars.

"We're gonna be dead like Butch and Sundance," Morty howled.

"And Sundance's mother," Edna Greene added.

Morty threw Stein's foot off his own, but there was nothing to do now but fly and hope that none of the six regiments of cops noticed them; and that the phalanx of sirens and motorcycles and patrol cars hot in their pursuit was a coincidence.

"It's ok. I know these people. Keep going."

"You know these people?" Edna repeated. "I feel really confident, now."

In the next moment the truck was enveloped by police vehicles. A voice boomed out of a bullhorn. "STOP THE VEHICLE. PUT YOUR HANDS ON THE DASH WHERE I CAN SEE THEM." Rifles were pointed at them from every direction, including from above, where Bayliss, having observed the chase and overheard the radio transmissions, had swooped down from the sky and landed in front of them. Dressed in his fatigues, Bayliss leaped out in a Prime Time news pose. When he saw that his quarry was Stein and Morty Greene, the catch he had already thrown back, he was furious that he had been diddled again and made a fool of.

"I swear to God you have fucked with me for the very last time in your life."

Up ahead, the Mercedes followed the rest of the procession up the hill and was now gone from sight. "Coach!" Stein yelled, then, humbly, "Chief. The killers are getting away."

With the door to freedom open, Watson sprang from Edna Greene's arms and bolted out of the truck and up the hill. "Watson!" Stein vaulted around to the driver's side of the truck and with the adrenaline rush of a pregnant woman, he shoved Morty to the passenger side and jumped in. He rammed the truck into gear, popped the clutch and held on. The rear wheels sprayed mud and grass and gravel, caught traction, and the truck shot forward up the hill.

Morty wrested the wheel away. "They're gonna kill us."

"They won't even chase us. They think it's a dead end."

Indeed, as Morty peered cautiously back, he saw that the police were exercising uncharacteristic restraint. The truck jounced up the rutted road, its smooth tires spinning them ass-left and ass-right as it tried to gain traction. A small turnoff to an unpaved road loomed ahead.

"Take it," Stein yelled. "Go right!"

Together they hauled the wheel right. Thistles and hedge whapped against both sides of the chassis.

"It's cool. I used to take Watson here when he was a pup a million years ago, before the mortuary bought the land. There's a back way in."

"Be more fun to reminisce if I had a cushion," Edna observed.

A quarter-mile further on, they found Watson sitting alongside a turnoff to a paved road, under a sign for the ETERNAL FLAME CRYPT AND CREMATORIUM. Orchards of young fruit trees swayed in the breeze on both sides of the road behind barbed wire fences. Morty was freaked out by the overly informational signage that described the high tech immolation units where controlled burns of ionized magnesium brought the kilns to temperatures of 4,000 degrees.

"I don't know about being cremated. Hate to wind up a plate of barbecued ribs."

"You'd be a lot less than that," Stein said. "Be a handful of talcum powder."

"No more of this talk," Edna scolded. "I thought Jewish people had issues with ovens."

Stein found what he was looking for, and parked under the sign that read NO ADMITTANCE. Morty and Edna passed a look between them that said it must be fun to be white and not have to obey signs. A trail led between the fences, uphill. "This path takes us to the mortuary side," Stein said. "Anyway, it used to."

Edna's hips weren't going to make that uphill climb and Stein asked if she wouldn't mind staying back here with Watson, which was fine with everyone. Morty's instinct was to stay with her, but she frowned on him. "Pay your debts on time or they gather interest." Morty followed Stein into the underbrush. The pathway made a tight double 'S' between two rows of tall bougainvillea, and emerged at the top of the hill into a broad, quite beautiful, sequestered dell.

The service for Nicholette was being conducted in a small amphitheater on the level below them. The arched portal and floor of the entryway were made of marble. The walls appeared smooth until you looked more closely and saw the hundreds of little sliding vault drawers that were built in. Morty shook his head profoundly when he realized what they were. Several hundred mourners were gathered on the grassy lawn looking up at a portly, white-whiskered Reverend Parsegian. Stein recognized him from late night cable TV. His voice was raspy with the ravages of non-filter cigarettes and Aquavit. He opened a small parcel wrapped in a lovely Indian cloth.

"Death," he intoned, "whatever we think it is, it's bound to be something else." He took a handful of what were presumably Nicholette's remains and scattered the ashes to the winds. "Let her beauty fill the world," he prayed.

"Any time you want to tell me what we're doing," Morty hinted.

Stein scanned the crowd below him intently. "I hope I'm wrong but I don't think I am."

"That clears it all up."

Stein sensed peripheral movement along the ridgeline. Fifty yards away, the diminutive figures of two mourners who had separated from the main body were absconding in rapid lockstep. Paul Vane was wearing a dark suit and designer sunglasses. Michael Esposito was in Hunter Thompson gonzo white.

"That's them," Stein whispered.

Michael was doing most of the talking. Vane listened like a child being told a harsh truth by a younger, wiser, crueler boy. Stein tried to penetrate through the pantomime. "I think they may have my daughter and my friend in their car."

After a brief huddle below, Vane and Michael Esposito departed in opposite directions.

"You take the little one," Stein ordered.

Morty bolted out of their little culvert in the direction of Paul Vane.

"No, the other little one," Stein yelled, but Morty covered the ground across the open field with amazing speed and was nearly upon him.

Michael Esposito had undulated along the back side of the marble wall and was out of sight. Stein gauged where he would emerge, and lumbered down the grassy side of the hill, still favoring his injured ankle. The grade was steeper than it appeared and the grass concealed uneven contours of the hillside. He couldn't break his hurtling momentum and had to throw himself to the ground and roll. The impact knocked the wind out of him and he felt like he had run into a stone wall. For a moment he feared he was paralyzed. He took mental inventory, discovered nothing was broken and pulled himself up by the handles of the sliding crypts.

Moments later Michael Esposito came around the wall and Stein stepped into his path.

"Hello, Michael," Stein said.

If the little shit were frightened he didn't show it. Stein grabbed him by the scruff of his shoulders and swore to him "If any harm comes to my daughter, I mean *any* harm, I will tear every inch of you apart, starting with your eyes. Where are they?"

Stein's threat was met with a smile, a killer's courtesy. "Lovely girl," he said.

Morty Greene pushed a miserable Paul Vane into the picture. Vane's eyes were red and he extended his hands to be cuffed. "I am the man you're looking for. Michael had nothing to do with it."

Vane's eyes were on Michael Esposito, imploring him to look upon him with favor, which he did not.

"Are they in the car?" Stein directed the question to the one place he thought he might get a straight answer. He thought he saw a sympathetic response from Paul Vane telling him "no."

Morty Greene's investigation went along less subtle ground,

He bent down and grabbed the elegant cuffs of Esposito's pant legs and lifted up and inverted the man several feet off the ground. He shook loose his car keys and quite a bit of pocket change, a nail clipper and silver flask of brandy.

"Easy on the rough stuff," Stein said. "He likes it too much."

The electronic key set the welcoming lights flashing on Paul Vane's Mercedes. They had parked it at the end of a row for easy egress. Stein ran to the car and threw open the doors to liberate his daughter and friend girl.

But the car was empty. He knuckled the hood of the trunk. He pressed the button enough times so it finally opened. He pulled up the platform that hid only the miniature spare tire, no prisoners

Morty was right behind him with the culprits in tow when out of the shadows of the "Walls of Eternity," David Hart emerged.

"Oh Good Christ," Morty gaped. "Another one."

"I thought I might find you here," Stein said.

"You should be more careful with the women you love," Hart advised him cooly. "That's three of them you've lost."

Vane beseeched Stein to believe him as he grasped for Michael Esposito's hand. "I never meant for them to put them in danger."

"Ironic, isn't it, how things work out?" said David Hart. And Stein watched as the picture was shifted one more time by the deft hands of the 3-card Monte dealer: Michael Esposito spurned the hand of Paul Vane and stepped into the embrace of David Hart.

"Did you think I was blind to your little game?" Hart flaunted his disdain at the flabbergasted and now twice-jilted Paul Vane. "You have such compassion, Paul. You didn't want to witness my humiliation. Compassion must be a quality that comes with age. And God knows you have oodles of that. *So* much age that it makes me wretch every time you touch me. Your old alligator fingers. Your old smell. And I've found someone who will take care of me in perpetuity."

David Hart kissed Michael Esposito on the face and neck, never taking his eyes off Paul Vane as he did. "You thought *you* were leaving *me?*"

"Oh my," Paul Vane breathed.

Morty pulled the smoochers apart. "That is really disgusting."

"You don't like to see two gay men kissing?" Esposito taunted him.

"I don't even like to see straight men kissing."

The picture manifested itself to Stein for the eleventh different time, but this time he knew it had come to rest. Stein realized that once again he had allowed all his conclusions to rest on the outdated karmic principle that good prevailed and that people got what they deserved. Hence his unchallenged acceptance of the notion that Paul Vane had been the one to leave David Hart. It was obvious now that the reverse had been true, that David had left him. David and Michael Esposito were the molecule; Vane was the odd man out, a stray electron spinning in lonely orbit around them.

Stein stepped into the narrow space between Hart and Esposito. "The very next thing that's going to happen is you are telling me where my daughter is or my homophobic friend will start bashing heads."

"Yes, that's very butch," said Michael, "but Let's talk about what's *actually* going to happen. Your daughter's safety is *time sensitive*. So the sooner we all agree, the happier we all are." He saw Stein's abhorrence and reveled in it. "You think you're smarter and morally superior to everyone. You're a joke. You're a minstrel show.

Everything you believe about the world is over."

Stein made himself play "Moonlight Sonata" in his mind. Fingers moving slowly up and slowly down.

David Hart got cranky. "Hello. I believe *I'm* here."

Michael smiled at his new lover then at the others. "In a few moments David and I are going to depart for destinations unknown, taking with us only the ten or twelve million we've garnered so far from our little moonlighting venture."

"*Our* little moonlight adventure," Paul Vane amended, with just a bit of irony. "You said you were going to let him down easy and come back to me."

At the end of every relationship, one lover is willing to take as many wrong roads as necessary to find the right way home; the other has already called off the search. Michael patted Vane's perspiring pate. "Look at it this way, sweetie. Everybody wins. Mattingly gets his whole company. David gets taken care of in perpetuity. In your old age you've had both me and David in our glorious youth. And now you get the pleasure of knowing you've brought the two of us together. You're thrice blessed."

"My daughter," said Stein.

Esposito went on with blithe unconcern "In an hour, when David and I are safely outside the reach of extradition treaties, you will be informed where to find your ill-mannered progeny and her disagreeable nanny, or whoever that cloying woman is."

Vane looked at Michael, still trying to salvage a way to think of him kindly. "My dear boy," he whispered, "you have to tell him where his daughter is now. An hour will be too late."

"I'm not dear, I'm not a boy, and I'm not yours," said Michael.

Vane turned to Stein. "I know where she is. I can take you to her."

"You don't know anything," David Hart spat. His hand flashed into his pocket and emerged with a snub-nosed .22 pistol. The report in the wide-open air sounded like a little pop. Vane clutched his chest and went down. Morty Greene engulfed Hart, took away his gun and then very nearly disarmed him in the literal sense. Michael tried to bolt, but Morty did a one-arm pushup, holding David to the ground and leg-whipping his fleeing accomplice. Small bodies lay strewn all about.

Stein knelt alongside Paul Vane and pushed a handkerchief against the wound to staunch the blood.

"Are you all right?"

"Just a glancing blow to the heart."

Now the entire landscape began to vibrate. The SWAT helicopter swooped in over the top of the hill. Chief Bayliss leaped out again, trying to understand through the tableau in front of him what might have taken place. He saw Morty Greene on the ground holding Michael Esposito down with his legs and David Hart down with his arm

Vane looked up at Bayliss from Stein's arms. "We need to get to Espé headquarters right away."

"Who is this?" Bayliss demanded to know. "Who are all of them?" David Hart and Michael Esposito and Paul Vane all began to speak at once.

"Sir." Morty Greene suggested politely. "Best you listen to the little bleeding one."

NINETEEN

THE POLICE HELICOPTER whizzed east over the Palisades. The cabin was filled with noise and activity. Esposito and David Hart were handcuffed in the tail of the craft amidst Bayliss and a dozen Special Ops. Paul Vane was wedged in the jump seat between Morty Greene and the pilot. A medic had dressed his wound. It was painful but not life threatening. Stein was an empty ghost, his face pressed against the plastic bubble, looking down over the terrain. Edna Greene sat alongside him and could read his thoughts. "Your baby will be all right," she said. "I don't believe any of these men would hurt a child."

Stein nodded thanks. But not because he believed her.

Paul Vane nudged the pilot's elbow and pointed down. "There it is." The pilot brought them down over the loading platform. The deck foreman who had taken over for Morty Greene was a muscular Italian in a formfitting undershirt with a marine buzz cut and bright corneas that made him look continually startled. Bayliss held onto the bulwarks and picked his way through the matrix of limbs and weapons, positioning himself to be closest to the exit when the bird touched down.

They alighted on the Astroturf front lawn of the executive wing. Bayliss leaped out first. The paramedic helped Paul Vane down. Aided by an adrenaline high and unmindful of his wound, Vane led the unit around to the elevated side of the building where the executive office wing fronted the warehouse silos.

"You know the layout?" Stein asked.

"I've been here once or twice," he said with a tight smile.

Inside, there were five corridors leading out from the central lobby. Bayliss deployed his men in groups to cover each artery of the wing. "The rest of you wait here," he directed.

"Like hell am I waiting here," said Stein.

"I'm not messing around with you, Howard. Stay out of the way!"

"This might be the time to mention that my name is Harry."

The paramedic who had taken Vane down the hall to the bathroom to re-dress his bullet wound now came running back in a state of agitation. "Somebody's locked in the girl's loo."

"Angie!" Stein bolted down the wing that the medic had just come from. The sound of muffled pounding could be heard from inside.

"Angie? We'll have you out in a second."

He tugged on the door but it was solid and locked and he couldn't budge it. He yelled down the hall. "Does anyone have a key?"

Morty Greene had gotten his mother comfortably seated in the ergonomic chair in the main lobby and now ran up to where Stein was tugging on the door. He extracted a skeleton key that fit into the lock.

"I'm not going to ask how you have that," said Stein.

"I appreciate that."

The thick double door opened and Lila sprang out, a total wreck After a moment's relief Stein looked past her. "Where is she?"

She could barely look at Stein, so wracked with guilt was she. "They wanted to take her picture."

"You let her go off with strangers?"

"I know where she is," said Vane.

Stein tried to hear relief in his voice but heard only restrained dread. Paul guided them through a door that looked like it led to an emergency staircase, but instead opened into a narrow corridor. It took a surprise dogleg to the left and seemed now to be angled upward. The perspective gave no evidence of elevation, but walking was more difficult. There was another security door at the end of the corridor. Stein's blood froze at the sound of running water. Steady. Unabated. Neutral. The way it had run that night at Nicholette's.

The doorway opened up onto a webwork of metal catwalks encircling an observation point fifty feet above an enormous open lake, two hundred feet around. One slender metal tightrope wire crossed above the center. Anyone traversing that bridge would feel like a Flying Wallenda. The bridge was vibrating.

A steady hum and splash emanated from the depths of the pit where epic-sized mechanical arms were rotating heavy steel mixing rudders through the liquid below. Through sluices at symmetrical points on the circumference torrents of ingredients cascaded into the lake. The roiling liquid formed a layer of foamy soap scum several feet high that looked like weary cappuccino.

"Daddy."

The sound of Angie's voice penetrated through every other sound, as it always had, all of Stein's life since she was born.

"There!" Lila pointed down into the lake where archipelagos of glycerin islands dotted the surface. The not very solid masses were diminishing in size, from large islands to very small ones, and then disappearing into the mixing blades. Angie was kneeling adrift on one of the tiny glycerin islands. Her legs and her arms were bound.

Vane melted into a pool of shame under Stein's horrified look. Stein could only choke out, "You weren't going to tell me?"

"He promised she'd be safe."

"Angie, I'm coming! Hold tight." In a spastic frenzy Stein tore off his shirt and ripped at his shoes, trying to pull them off without untying them.

"Leave them on," Vane instructed. "The glycerin-alcohol tincture is more buoyant than water. You need the ballast. You have to pull her down to the bottom. Then swim through the drainage pipes." Stein listened carefully. "You're going to be under for at least sixty seconds. Tell her not to take too deep a breath. You won't be able to get down deep enough with too much air in your lungs."

"Hurry, Daddy."

Stein maneuvered slowly out over the thin, vibrating, wire bridge. When he was positioned nearly above Angie he closed his eyes and plunged. Feet first. Stein had never learned to dive; he had never liked water. At the moment of impact he curled his knees to his chest, gulped a breath and cannonballed through the surface of the viscous liquid.

At the bottom, the tubes, like two giant nostrils, snorted out the impurities from the pool; the ferrocycrosulphate, the flecked mica flecks of phenol2Yisobutyltryptophane. He could do this, he told himself. He would propel himself up to the surface now.

The first twenty feet up was dessert pastry. Easy. Sweatless. He was a seahorse, bobbing to the surface. Squinting, he could see the outlines of the bottoms of solid mass. The hype about the sham-

poo was right in one regard, it didn't sting his eyes. He could see
translucent outlines. Then he hit the glycerin level. It was like
swimming through a five hundred foot clam. He had no more
breath and began to flounder. His body thrashed. His neck arched,
desperately pushing his nose toward the surface. At last, with a
thwop, he surfaced through the membrane into fresh air.

Soapy bubbly air filled his nostrils. He coughed and gagged
and nearly puked.

"Daddy, here."

Her little iceberg of glycerin had dissolved into a smaller islet
and was drifting inexorably toward the lip of the upper level of
the pool, from where it would plunge into the mixing section,
where the steel blades whirred.

"I've got you, honey. We're ok."

Stein maneuvered himself to her and bit through the duct tape
used to bind Angie's arms. The shampoo made it come off a little
easier. When he had pulled the tape off her hands and feet he held
her face in his hands. Her eyes were wild like a deer trapped in a
forest fire.

"Are we going to die?"

"Remember the time I pulled that cactus needle out of your
eyelid and you had to sit perfectly still? And I told you it would
hurt like hell for ten minutes and then it would be ok?"

"You pulled it and it bled and we had to go to the hospital."

"This time it'll be different," he smiled.

He reached his arms out and eased her down into the lake.
They held onto their dissolving life raft. "Get your clothes all
heavy and goppy," he said. "We're going to take a deep breath and
dive down to the very bottom. We're going to see a couple of tubes

and we're going to swim right through them, until we get to the other side. We'll have to hold our breath until we count up to sixty nice and slow in our minds and when we get there, we'll be fine. Are you ready?"

"The same tube or different tubes?" Her voice was tremulous.

"What do you mean?"

"Do we both go in the same tube or different tubes?"

"You pick."

"Same."

"That's just what we'll do. Are you ready?"

She nodded, yes.

They breathed, they held hands, they jack-knifed their bodies, and they dove down. Stein counted his fingers off in front of her face as they descended. One, two, three, four. They reached the bottom at ten. The water was less viscous but darker down here. He could sense only the dark shapes of the open pipes. He pointed at the openings in front of them, to the tube on the left. She swam toward it, her hair pasted to her neck like a mermaid. She lost heart for a moment. Stein pushed her by the heels and propelled her in. And he followed.

Stein thought of the seals he used to watch frolicking in the pool in Central Park Zoo, where Stein Senior had taken him on occasional weekends. One cub was Stein's favorite. He was rambunctious, with whiskers only on one side of his mouth. Maybe the other side had been bitten off or never grew in, but it gave him an air of amused contemplation, as though he were thinking what prank he could pull next. He loved to waddle up along the hot rocks and get behind anyone who was snoozing in the sun, snuffle his snout down in good leverage, and shove his victim rolling fins-over-flippers into the cold water. Elder seals barked at him and tried to discipline him but he was incorrigible, and whenever they got too close, he'd dive into the water himself and become pure exuberant motion. That was how Stein tried to envision himself now, that every moving part of his body was an act of propulsion.

He kept mentally counting. At forty-two his lungs began to implode. He could see, he thought, a lightening at the end of the tunnel. Forty-four. Forty-five. He reached forty-eight knowing it was over for him. He saw himself at the zoo. Where Stein senior had died. At age forty-eight. He visualized Angie standing there with him watching his father die. He knew that couldn't be possible. She wasn't born yet when his father died. He dreamed that he tried to yell to her to swim on without him. But the power in his brain shut down. The screen went black.

He never felt himself being grabbed by the hair and pulled through the last few feet of the pipe and lifted out onto the casement alongside the purification tank. He was unaware of the EMT giving him CPR or of the expulsion of liquid from his lungs. He was aware of Lila taking his hand and helping him up to sitting position, and when she saw that he was all right, she nodded to Angie, who was able look at Lila but not at her father until she knew.

Lila helped Stein to standing. His feet squished in his shoes. He could still barely breathe and the world was pixilating through the membrane of placental soap that still surrounded him. "I don't mean to trivialize what you've been through," Lila said, "but your hair looks absolutely lustrous."

TWENTY

STEIN WAS NOT AN ARDENT OBSERVER of Nature but it always amazed him when the same kind of tree burst into blossom simultaneously all over the city. In late winter it was the heady mock orange blossoms. In spring the purple jacaranda flowers carpeted the streets. And all through the year, a bunch of other stuff whose names he didn't know. He wondered how they all got the signal. What was the trigger? He was reminded of this phenomenon now as he drove across the city and saw one after another after another of newly exposed billboards for Espé New Millennium Shampoo.

Each was ingeniously comprised of a three-dimensional reproduction of the bottle, which in itself was a generation of Nicholette Bradley's sumptuous body. As though she had been regenerated. Become a milkweed, seeds of her new life spread by the wind after death and desiccation. Being surrounded by all these pictures of Nicholette made it harder for Stein to let go of her. He didn't want forgiveness. There was too damn much forgiveness in the world. Emotional pedestrian crossings. If we learn anything at all in this life it is through enduring the consequences of our worst mistakes. The moment Stein had stopped believing that one man could make a difference, Nicholette had died. He resolved never to forget what Shmooie the Buddhist always said, that we had to keep doing the best we could all the time, even if no one was watching.

What also pissed him off was that he had been yoinked once again—swallowing the whole story about Alex being the new Espé model when obviously she was not—and never catching even a whiff of the lie. At least he had been right (*after how many wrong guesses?*) about David Hart and Michael Esposito being the killers, so that was something. He had just come back from the homecoming of Goodpasture's orchids, which had taken place at the edge of the Los Padres National Forest (which in Los Angeles resembles a forest as much as the Gobi Desert resembles a ski resort). The weed had been flown commercially from Amsterdam to Ottawa, Fed Ex'd to St. Croix, yachted to Santa Barbara, taken by HAZMAT truck down to L.A. and now, concealed amongst ten freshly cut California Spruces that were loaded onto the open flatbed of a lumber truck which would carry them up north, carefully swaddled in burlap so as not to disturb the cones of gorgeous green sinsemilla that hung from the branches like festive ornaments.

Stein watched the proceedings but had little to say to Goodpasture or Schwimmer, nor they to him. There was muted joy in the triumph. More and more, the fight was exhausting just to get back to even. Stein found it depressing that they were still considered outlaws for aiding people at the end of their lives. Maybe next year when Al Gore was elected president and we put all the Clinton blowjob stuff behind us, the country would get back on track and Stein would feel a part of something again.

Paul Vane was being discharged today from Cedars Sinai, the gunshot wound, as he had accurately self-diagnosed, a mere glancing blow to the heart. He was sitting primly on his hospital bed as Stein entered the room. It was filled with flower arrangements, beautiful, unusual, thoughtfully constructed poems of flowers. In his bright yellow shirt and brown silk pants, Vane looked very much the pistil of the flower. His weight barely made an impression on the hospital mattress. He looked his age. He looked beyond his age. He looked fossilized. He pretended not to have been looking at the newspaper strewn across his bed carrying the sordid tale of his two former lovers.

Stein put his arm around Vane's shoulder. "You just bet the wrong horses."

"Story of my life."

"You only *bet* the wrong horses. They *are* the wrong horse."

"Sometimes it doesn't feel any different."

A pudgy bespectacled man shaped like a bowl of mashed potatoes came into the room. He was wearing white, which even Stein could see was an unfortunate fashion choice. He had brought Vane a candy bar and Stein was glad to see the staff was caring and personable. "They didn't have Twix so I got you Almond Joy. I hope that's close enough."

"My two heroes," Vane announced. He introduced Stein to the man Stein first thought was an orderly but who was not an orderly at all, but the photographer Ray Ramos.

"You did the shots of Alex for the Espé box," Stein said, recognizing the name as soon as Vane spoke it

Ramos smiled, while he went about the efficient scouting of all the hidden crevasses in Paul's room where items might accidentally be left behind.

"What was that all about?" Stein persisted.

"That story is best left in the vaults of industrial secrecy," Ramos said as he puttered.

"I think he's earned it," Vane purred.

The story was revealed, and as Penelope Kim so aptly observed, truth kicks fiction's ass. The plan had never been to replace Nicholette as the New Millennium girl. The plan had been to leak a plan of disinformation that she was going to be replaced and generate the tremendous buzz around who the new girl would be. Of all people, it had been Mattingly who came up with the brilliant idea to make it a fake replacement and to stay with Nicholette. Whether that demonstrated tremendous imagination or tremendous lack of imagination can be debated. The results were that with the arrest of Michael Esposito, Mattingly was once again the only unindicted survivor and would now be sole owner of the franchise.

The last pieces of information came out, and it was as if a chiropractor had made one last crack, and the pain and chafing that had plagued Stein's neck at last abated. At the time of the photo shoot for the New Millennium package, Ray Ramos was among the very few people who knew the secret plan. He knew that the shots he did of Alex would never be used, so to save money and not waste good stock, he had used film that had been degraded going through an airport X-ray scan.

"Imagine Ray's surprise," Vane elaborated, as he told the story with great relish, looking younger with each level of embellishment, "imagine his surprise when the next morning his gorgeous, eager, young assistant David Hart presented him with twenty rolls of perfectly shot, perfectly exposed images of Alex."

"Which he knew could not have been perfectly exposed," congratulated Ramos. "So you had to know something was up."

"Something is always up," Vane purred. The question is up whose?"

"Don't you love him?" Ramos smiled

It was nearly time to pick Angie up at Lila's. They were going to meet Hillary for lunch and attempt to mediate the standoff. Hillary would have full custody if she got her way. Stein would have full custody if Angie had her way. Both prospects terrified him. Lila had left a note for him on her front door saying that she was out back and that Angie was upstairs waiting for him. Stein punched in the code to her alarm system. She had given him the combination to her wall safe and her internet passwords.

She trusted Stein with everything she had. Inside the dark oak and stucco Spanish entranceway Stein called out Angie's name. God forbid she should ever answer him without his having to climb a flight of stairs. He climbed the spiral staircase to the second floor. Angie had a funny look on her face when she opened the door.

"What is it?" he asked.

"Oh, nothing. Lila washed your clothes from Amsterdam. Look what else we found." Sitting on top of the neatly folded pile of laundry was Yosemite Sam's silver bud holder.

"It's not mine," he explained with lame sincerity.

"Good one, Dad. Very original."

He told her to meet him out at the car.

"If you want to marry her it's cool," she said.

Stein nearly wept. She never said anything to him that indicated she thought about his life in any way. Maybe what Lila said about her in Palm Springs was true.

He combed his hair back and tucked in his t-shirt and came out of the house into the yard behind Lila. She was lying on the chaise alongside the pool, with her back to him. She was wearing a big straw hat tied under her chin with a ribbon, sunglasses, a pair of white shorts and a halter-top, sunning herself while reading a magazine and partially absorbing her Italian lesson on her earphones.

A wave of nostalgia for Lila swept over him. He thought about what life would be like with a woman who loved him unconditionally. No financial worries. A stable home for Angie. A strong role model. Lila did not hear Stein approach. He had perfect position two steps behind her. She was defenseless. He could do anything to her he wanted.

If only love was like unleaded gas, and didn't matter whether you pulled into ARCO or Mobile. You filled up your tank, it ignited your spark plugs, torqued your engine and it got you where you had to go until you were empty again. But with love, all that matters is the pump. And because Stein did not love Lila the way we all yearn to be loved, deserve to be loved, believe that some day we will be loved, he did not swoop her off the lounge and hurl her into the pool, sending her magazine and tape machine flying out of her hands in all directions, her arms flailing at her straw hat, a scream of exultation caught in her throat, her eyes wild with glee.

A preview of the next
HARRY STEIN SOFT-BOILED MURDER MYSTERY

STEIN, STUNG

SPRING 2011

ONE

DISNEYLAND BY DINNERTIME was the rallying cry. Ned Peering had his family up and out of their motel room by seven-thirty sharp and marching to their Range Rover with a jovial *hut hut hut.* He was a man who mistook enthusiasm for infectious good cheer, and dressed like a member of the Chamber of Commerce too. His wife Barb, a librarian in the Sacramento school district, had grown tolerant of him during their nineteen years together. Tolerant was not what she had hoped for when she married him. She had felt something more powerful and had foreseen that the feeling would deepen and widen over time rather than recede.

Ned's goal for the week was to visit or at least to pass through as many of the state parks and attractions listed in the guidebook as they possibly could. He excelled at projecting ETAs, not only for a trip's final destinations but for a series of interim checkpoints along the way, mentally celebrating at each one how nearly perfect his estimation had been. Sanford, their fifteen-year-old son, who was called Skip because he had skipped first and fifth grade, was often right in tune with his dad and would ask, "Did you hit it?" which pleased his father greatly. Like his father, he was wearing Bermuda shorts and a California Angels baseball cap. He enjoyed road trips with his family and was a repository of answers to arcane questions no one would ever think to ask. *According to Olympic rules, what is the greatest number of feet that an athlete can have off the ground and still be considered walking?*

Sitting alongside him in the back seat—or rather, slouched into an impenetrable C-curve—was his sister, Sabrina the Ice Queen, futilely desired by a long skein of ardent males who had attempted to melt and mate and meld with the delights of her erotically sculpted body. She wore spandex shorts over tights and a leotard. She was like a perfectly mown lawn with TRESPASSERS WILL BE KILLED signs.

Behind the wheel with his window rolled down, Ned breezed his family through the redwoods, secanted through two points on the circumference of Yosemite so he could check that off his list, and began the climb up the eastern side of the Sierras that would carry them down into the San Joachim valley on the way to Los Angeles and Disneyland. But first there was lunch to be had, and he pulled into the pre-designated rest stop within ninety seconds of his ETA, which was exceptional even for him. He glanced hopefully at Barb for a nod of approval but she was using the side view mirror to refresh her crimped blond hair.

There were vacant spots closer to the restaurant but Ned prudently parked in a shady spot under a stand of eucalyptus. His family would be comfortable when they came back to the car, not like these others parked under the direct sun. It was one of the many anonymous good things he did for which he sought no acknowledgment. Country music was playing on the jukebox as they were led to a nice semi-circular booth. It was a family place with a western feel. Dark wood paneling. Large framed oil paintings of men on horseback in the days before the valley had become agrobized, and where in place of wild grass and cottonwoods, now mile after mile of orderly positioned almond orchards stood.

An eighteen-wheeler happened to be maneuvering laboriously into the parking lot odd the weigh scales as the Peerings were being seated. The chintz curtains covering the widows behind their booth happened to be pulled open and it was no more than the co-incidence of motion of the truck that caught their eye. It could have been anything, a flock of birds, or nothing at all. There was a belch of black smoke out of the pipe as the diesel engine cut off. Nothing else was remarkable, and there would have been no par-ticular reason to notice the stiff-legged gait of the driver as he checked the security of his load of neatly stacked white wooden boxes, all of uniform size, perhaps two feet-by-three feet, and made his way across the gravel-strewn parking lot to the café.

Skip noticed it had South Dakota plates and his mind imme-diately spit out its capital, Pierre, pronounced Peer, its exports, wheat and sunflower seeds and that its state's bees produced the highest yield of honey per colony. Sabrina noticed the driver was tall with raw bony shoulders atop a body that once had been leaner. That he walked like a bronc rider who had been thrown a few times too often, and probably gobbled down a handful of Advil in the morning with his black coffee, bourbon and orange juice. A man who could teach a woman things she oughtn't know. On the outside she just looked bored when her mother nodded toward the menu and asked if she saw anything she liked.

They were all on different diets or body times. Skip was still hungry for breakfast and ordered bacon and eggs and white toast. Barb felt lunchy and ordered a steak sandwich. Sabrina didn't care.

Her mother said she had to eat and suggested cottage cheese and fruit. Ned surprised everybody who expected him to have his usual grilled cheese and tomato by ordering a banana split.

"No, dad," Sabrina said, because she recognized that look in her father's eye when he noticed that the paper place mats had a map of the states, and foresaw that he was going to suggest a game of naming the capitals or coloring in every state whose license plate they had seen. "I'll play," Skip said, which made Sabrina squint at him caustically and ask if he were fifteen going on eight.

Their food came, nestled up and down the length of Mavis's pudgy right arm. Her uniform color was pastel orange. Her hair had some gray. Ned posed with two utensils held above his banana split like it was a ground breaking. "Last chance," he crooned. "Can I tempt anybody?" He leveled humorously intense looks at each of them in turn. There were no takers. "You've been very quiet this morning," he said to Barb. She smiled back pleasantly and said she'd been enjoying the sounds and the smells and the scenery and that satisfied him. Sabrina flipped through the ten pages of jukebox selections mounted above their table. "See anything you like?" Ned encouraged, reaching for pocket change.

Her father's interest instantly sapped hers. "Country," she said, and stopped looking.

"Country can be good," her father said with vacant cheer. And then backed up his claim by referring to the person who happened to enter his visual frame.

The driver they had seen out in the parking lot must have had gone directly into the bar area through a separate outside entrance. He emerged now into the dining room with a drink in hand, a little tipsy—or maybe it was just the contrast to the sudden brightness that startled him and made his first step look unsteady. He located his destination and serpentined his way amongst the bustling waitresses and noisy lunchtime crowd toward the men's room. "I bet *this* guy likes country," Ned said in his wide-open, affable voice. "Am I right, Jimbo?" He read the name stitched above the pocket of the truck driver's dungaree jacket.

The driver cocked his head to one side and looked down from his six foot two inch natural height, enhanced by the heels of his riding boots. "Do I know you?"

Ned ignored Barb's warning pressure on his left arm. He knew an invitation to conversation when he heard one. "My name is Ned. I was just telling my family that you probably liked country music."

"Is that right, Ned?" The driver looked down at each member of Ned's family. His gaze did not linger long on the side of the banquette where the men sat, but it did on the other, occupied by mother and teenage ice queen, whose acetylene grey eyes were burning hotter.

"What would make you think I like country music, or are you just one observant as hell kind of cowboy?"

"I'm certainly no cowboy," Ned chuckled, wishing the man had just said yesiree bob and kept moving. But now he had set his drink down on the leatherette bolster behind Skip's shoulder.

There was a lull in the jukebox music so people at other tables looked around. "What else do you know about me?" Jimbo asked. "That I cheat at cards? That I have a knife in my boot and a hunger for pretty women?"

Ned may have been the last person in the room to feel the undercurrent but he felt it now. "I certainly didn't intend to be rude," he said.

"Do you think I like to dance?"

"We really just want to finish our meals and get to Disney-land. I'm sorry if I gave you any offense."

"You're absolutely right," the driver said and clapped Ned's shoulder with a grip that nearly paralyzed his left side. "I do like to dance. He reached into the tight right hand pocket of his blue jeans and spattered some change across the table in Skip's direction. "Play E-9," Jimbo said.

Skip had already memorized the songs. "E-9. *If I Said I Liked Your Body Would You Hold It Against Me?*"

"That's the one," Jimbo said. His eyes were drawn to the heat of the Ice Queen's young eyes, which were only partially averted as the whine of the steel guitar penetrated the air. But it was not her hand that he took. It was Ned's wife Barb whom he led from the booth to the center of the floor, held her against him, the rim of his hat so high above her head it looked like a halo, her eyes closed in surrender, her cheek against his beating heart for the whole of that the slow sinuous country song.

The stunned silence in the aftermath of what had happened was as mesmerizing as the event itself. The bourbon poured into the partially eaten banana split left its bitter reek over the entire booth. In the physical sense Ned had not been assaulted. He had not been struck. No ice packs would be needed to bring down any swelling, nor bandages to staunch the flow of blood. It was more that the bandages he had always swathed himself in to conceal his true nature had been stripped away, revealing to the room full of strangers who would soon forget, and to his wife and children who would forever remember, the cowardly man he had always known that he was and wished he were not.

The driver sauntered across the gravel covered parking lot, his hands tucked into the back pockets of his straight-legged jeans. He didn't have to look back to know if they were watching him through the parted curtains. Sabrina was fixed on his back pockets, imagining how those muscular haunches would feel if they were her hands tucked into his pockets. Skip was more curious about the truck and counted the wheels to verify that there were eighteen. Perhaps his leg had tightened up on him or he was exaggerating for effect, but the driver sauntered around to the back of his rig and opened the canvas tarp to check on his cargo. It was fully loaded, front to back and stacked four high, with two-by-three foot white palates, easily a hundred of them, maybe more, all carefully tied down. He checked that the bindings were taut like a cowboy would check the cinch belt on his palomino before mounting his saddle, then with his left foot first on the bottom step, grasping the roof with his left hand, he vaulted into the cab.

Ned was not looking out the window. His index fingers were on opposite sides of his orange juice glass, intently studying the geometry of the fragments of pulp and wondering if his wife would ever get over the feeling she must harbor for him now. His ears were attuned to the sound of the throaty gargle of the diesel engine starting, the grinding engagement of its gears and the gravel being crunched under the weight of its tires.

Only after the last vestige of sounds had receded did Barb return from the ladies room. Her slender body recomposed, her jacket back in place. Skip greeted her in his oblivious upper register. Sabrina glared with resentment, but it was resentment tempered with some grudging respect, for through the entire incident her mother had never lost her dignity. Her own dignity, Sabrina knew, would have drowned in desire.

"Are you all right?" Ned asked, daring to seek out her eyes.

"Am I all right?" she repeated.

They delayed their departure over the semblance of coffee. The sun had shifted position and the anticipated shade from the eucalyptus trees was gone. The interior of their Rover was a kiln. Sabrina complained that they needed the air conditioner. "Not going uphill," her mother said, keeping in place their rules of the road even if everything else had been tattered.

"It's all right," Ned murmured. He reached for the dial. Their finger and knuckle met briefly at the dashboard, where he waited to measure whether the current in her hand carried solace or repulsion. Reaching the summit of the eastern crest, an ovation of sunlight bathed the expanse of the San Joaquin Valley below them. February meant something entirely different here than in the rest of America. Here, two hundred and fifty miles of almond trees stood poised to set blossom. "The San Joachin valley is named after the father of the Virgin Mary," Skip informed everyone.

The vista of farms under cultivation was marred only by a mysterious dark, palpitating cloud that gyrated and changed shape below and ahead of them. From their angle and altitude, perspective played tricks with the eye. The phenomenon could have been small and nearby or a distant monumental cataclysm. Skip grasped the back of his mother's seat for leverage and pulled himself forward for a better look. "What is that?" he asked. Their attentions became riveted upon the swoops of kaleidoscopic motion. The dark cloud hovered in place, then thinned into a long chain, rose up, gained altitude, broadened, flattened, expanded into a long streak of black lightning, then disappeared, as if the entire elaborate display had been a stage effect or hallucination.

Ned took each of the next three hairpin turns with emboldened speed, bearing into the turns like he had a sports car under him rather than a top-heavy vehicle with a propensity for rollovers. "Evel Kneivel," said Barb.

"We're behind schedule." But he braked down to an obedient twenty, causing Sabrina to slump deeper into her seat, sensing that the diminished speed meant more time having to be spent with these people. It was from this angle that she glimpsed down through the tree line to where the road emerged below after its next curve. "Shit!" she exclaimed.

The Rover skidded to a long sliding stop thirty feet from what looked like a felled brontosaurus splayed across the road. Twin geysers of diesel smoke billowed up from the eighteen-wheeler's engine and exhaust. The four hundred white boxes that had been tied down and packed with such precision now lay strewed and broken across the road. The four doors of the family's Range Rover opened in cautious unison. The rear guard advanced first—Ned cautioned them about going any closer, but his authority was gone.   The children went forward, outflanking their father's extended arms.

It was the ice queen who lost her cool. The truck's cab had separated from the rig and was bent over on its side as though its neck had been twisted off in the jaws of a ferocious beast. Out of the open window, resting on its lower frame looking ready to guillotined, the neck of the driver hung in an impossible angle. The expression on his face, which had been so fiendishly cocky when he had tousled the Ned's hair and summoned Ned's wife, was now distended beyond recognition. His cheeks were four times their size. His forehead bulged off its cranium. His eyes were ghastly open but nearly covered with distended flesh.

"Look." It was Sabrina who saw the orange and black striped body crawl feebly out of the trucker's open mouth. "It's a bee," she said, and drew back.

"Honey bee," her brother verified. "Apis mellifera."

It beat its wings twice, toppled in a vain attempt to fly, tried once more and then sat motionless, corpse on corpse. An electronic hum began to fill the air. So transfixed were the foursome that it took several moments of the sound's approach before they noticed and looked up. At first nothing was visible. It sounded as though police helicopters were approaching from just over the other side of the mountain. And then the sky darkened above them.

Ned rousted them to run like a cowpuncher stampeding a herd. The four open doors were at first a barrier to their safety. Sabrina stumbled and slipped to the hard ground. Her brother did not stop. Her father lifted her to her feet, escorted the others to safety. In an effort to regain what he had lost, he remained a sentry until his family were inside and their doors slammed shut. The shadow descended toward him like a pterodactyl, then partitioned into hundredths, a horrifically beautiful still life of dense, hanging clusters.

The first swarm settled on his back. He felt its vibrating weight like a rear-mounted engine. The next one wound itself slowly around his right leg. He stood without moving. Inside the car, his horrified family watched. His other leg was now covered. Slowly, excruciatingly, he reached out his arm, indicating them to shut the one remaining open door. His outstretched arm was surrounded. Then the other. Sabrina whimpered. "What are they doing to Daddy?"

"They go crazy for bananas," Skip replied.

The soft scarf of organic life revolved itself upwards now around Ned's chest, then higher until it covered his throat, his mouth, his eyes. It encased him. Inside the whirling darkness the buzzing filled his senses. It went beyond hearing. His entire body buzzed. He was a tuning fork in sympathetic vibration with the universe. He felt an eerie nostalgic ecstasy as though he were two hundred fathoms beneath the sea. The rest was silence.

HAL ACKERMAN has been on the faculty of the UCLA School of Theater, Film and Television for the past twenty-four years and is currently co-chair of the screenwriting program. His book, *Write Screenplays That Sell…The Ackerman Way,* is in its third printing, and is the text of choice in a growing number of screenwriting programs around the country.

He has had numerous short stories published in literary journals over the past two years, including *New Millennium Writings, Southeast Review, The Pinch, Storyglossia,* and *Passages.*

His short Story, "Roof Garden" won the Warren Adler 2008 award for fiction and is published by Kindle. "Alfalfa," was included in the 2006 anthology, *I Wanna Be Sedated…30 Writers on Parenting Teenagers.* Among the twenty-nine "other writers" were Louise Erdrich, Dave Barry, Anna Quindlen, Roz Chast, and Barbara Kingsolver.

TESTOSTERONE: How Prostate Cancer Made A Man of Me won the William Saroyan Centennial Prize for drama following its theatrical run in Santa Monica, CA and is currently being mounted for a New York production.